City of Others

"Urban fantasy that vibes like X-Men meets *Parks and Recreation*? Sign me up! I love it when a book makes me think, 'I have never read anything like this before.' *City of Others* is that book."

—Megan Bannen, *USA Today* bestselling author of *The Undertaking of Hart and Mercy*

"Delights and charms with a ragtag group of magical bureaucrats. Poon seamlessly blends action, magic, and romance. I absolutely adored this!"

—Andrea Stewart, author of *The Bone Shard Daughter*

"An absolutely delightful mythological smorgasbord bursting with wit, humor, and a cast of vibrant characters that warmed my heart."

—Sophie Kim, *Sunday Times* bestselling author of *The God and the Gumiho*

"A wildly fun ride—equal parts supernatural mystery and heartfelt workplace comedy. Full of twists, wit, and heart, this is one utterly unputdownable story."

—Kyla Zhao, author of *The Fraud Squad* and *Valley Verified*

"Full of wonder, tenderness, and breathtaking adventure, *City of Others* is a fresh and captivating fantasy that will grow roots in your heart."

—Kylie Lee Baker, *Sunday Times* bestselling author of *Bat Eater and Other Names for Cora Zheng*

"A whip-smart urban fantasy humming with the vibrant energy of Singapore and its chaotic magical inhabitants. This found family will welcome you in with open arms (and tentacles)!"

—Molly O'Neill, author of *Greenteeth*

"Heartfelt and laugh-out-loud. Filled with Southeast Asian folklore, an eclectic cast of outsiders, and a thoroughly satisfying takedown of bureaucracy; I smiled my way through this entire book."

—Eliza Chan, *Sunday Times* bestselling author of *Fathomfolk*

"A wickedly funny take on paranormal government bureaucracy. Warmhearted and delightful."

—P. H. Low, Locus, Ignyte, and Rhysling–nominated author of *These Deathless Shores*

CITY OF OTHERS

The DEUS Files: Book One

JARED POON

orbitbooks.net

This book is a work of fiction. Names, characters, places, and incidents are the product of the author's imagination or are used fictitiously. Any resemblance to actual events, locales, or persons, living or dead, is coincidental.

Copyright © 2026 by Jared Poon

Cover design by Alexia E. Pereira
Cover images by Shutterstock
Cover copyright © 2026 by Hachette Book Group, Inc.
Author photograph by Jared Poon

Hachette Book Group supports the right to free expression and the value of copyright. The purpose of copyright is to encourage writers and artists to produce the creative works that enrich our culture.

The scanning, uploading, and distribution of this book without permission is a theft of the author's intellectual property. If you would like permission to use material from the book (other than for review purposes), please contact permissions@hbgusa.com. Thank you for your support of the author's rights.

Orbit
Hachette Book Group
1290 Avenue of the Americas
New York, NY 10104
orbitbooks.net

First Edition: January 2026
Simultaneously published in Great Britain by Orbit

Orbit is an imprint of Hachette Book Group.
The Orbit name and logo are registered trademarks of Little, Brown Book Group Limited.

The publisher is not responsible for websites (or their content) that are not owned by the publisher.

The Hachette Speakers Bureau provides a wide range of authors for speaking events. To find out more, go to hachettespeakersbureau.com or email HachetteSpeakers@hbgusa.com.

Orbit books may be purchased in bulk for business, educational, or promotional use. For information, please contact your local bookseller or the Hachette Book Group Special Markets Department at special.markets@hbgusa.com.

Library of Congress Cataloging-in-Publication Data
Names: Poon, Jared author
Title: City of others / Jared Poon.
Description: First edition. | New York, NY : Orbit, 2026. | Series: The DEUS files ; book 1
Identifiers: LCCN 2025035852 | ISBN 9780316585477 trade paperback |
ISBN 9780316585484 ebook
Subjects: LCGFT: Paranormal fiction | Novels | Fiction
Classification: LCC PR9570.S53 P66 2026
LC record available at https://lccn.loc.gov/2025035852

ISBNs: 9780316585477 (trade paperback), 9780316585484 (ebook)

Printed in the United States of America

LSC-C

Printing 1, 2025

To those who keep the world turning:
the public servants,
the gardeners,
the delivery drivers,
and the gnomes who turn the secret cranks

CHAPTER ONE

So there I was in the office, processing paperwork to register a batch of undead ducklings.

Four of the yellow fluffballs crowded the scarred table in front of me, the glint of malevolent intelligence in their beady eyes the only clue that they'd been raised through black magic to serve as familiars. Three were angrily testing the boundaries of the ward circle that kept them penned in, while the fourth fought valiantly to stay awake. None of them were having much success.

Across the table, Seng—short for Chong Jun Seng—watched me, smiling with irritating familiarity. He was a licensed necromancer and the CEO of one of the largest funeral services companies in the country, distractingly handsome, with the slight build and fine, classic features you'd expect from a leading man in a period drama. His charcoal suit and gold watch probably cost more than several months of my salary, their quality a sharp contrast to the worn-out conference room with its wheezing air conditioning and herd of broken office chairs in a corner. New money juxtaposed against the miserly prudence of the Singapore public service.

"Seng," I said, clicking through the Ministry's slow, outdated form system on my laptop and consciously unclenching my jaw. "You can't just walk in here. Appointments exist."

"Come on, Ben," he said. "Friends, right? Us against the world and all that."

Friends. That word. Our families had been neighbours and we'd played together as kids, gone to the same primary school. Back then, he'd made me help him with the most random things. Mosquito bites. Maths homework. Rehearsing talking to a girl he liked. Having his back when he—

I didn't want to think about that right now.

Later, we even served in the same unit in the army. Since then, we had drifted apart, perhaps because of his not-fully-legal use of necromancy to build his fortune, perhaps because that was just what happened to adults. You lose friends, to death or to life.

I hadn't heard from him in years, but some things, it seemed, hadn't changed. He was still making me fix his messes.

And this time, the mess was four baby birds giving me the stink eye.

The ducklings had apparently come to the conclusion that I was responsible for their predicament and were glaring at me with seething fury from inside the hastily drawn boundary of the ward. One of them was obviously trying to memorise my face for later revenge. Even the sleepy one was trying to join in, but its head kept drooping mid-glare, only to snap back up with a stiffness that didn't seem quite natural.

I ignored them the same way I was intently ignoring the notifications blinking in the corner of my screen—colleagues from my other meeting, I assumed, frantically messaging to ask why I wasn't there. But I couldn't very well leave Seng wandering around here unsupervised with this cargo.

"So, let me get this straight." I squinted at the screen and navigated yet another sluggish drop-down menu. "You want to transfer ownership of these... What are they even?"

"*Toyols*, technically," Seng said. "Used to be made from human fetuses, but I don't do those these days. Ethics and all that. Ducks are more loyal, anyhow. If you want, I can—"

"You're probably thinking of geese. Titus Livius actually credits them for saving Rome from the Gauls—which is apocryphal, obviously, but... You know what, it doesn't matter. You want to give these *toyols* to your nephew so he can... impress some girl?"

"It's not just *some* girl. Her family's important. Powerful."

"And you thought a set of postmortem poultry was the solution."

"The family," Seng said, glancing away as if embarrassed. "They're *jinn*. Wei Jie's got nothing compared to them. And her family..." He hesitated. "They're already talking about forbidding the match."

Of course. The jinn were big players, notoriously mercenary in all their dealings. I could see why they'd not approve of one of their own hooking up with some human nobody, and why Seng might have thought that a retinue of *toyol* servants would give his nephew some supernatural cachet.

And I could see why Seng would want this. A connection like this could mean security, legitimacy, maybe even a little respect. For Seng, these were worth almost anything.

I set my laptop aside and took off my glasses, already feeling the beginnings of a headache. "Look, I can do the paperwork to make sure these get proper IDs. The permits should come in within a couple of weeks. I can help you with the transfer forms after that, but I'm really not sure saddling the kid with zombie ducks is the way to go. Please tell me you asked him."

"No, but—"

Of course not.

"Listen." I slid my glasses back on. "This isn't going to solve your problem anyway. You think the jinn family is going to respect your nephew just because he's got a bit of power from his uncle?"

Seng started to argue, but I held up a hand to stop him. "And you know what's likely to happen? Wei Jie is going to do something stupid with these things—blow shit up or demonstrate his love or even worse. You remember what jackasses we were back when we were teenagers. Someone's going to get hurt—maybe the jinn girl—and then the family will escalate, and then my Ministry will have to get involved, and then it'll end up on my desk next week as some sort of diplomatic incident."

I sighed, softened at the look on his face. The confidence he always wore like armour—it was cracked at the edges. He had looked like this, that one day when we were thirteen. He'd asked me for help then, too.

"Look," I said. "What we... what you need to do is have a little faith. Let the kids work it out themselves. In the meanwhile, I can reach out to the jinn side, see if there's a way to nudge them in the right direction. It's way above my pay grade, but I'll see what I can do."

Seng's shoulders relaxed a fraction, and he gave me a small smile. "I knew you'd come through for me."

"I haven't come through yet," I said.

"You always do, Ben. I don't know what I would do without you."

And there it was. He'd been saying versions of that since we were kids. Most of the time, I'd indeed come through for him. But we both remembered the one time I didn't.

He'd forgiven me. I hadn't.

Seng left without looking back, taking the ducklings with him. As the door clicked shut, I wiped the ward circle from the table and slumped back in my chair, a familiar tug of resentment twisting in my chest. It was a sharp-edged feeling, a thorned weed I had to burn out before it took root.

Seng shouldn't have put this on me. But he also knew I couldn't turn him away.

So that was one more thing on my plate. I eyed my laptop screen, the accusing blink of notifications, the column of tiny red flags marking out emails I needed to respond to today. A few from the Strategic Planning team, requesting inputs on the workplan slides and how our projects for the next year would fit into the key pillars of the Ministry's work. A couple from the Heritage Sites division, who were in charge of this year's Ministry-wide Sports Day, asking me to make sure the team signed up. More from our PS and DS—Permanent Secretary and Deputy Secretary, the head honchos around here—with PDFs of articles on psychology or philosophy or leadership they thought we should read. One from Rebecca, my boss, asking about the status of this email update I'd been working on.

I felt my headache get worse. The update was our quarterly report to Minister, who for all intents and purposes seemed like a very nice, very reasonable man. The problem was that Rebecca was his gatekeeper, convinced that he would be scarred by any contact with inconsistently indented paragraphs, the active voice, or reality. We were now on our fifth round of edits, each iteration improving in elegance of phrasing but diminishing in actual content.

I thought I could catch the tail end of the meeting I'd missed, so I could at least know what next steps they'd agreed to. Then I could get those edits for the update to Minister done in an hour or so. After that, if I skipped lunch and really focused, I might be able to give everyone the replies and inputs they needed by five. Then I'd have the last part of the day to do the part of my job I actually cared about—what I'd done for Seng, if I was being honest with myself. Not bureaucratic bullshit but something more tangible.

On my list, there was a minor avatar of the goddess Annapurna, who'd put her pride aside to ask for help with racist landlords, and a goblin family who couldn't get their kid into any public schools but also couldn't afford the exorbitant fees for a private school. I could help them navigate the bureaucracy, get their issues seen by the state, as long as there were no last-minute interruptions—

A knock on the door of the meeting room, and then, without waiting, a young woman poked her head in. She was maybe twenty, short, her T-shirt printed with some anime thing and the tudung that hid her hair an alarming shade of pink. Her smile was bright but uncertain.

"Sorry! Mr. Toh? Ms. Saanvi from HR said to find you here."

"Wait, who are you?"

"Oh! Sorry, I'm Fizah. I'm here for my internship?"

Right. The new intern—jinni, if I remember her application correctly. *Jinni*, like the girl Seng's nephew is dating.

I blinked at Fizah, staring for a fraction longer than I meant to. What were the odds…? No, it couldn't be. There were enough jinn families in the city that jumping to conclusions would just make my headache worse.

Coincidence, I decided. I was overthinking things again. With all my other work, I'd forgotten she was starting today. Jimmy was supposed to be in charge of the internship programme, so it really should be him giving her the onboarding talk, but this poor girl looked frazzled enough as it was, and

I didn't want her first experience with us to be getting turned away. My day was probably shot anyway.

I set aside my headache and pushed my laptop away, composing myself, with some effort, into a semblance of friendliness.

"Come in," I said. "Let me tell you about the team."

My team was the Division for Engagement of Unusual Stakeholders, or DEUS—the post-colonial irony of a government team with a Latinate acronym was not lost on any of us. We were part of the Ministry of Community, the MOC, and I suppose it was a quirk of history that we were here instead of, say, the Ministry of Home Affairs or the Internal Security Department. Unlike most other developed nations, Singapore had quickly made it policy to count our spirit mediums and sorceresses, our *hantus*, our *devas* and *asuras*, as citizens to be served and regulated rather than monsters to be suppressed. This didn't spring from particularly liberal ideals about equality or moral community. Rather, it came from anxiety about Singapore's lack of natural resources and the pragmatic conviction that we needed everyone to work together if we were to survive. We could not afford to completely sideline our traditional gods and demons. We needed them to contribute to our nation's *actual* gods and demons—our government, our economy, our security, our new Leviathan and Moloch.

The job of DEUS was straightforward—keep the weird people content, get them to be productive members of society, and keep them out of sight. That is, don't bother the good, normal citizens of Singapore with disturbing things, and certainly don't bother your bosses (or other Ministries) with that stuff. They had more important things to worry about.

Thankfully, keeping the supernatural from normal human beings and senior management wasn't hard. People don't see what they don't want to see, and our minds are marvellous confabulators.

That lady on the MRT with frangipanis growing where her eyes should be? Don't look at her face, don't remember seeing her, focus on your phone and the K-drama you're watching.

That temple near your old house, where you've only seen people leaving but never entering, where you've seen something enormous and many-limbed and *holy* dancing inside? Well, it's usually dark, and it could have been something else.

That canteen stall you went to all the time in primary school, where you could pay with promises and the food tasted like thunderstorms? Your friends don't admit to recalling anything like that, so you probably just misremembered. You know how fanciful children's imaginations can be.

So we whistle to ourselves as we walk deserted streets home at night, singing tuneless little songs, our brains protecting us from the horrors around us. Officially, this phenomenon is known as Deviant Occurrences Blind Eye Syndrome, or DOBES, following the British government's understated (and poorly chosen) name for it, but no one calls it that except in official reports, not even the Brits. They call it "the jumblies," I heard, and here in Singapore, we call it the DKP effect. Don't *kaypoh*, don't be a busybody, mind your own business.

The DKP effect did make life easier for those of us who had to manage the supernatural stuff, that being the four of us on the team. Jimmy was our resident goofball and psychic—precognition, psychometry, all the usual. He spent an hour every morning, after his tea break, contemplating a printed map of Singapore and using a dowsing pendulum to sniff out neighbourhoods with unusual supernatural activity. Mei was our spell-slinging *bomoh*, always perfectly poised in her enchanted heels, and she had been doing this for a long time—don't let her pixie haircut and apparent youth fool you. Rebecca was our boss, the head of the department, but she also double-hatted with two other teams, so she was always at other meetings and never around. I was a Gardener and our ersatz field agent, for whatever that was worth.

And now, we also had a jinni.

"Technically, half-jinni, um. Sorry. My dad's just a teacher," Fizah said, fiddling with the edges of her notebook. "How old is Mei, anyway? I mean, because..."

"Probably not the best idea to ask," I said.

"Sorry, sorry!" She flipped through her notes, her handwriting neat and perfectly aligned. Perhaps there was hope for the next generation yet. She looked up. "Um, so what do I, like, do around here?"

It was a valid question.

"For today, why don't you go check with Mei or Jimmy and see if they need any help." I knew real work was unlikely to get done—Jimmy would brag about his daughters, Mei would rant about third-wave feminism and the societal pressures forcing her to use magic to look young, and then they would all go out for cake. But hopefully that would give me the space to clear my emails, check in on Mdm. Annapurna and the goblin kid, and tackle that damned update in the evening.

Her face lit up at my suggestion. "Okay! Should I introduce myself, or—?"

Before I could answer, my phone buzzed. Against the sandy landscape that was my lock screen—a photo of Mars taken by the ill-fated rover *Opportunity*—notifications blinked. Missed calls from an hour ago from my father and from Adam, this guy I was seeing, and a message from Jimmy on the DEUS group chat:

Ghost cat! L3 pantry, come now!

We threaded our way out through the labyrinth of cubicles that made up the third floor. This close to lunchtime, every department had bifurcated into two camps. First: the sprinters, desperately trying to dash off their last four emails or final annex to a paper so they could leave. The second: the defeated, so far from the finish line they'd given up on leaving for lunch, picking at cold noodles while staring at their screens with dead eyes. They don't call it a rat race for nothing.

By the time we reached the pantry, Jimmy and Mei had cleared the area, blocking it off along with a whole section of the adjacent corridor with signs that said SENIOR MANAGEMENT FILMING IN PROGRESS.

Clever. There was no better way to make civil servants avoid a place than with the threat that their bosses might be there.

"Get me a cup," Mei said the moment we stepped in, her manner imperious. "Quickly. Water from the tap will do." She had her back to us and was spreading her scarf—peacock green and gold—on a table. Jimmy waved a broom around threateningly.

There had been rumours about this cat for months—gossip about scratching in the walls once the sun had set. How stationery on your desk would wind up in a different place from where you left it. How papers sometimes looked like they had been chewed on. Sok Ling, from Legal, was convinced that the perpetrator was the ghost of her cat's late best friend.

Hauntings like these were fairly common where we worked. We were in a heritage site that used to be a police barracks, and people said that terrible things happened here when the Japanese occupied Singapore during World War II. The occupation only lasted for about two years, but the pain, fear, and depravity that soaked into the brick and plaster during that time remained. Supposedly the building sat on a conjunction of ley lines and dragon meridians, and so the structure itself stayed, even as everything else around was torn down and rebuilt into shopping centres and skyscrapers, becoming a powerful node for spirits of the darker kind. Or so I have been told by those knowledgeable in such things. History speaks. Stones remember. Buildings accrete memories and excrete ghosts.

But now the inside of the building had been remodelled into air-conditioned government offices, rows of cubicles and meeting rooms, and it was civil servants instead of prisoners of the regular variety who spent their days there. The torture had gotten slightly more sophisticated, the shootings had become (for the most part) metaphorical rather than literal, and we had Wi-Fi. But the decor hadn't improved much, and now you had to buy your own snacks. So, you know, win some, lose some.

The cat didn't seem to think we were winners. It turned out to be a small tabby, one of those *kucintas* you'd find lounging around any housing estate—except this one was sitting very securely about two metres off the floor on absolutely nothing. It glared at us, slow-blinking with supreme indifference—at me, at Mei bent over her scarf and muttering, at Jimmy brandishing a broom, and at Fizah grinning with open delight. Then, as if to underline just how little it cared, the cat started licking a paw. It was a little insulting being ignored like that, to be honest.

I edged past Jimmy and got Mei her cup of water, which she placed on her scarf. The water gleamed momentarily, opalescent.

"Can we help?" I asked.

Mei shook her head, not breaking off from her chanting. Fizah came over to peer into the mug, then up at the cat, then into the mug again. She was practically vibrating with excitement.

"It's so cute!" she squealed. "And this is all so cool. Maybe it's not the only one—maybe there are, like, ghost kittens? Do you think there might be ghost kittens? Could we keep one? Like, what would we do with ghost kittens? Is there like an SPCA or . . . wait . . ."

She looked at Mei's water, a look of dawning horror on her face. "Are we . . . ?" she said, swallowing. "Are we going to exorcise it?"

All right, that was enough. Mei needed space to do her work.

"Hey, Fizah," I said. "Can you help guard the entrance? No, the other one. We need you to watch and see if PS or DS pass by, and distract them if they want to come in. Can you do that?"

We had to get this done under the radar. If Rebecca found out we were doing exorcisms without official clearance and a risk management plan, there would be hell to pay.

Fizah parked herself dutifully at one of the doorways, but she looked a little glum, her earlier enthusiasm for the work dampened now that she knew what Mei meant to do. All this on her first day. I'd have to find a time later to explain that ghosts were just echoes, not conscious things, and exorcisms were less like murder and more like wiping a cassette tape. Not that someone her age would even know what a cassette tape was.

Throughout all this, the cat remained unconcerned by what we were doing. It blinked slowly at us, then rolled over in mid-air, exposing a fuzzy white belly.

That was when Mei threw the cup of water on it, and all hell broke loose.

The cat yowled and shot straight up, tail rigid and bushy with indignation. It bolted through the air, landing on the back of a couch before springing to a table, Mei's scarf getting caught in its scrabbling claws. Then it launched itself onto a shelf, knocking off a tower of plastic cups and piles of mismatched paper napkins. Amidst all the clattering, the cat took a moment to turn and scowl at us before walking with injured dignity through the back of the shelf. We watched as the scarf disappeared behind it.

It was *definitely* a ghost.

"It is not a ghost," Mei announced. "It is something else."

"It walked through a wall!" Fizah said. "I mean, that's a ghost thing, right?"

Mei shook her head, patting her hair back in place. "It is not a ghost. If it were, my Working would have dealt with it. Few ghosts can ignore the blessed waters or have enough physical presence to tear up a couch like that. Jimmy, Fizah, come with me. We must figure out what it is.

"We will find it," she declared, her sharp glare making clear her new personal vendetta. "I *will* get my scarf back."

I was just about to add "scarf retrieval" to my very reasonably sized mental task list when Jimmy lowered the broom and turned to me, his expression serious.

"Hey, uh, boss," he said. "Since I have you here. I got a signal earlier. Clementi, Block 375. Energy spike. Ghosty one."

I froze for a moment. Jimmy's morning dowsings didn't catch everything, but what they did catch we couldn't afford to ignore. Especially not in a residential housing district.

"Define *ghosty*," I said.

"I'm not sure. Something dead and left over, maybe? It showed up for a few minutes, then disappeared. Not like a normal haunting. Felt... deep, but not strong. Not old, not big. You know what I mean?"

"Nope." I pinched the bridge of my nose. "I'll go over there tomorrow morning and take a look."

Fizah was still staring at the spot where the ghost cat had vanished, looking shell-shocked and lost. Her notebook was clutched tightly in both hands.

"How do you feel about coming along?" I said.

She blinked at me. "Me? For real?"

"Yes, for real," I said. "Clementi, tomorrow. Ghosts aren't dangerous, and it sure beats sitting in the office on your second day. You're just there to observe, but you might learn something."

Jimmy snorted. "You'll learn that Ben is entirely too chipper in the morning."

Fizah's grin was so wide I briefly worried that she might spontaneously combust. "Thank you, Mr. Toh! I'd love to!"

I sighed, already regretting my decision. *Ghosty* was new, and the last time Jimmy had invented a new word to describe something weird, it had cost me three nights of sleep, four email reports, and one pair of perfectly good shoes.

Surely this couldn't be *that* bad.

CHAPTER TWO

I was operating on five hours of sleep when I arrived at Clementi. The whole intern and cat thing had thrown off my schedule the day before, so by the time I had finished up in the office and gotten home from the gym to the apartment I shared with my father, he was already asleep. In the relative quiet, without the distraction of small talk, I had ended up clearing a few more emails at the kitchen table. Someone had to protect the team against requests to sign up for this course, or to file your emails in this new way, or make a banner for Sports Day, all coming from well-meaning but overzealous colleagues.

Speaking of overzealous, I found Fizah already waiting for me at the site when I arrived, sitting at the playground on a plastic pogo-pony. The playground nestled in the open space between older flats, one of those modern designs with primary-coloured synthetic surfaces and spongy rubber flooring. A fort took pride of place in the middle, a series of raised platforms and low walls that allowed children to pretend at being medieval European knights. The wear marks and the scuffing on the equipment indicated that this playground was well-used and well-loved, but at this time of morning, with the kids in school, things were quite peaceful. A few domestic helpers were about, walking dogs, carrying groceries, taking the chance to catch up with friends. An older couple sat on the swings, giggling. Someone on the higher floors of one of the blocks was hanging up blankets to sun, laying them over the parapet of the common corridor, splotches of bright colour against the cream of the flats.

It was all very normal, suggesting that whatever occult thing Jimmy had detected was likely to be minor. Something good to ease Fizah into her first day of fieldwork.

She jumped to her feet when she saw me, leaving the pogo-pony to wobble absurdly behind her. "Mr. Toh! Oh no, I didn't know I had to dress so formal," she said. "Sorry, sorry, I can go home and change."

I looked at her, in her graphic tee and jeans, then down at myself. Tailored blue shirt, chinos, brown belt, sturdy Oxfords, navy blazer. I had fourteen sets of the same shirt and pants at home, and three sets of belts, shoes, blazers. It just kept things simple to rotate through them and not have to think about what to wear every morning. I supposed I was a little overdressed for today, and maybe would have taken off my blazer if I'd been alone. But now I was committed, so the blazer stayed on. "No, it's fine. Wear whatever you want. And call me Ben, please."

"Okay, sorry. What do we do now?"

"Let's go look around, see if we can figure out what's going on. Shall we?"

OAR—Observe. Analyse. Respond. That was the DEUS framework for field observations around deviant phenomena. There was even a very nice set of slides, featuring clip-art people rowing a kayak together, that showed how the OAR framework could help us navigate complex situations. Naturally, Jimmy and Mei ignored it despite my nagging, but today was a good opportunity to show Fizah how it was properly done.

First, *observe.* Pay attention to the small things—the iconography on dropped pamphlets offering salvation through Jesus. Footprints in the ash of burnt paper offerings. The presence of banana trees. Something would reveal itself. If you looked hard enough, something always did.

Fizah trailed me as I wandered around the area, just getting a feel for the place. HDBs, or public housing built by the Housing Development Board, were where the vast majority of Singaporeans lived. Common areas like this playground and park were the government's attempt to replicate the fabled olden times when Singapore was a fishing village and everyone was friendly and outgoing instead of hiding at home watching Netflix. Of course, the government never could resist an opportunity to educate, so there were little plaques everywhere explaining things—the name of this flowering shrub, which philanthropist sponsored this bench, what the fine is for littering. Walking around and pretending to read these signs gave us the perfect excuse to investigate everything.

We eavesdropped on the elderly couple, but based on what little I could understand with my rudimentary Cantonese, they were just trading dirty jokes. Nothing supernatural there, unless it was about how love could persist across decades. A group of four women jogged by, middle-aged, slightly out of shape, all wearing new shoes. They were sweating hard, footsteps heavy, clearly pushing themselves.

Fizah grunted once they were past.

"They have the same haircut. And they're wearing the same clothes," she said.

"What?"

"I mean, clothes from the same place."

"What?"

"Actually, those ones over there, too. And over there." She cocked an elbow to indicate another two clusters of women. "Love, Bonito."

"What?"

"It's, um, a Singaporean designer—"

"I know what it is. All of them?"

"Yeah. All newly bought on clearance, too—I thought I saw a tag. That's weird, right?"

"Yes. I think so. Let's think through this."

OAR. Next step was to *analyse.* I chewed on my lip, mentally scanned through the DEUS Fieldwork Playbook that I'd, as part of my duty, committed to memory. Similarity in dress was flagged in a subsection under Section 4A: "Indicators of Deviant Phenomena," with subcategories ranging from low-level cult activity (see Footnote 3) to metaphysically significant—

Out of nowhere, a deluge swept over us, an ocean of water dark and cold.

Sound vanished. We were submerged in crushing depths, the morning sunlight suddenly refracted and filtered to dim shadows as we drowned in an impossible sea. Brutal, chest-squeezing pressure. Cold. The taste of brine, burning my eyes and throat. Tugged by unseen currents in water that was somehow abstract, surreal, like from a nightmare, something from a different reality.

This colossal wave rolled over us, washed over the world, a long, slow ripple, alien and freezing, a lazy shrug in existence that turned everything strange. The world around us was sinking. Everything was deforming under a crushing tide. Beneath us, the sidewalk we were on twisted, curled down to somewhere unfathomably far away. A nearby tree split from the pressure, a crack like a gunshot, and inside were masses of roots or tentacles, massive as mountains, each strand somehow larger than the tree itself.

I tried to turn, to shield Fizah from whatever this was, but movement was for when the world made sense. I was suddenly and hideously aware that I was but a node of flesh, a polyp dangling in a deep and incomprehensible ocean, my too-many limbs spastic and flailing in cold currents. I was bloated and elongated across benthic dimensions, suspended like an insect in taffy. The air was simultaneously too thick and too thin. It was hard to breathe. And getting harder.

I'd heard people say that drowning was a good way to go. Peaceful, they said. But this felt anything but. There was no grace here, only the need for oxygen clawing from my chest with increasing madness, only my desperate and futile fight to place myself between Fizah and whatever this was.

In that frozen moment, something wavered above us. It was the floor with the brightly coloured blankets—the sixth storey, I counted—blurry and shifting as if we were looking at it through water. Another slow ripple, and it receded in a way my mind could not grasp. Like a sinkhole collapsing, but the perspectives were all wrong, like the horizon was too close. The blankets, the corridor, the flats on that floor, they grew distant, sank incomprehensibly into nothing, and vanished.

Nothing made sense.

Then.

The wave receded partially, and the pressure eased. Sound returned, but muffled, like when you have water in your ear. A dog barked. The sidewalk was only slightly skewed, mostly obeying the rules of Euclidean geometry. The split tree remained split, but inside it were merely regular-size splinters and torn wood.

A gasp, two. I could breathe.

The hammering of my heart slowed only when I saw that Fizah was next to me, wide-eyed, gasping but unharmed.

Thank god. I didn't know how I would have lived with myself otherwise.

But what had just happened? It was clearly no mere haunting. My brain raced. A natural phenomenon? The doing of a paranormal beast? Some sort of black magic? I didn't know. But whatever it was, it was something new, non-routine, and definitely dangerous. Bringing Fizah along, it turned out, had been a terrible idea. Guilt sprouted inside me, a familiar plant, but I quashed it. No time for that now.

"Should we go?" Fizah said. She was looking up at the missing sixth floor.

"No," I said. "Absolutely not. Go back to the office."

"I'm coming with you."

"I'm ordering you to go home."

"I don't care."

"What?"

"You can't order me to do anything. Um. Anyway, you might need help."

These goddamn Gen Z's, I swear. I thought about physically bundling her into a taxi and must have made some frustrated sound as I considered the logistics of kidnapping a teenager, even if it was for her own safety.

"I'll be careful," she said. "Promise."

I sighed, beaten. What else could I do? "You run the moment anything funny happens, okay? Don't be a hero."

We jogged over to the block with the missing sixth storey, though it felt like wading through shallow water. The noticeboard in the lift lobby was plastered with flyers. A poster from the town council warning residents about mosquitoes that carried dengue fever. Five or six different advertisements offering piano lessons for children. Someone with a lost parakeet. Fairly normal stuff, no real clues.

The lift smelled like bleach with a hint of old cigarettes, and the button for the sixth floor was missing, replaced by smooth metal. We hopped off at the fifth floor and hoofed it up the stairs. The plastic sign on the walls said 5, then up one flight of stairs, 7. Nothing in between. No seams in space-time, no portals, nothing. Just stairs and railings and then those two damn numbers. How do you investigate something that isn't there?

And then it was. The wave of unreality ebbed further, and the sixth floor re-emerged like a rock at low tide. Between one step and the next, it was just there, as if nothing had happened. The staircase contained a pair of someone's discarded slippers. The common corridor had someone's plants, and a bicycle locked to a rack, and some brightly coloured blankets draped over the parapet. A cat looked at us through the grille of someone's front gate. The only evidence of anything strange was a lingering smell of something sweet, almost rotten.

Of course, none of the residents remembered anything when Fizah and I spoke to them. They were friendly enough, and several invited us inside their homes when we said we were from the (made-up) Singapore Heritage Youth Community, interested in the history of the place. An older *makcik*, eyes enormous behind thick glasses, offered us freshly made kuehs, telling us about other people who had visited recently—some guy ("Like you, very handsome," she said) who was thinking of moving to the area, and also NEA officers who had been by recently to check for mosquitoes. Another auntie asked us, weirdly enough, where she could buy a piano. An old uncle gave us tea and told us about his grandchildren studying in Australia, his time as a firefighter with the Singapore Civil Defence Force, and his late wife's favourite stalls at the nearby hawker centres. It was all a lot of useless information, and nothing about the unreality wave that had swallowed parts of the urban landscape.

I mean, how do you even begin to ask about that? "Hello, ma'am, do you remember not existing for a few minutes earlier this morning?" What we needed, I realised, was someone who wasn't subject to the DKP effect. Someone who could remember what happened.

We needed an Other.

Others was what we called people like Fizah, Mei, Jimmy, or me. No one really knew who originally coined the term—it's been attributed to Rajaratnam, to Edwin Thumboo, to William Farquhar—the usual big names of Singaporean history. The way it was widely understood, correctly or not, was that it was based on CMIO—Chinese, Malay, Indians, Others—the racial classification first designed by the government as an administrative tool, quickly internalised by the public and ossified into identities. We, of course, were in the last category, which included *jiangshi*, diviners, and elves right alongside Eurasians, Filipinos, Arabs—all the ones who had to tick a special box and fill something in when they entered National Service or applied for an HDB. Over the decades, as different ethnicities found their identities as Singaporeans, *Others* had come increasingly to mean just those of us who lived halfway in the world of the supernatural.

And because we were halfway in, we couldn't ignore the strange things that regular people might overlook, and the DKP effect was muted on us. An Other would be able to give us more information about the wave.

"Come on," I said to Fizah. "Let's see if we can find someone who remembers something."

We walked downstairs and looked back out at the playground. The sun was a little higher now, starting to burn away the cool morning damp from the air. Fizah pointed towards a group of women huddled together, several of them with plastic bags of groceries. In the middle, half-hidden by the rest, was someone crying.

"They look fine," I said. There was no indication any of them were Others. And public displays of emotions like that . . . ugh.

"She's, like, freaking out," Fizah said. "And you said we had to pay attention to small things."

"Fine," I said, trotting over. "Could be dangerous. You wait here."

"Sorry, nope," Fizah said, and followed.

The person crying was a woman, a little younger than the ones around her, dressed in a loose T-shirt and paisley shorts. One of our migrant domestic helpers, if I had to guess. She squatted on the ground, sobbing, stroking a dog...or what used to be one. Extrusions like fingers erupted from the side of the poodle, and its back half seemed diminished in a way strangely hard to focus on. The dog was vomiting up what looked like water but clearly wasn't, likely the same unreal fluid that made up the wave earlier. I thought of that feeling of drowning, the sense of extra parts, of being extended. I thought of the sixth floor of the flats, withdrawing and disappearing. Was this what it was like to be taken by that wave?

The women around us steadfastly paid no attention to the dog's oddities, making calming sounds and speaking in what sounded like Bahasa.

"Are you okay? Did something happen?" I said, keeping my voice level, professional. Just find out what happened and move on. But no one paid me any attention.

Fizah squeezed past and knelt by the crying woman, taking her hand. She said a few soft words, then turned to me before giving a significant look at the ground. That's when I saw it—the tears never made it to the pavement, instead transforming into moths mid-air. This one, she was Other.

"Ask her what exactly she saw," I said.

Fizah ignored me, let the woman clutch at her hand too tight and gasp out some words.

"She says her employers don't see the sickness," Fizah said, translating for my benefit. "Won't let her take the dog to the *dukun*... the medicine man. She says it got worse each time."

"Each time? What do you mean each time?"

"She says—" But the rest of Fizah's translation was lost as the dog retched again, gave one last confused whimper, and slipped away before our eyes, front paws and head receding in the same way its back legs already had, the same way the flats had. In a moment, it was gone, and the young woman let loose a wail of grief.

I stiffened, useless. What do you even say in the face of this?

Then the woman started whispering something, voice dulled with loss. All I caught was *tiga*, *tiga*, *tiga*.

"What's she saying?" I asked. We needed to know.

"She says we mustn't tell her employer. She says..."

Fizah looked up at me, eyes wide with dismay.

"She says this was the third wave this month. She says the sea will come again, and sweep us all away."

CHAPTER THREE

Next to the office were a few shopping centres. Naturally. This was Singapore, where we had shopping centres the way other countries had forests and fields. If *The Lord of the Rings* had been set here, the journey to Mordor would have involved a lot more escalators and air conditioning.

These shopping centres all had their niches. One catered to people looking for high-tech gadgets and electronics, another to the Japanese diaspora. Yet another was filled entirely with stores that sold cameras, sound systems, and ritual implements—zoom lenses, subwoofers, small urns for home use, big urns for temples, prayer mats, crucifixes, crystal geodes, painted gods, reflexology charts. This last one always smelled like incense and piss, but it was our favourite. The kind of team that we were, with the kind of work that we did, we felt a kind of warm kinship with a place so strange and so incongruous with the modern vision of Singapore.

On the second floor of this mall, tucked away in the back

between a reiki practice and a gong shop, was a small eatery. It had four plastic tables and the coffee was a war crime, but it was open around the clock and had very adequate biryani. It also had a small window, which was useful for reminding us when it was dark outside and that we should go home. This little place was our go-to for team meetings, and sometimes we would spend hours there under those fluorescent lights, convincing ourselves that maybe the coffee was actually only a minor infringement to human rights and arguing about the best way to respond to an email from senior management.

This time, it was just Jimmy and me, catching a quick discussion before I had to go for my late-afternoon meetings. Earlier, I'd taken Fizah to Dr. Kamini and Mei, the former to check her for physical aftereffects of yesterday's incident, the latter to check for supernatural aftereffects. Mei had then taken advantage of Fizah's presence to try using Fizah's jinn energies for a tracking spell for the missing scarf, which was why the two of them were off in some meeting room doing magic.

"Fifty bucks says they'll trip the fire alarm," Jimmy said, sipping his coffee.

I considered my own and thought about whether I was desperate enough to drink it yet. I wasn't. "Mei knows better than that."

"She's never used a live jinni before. Can you imagine? Don't you want to—"

"No," I said, already pretty worried about it. "Absolutely

not. Can we get back to this?" I gestured at the heap of off-brand Ziploc bags on the table, nestled in the space between our laptops and coffee cups. Each bag contained something small I had filched from the Clementi incident site, fodder for Jimmy to do his thing. A splinter of wood from a ruptured tree. Some rust scraped from a bicycle spoke. Sand from the playground. A more professional department with an actual budget might have used actual evidence bags, I guess, based on what I see on TV, but this was just DEUS. We made do with cheap bags from the supermarket.

Jimmy poked at one of them, brought it up to his nose, and grimaced. "These all smell funny. I don't know how to describe it. Like the sea. Like they're... damp."

My turn to make a face.

"Damp. Like, you know, moist."

"Stop it."

"But seriously, these feel like they'd been submerged. Somewhere deep."

It made sense, inasmuch as anything did. The experience had felt like drowning, and the dog-lady had talked about some current. But what sort of water swallows dogs and HDB flats, and feels wet only to psychics? The DEUS databases might have something helpful.

"Have you checked—"

"Binder Two? Yes, obviously," Jimmy said. "I spent all day looking, while you were taking Fizah to Dr. Kamini. System must have crashed on me twenty times. What's the point of making us do all this filing and note-taking if the stupid search doesn't work? It's ridiculous."

"Okay, okay, I know. Find anything useful?"

What was unspoken was that our databases were barely worthy of the name. Even putting aside the inadequacies of the last-decade software, the information we had in there was pathetically meagre. Sure, we had thousands of filed minutes of meetings and Steering Committee decisions and programme after-action reviews, but real data about Others? Like, say, statistics on frequency of deaths resulting in *hantus* versus reincarnation versus moving on? Or a needs analysis of gaps in our service provision? Nothing at all. We just didn't have the resources. No time to read the books put out by the more esoteric publishers, no funding to commission research by the more open-minded professors of sociology, no mandate to get the data we needed from other Ministries and Statutory Boards. We made do as best we could with Mei's knowledge and Jimmy's sensitivity. Still, we had to check Binder Two, just as part of due process.

Why Binder *Two*, you ask? Binder One was a stone. Well, a magic stone that could literally bind you to oaths, something we reserved for emergencies. There was no Binder Three.

"Actually," Jimmy said, "I found a few old reports of similar incidents. There was that guy importing 'Monkey King Invisibility Pills' from Hong Kong, back when the martial arts movie industry was big there. Apparently they worked—really well—but came with a side effect of mischief, so we had to ban them. Or, going further back, the whole *koro* thing in the sixties. You know the one, with people thinking that their genitals were vanishing."

"This incident isn't a penis, Jimmy. And it wasn't a case of invisibility. The whole HDB floor wasn't there. The dog was trailing weird tendrils, and at the end it was just *gone*."

"If it wasn't there, then it wasn't visible, was it? Wouldn't that mean, then, that it was invisi—"

"Stop, Jimmy. This is serious."

He sobered. "What do you think this is, boss? Deep ocean, massive power... a sea god?"

"That's the right level of strength, but Block 375 isn't close to any major body of water. And why that one particular floor? What were those tendrils or roots or whatever they were? The specificity has got to mean something. What was it you said you sensed, when you sent us there? That it was 'ghosty'?"

"Oh yeah. That spot on the map had felt like... like something should be dead there but isn't quite. Felt it again when I checked this morning."

This didn't make sense. No ghost would be strong enough to cause the sort of large-scale phenomenon we observed. Or at least, I corrected myself, no single human ghost. An organised legion of the dead? The fading echo of some fallen deity? I considered for a moment the possibility that these were separate things, the ghost and the unreality wave, but dismissed it. Occam's razor and all—don't multiply entities beyond necessity. But I really didn't have confidence or clarity in my deductions. There was just so little information. No choice, though—I couldn't let the lack of quality information hamstring us.

"Let's focus on looking for a ghost," I said, taking a gulp of the coffee and regretting it immediately. "Or ghosts, localised to a particular block and floor in Clementi, and connected to the sea in some way. Can you poke around online and see if you can build up a list of people who live in that block? Especially people with family members who've passed away, *especially* if they died at sea. I'll draft up emails to HDB and the Marine Coast Guard, see if they can send us records."

I wasn't hopeful about this last part. Data privacy laws meant it would be months of back-and-forth before they decided we didn't need that information.

"Sure thing," Jimmy said. "Is this like... *urgent* urgent? Because I still have those notes I have to finish up from yesterday's SMM, and you-know-who will be pissed if we're late on those."

Rebecca. Our boss. She loved her senior management meetings, and always wanted more time with the minutes so she could edit them to make herself sound insightful. If we didn't get those to her as soon as she'd like, she'd want to know why, and then she would find out it was because we were working on this Clementi incident. She'd overreact for sure and blame it on her bogeyman of the week, whichever group of "dangerous Others" she'd decided were to blame for everything, evidence be damned. And then we would have to come up with new regulations to clamp down on Other activity, just so something like this doesn't happen again. Never mind the cost on justice or equality, or the fact that these policies would make the communities more suspicious of us and our engagement work more difficult.

On the other hand, if we didn't get a handle on the Clementi thing and it blew up, Rebecca would hear about it anyway.

"You know how it is," I said. "Everything is urgent. Why don't you focus on the SMM notes first, get that out of the way..." Just then, my phone buzzed once, twice, but I studiously ignored it. I was trying to divide up the work fairly. "I'll get started on that list of residents and those emails to agencies. Then I have to go for that IT briefing for middle managers, but after that I can— *What?*"

Jimmy was peering at my phone from across the table and making a big show of waggling his eyebrows. I glanced down at it—Adam was calling, his picture smouldering at me. And it was definitely a smoulder. On our first date (a few months ago now), he had asked to choose his own picture for my contact list, and had picked something from his own social media, a photograph of him emerging like Aphrodite from the ocean somewhere with white sands and blue waters. It was, I'll admit, a heck of a picture.

Jimmy was mouthing "pick up, pick up," so I glared at him again and picked up the call. My tirade had already been interrupted, anyway.

"Hey," I said. "What's up?"

"Hey, mister! You ignored my text, so now I'm escalating. Anyway, we're playing tonight—that band I pretend to be cool in? It's at Mohamed Sultan. You should come!"

"Oh wow," I said, somewhat awkwardly with Jimmy right there. "Yeah, that's awesome. But, I don't know. I've got... um, work."

"Aw c'mon, just come! We'll even play some of that basic bro music you like, just for you. Ed Sheeran or something."

We had bonded over a shared love for superheroes, trashy fantasy novels, and Disney music on our first date, him making fun of my love for outer space and me making fun of his obsession with cheese. I had made the terrible mistake of telling him I kinda liked that one Ed Sheeran song.

"I'd love to, I really would. But I can't."

He was quiet for a few heartbeats. "That's all right," he said. "Good luck with your work thing. But I'd really like to see you soon, okay?"

This guy. We had matched on a dating app, then discovered that we had gone to the same secondary school but just never really noticed each other back then. He was a photographer and personal trainer and football coach for kids, from an old-money family. He did rock climbing and scuba diving for fun and I was just a boring bureaucrat, but we somehow really hit it off. It'd only been a few months, but it felt like it was going somewhere. And that felt exciting, if not mildly terrifying.

"So..." Jimmy said. "Is that the guy? Adam?"

"It's none of your business."

"Is he Malay? He looks Malay."

"Still none of your business."

"Do you two work out together? Because... Okay, none of my business, I know. But you should go tonight. In fact, I want to come, too. I love live music."

"What?" Was he reading my mind? This was totally unaccepta—

"Your volume was turned up very loud. I heard everything."

"We need to work," I said, tapping on my laptop touchpad to wake it back up. On the screen, the galaxies of the Hubble Ultra Deep Field glimmered at me.

Jimmy rolled his eyes. "Look. I know you'll have the emails done and the Excel sheet filled out in the next hour. Then you'll be checking your inbox twice a minute, even though you know HDB and the Coast Guard won't get back to you by today. You'll just sit and fret and get nowhere."

Not true. Sometimes I stand and fret.

"I'll go back to Clementi," I said. "Talk to more people, see if—"

"After your meetings? At, what, seven? Eight? You want to deal with a haunting just as the sun is setting? Anyway, no one will believe you're on legit government business if you knock on their door at night."

I hated it, but he was right. It made sense to hit Clementi tomorrow. For today, all we could do was sit on our hands and twiddle our thumbs, though probably not in that order.

Also, it would be nice to see Adam again.

"Come on," Jimmy said. He must have picked up on my wavering resolve. "I have the scent now, from all those moist things you found, and I'll keep my nose out for sea ghosts. Promise. Oh, and the wife and kiddos are off in Bali for the week, so I really want to get a drink, just us guys. And you can introduce me to your new man, ya?"

"Okay, fine. The plan is you tell me the moment you smell anything, right?"

"Yes, boss." Jimmy raised his hand to his forehead and waggled his fingers at me. "If I get the tinglies, you'll be the first to know. But for now, I'll go back to the office to finish up those SMM notes. Send them to you by end of day, okay?"

I nodded. "I'll text you the name of the place. See you tonight."

With Jimmy gone and the proprietor off in the back doing whatever it was she did, I was the only one in the eatery. The fluorescent lights overhead were steady and bright, my coffee on the table was untouched and cold, and next door, someone was testing out gongs. No one would have called the place charming, bucolic, or even quaint, but it was familiar and oddly comforting.

The plastic chair creaked alarmingly as I leaned back and rubbed my eyes. A deep breath, an exhale, and I sank into the Garden in my soul.

We all have spaces in our souls. If you looked inside, you

would find it—the place where all your hopes and fears and wonderings are, where you hide the pain of heartbreak and the scars you can't show to the world. It's the hole where that catchy song you can't stop thinking about takes root; it's that channel through which a memory of your first pet can still reach through like vines and grip you by the heart.

For most of us, our private places are graveyards of scraggly weeds. Old dreams wither on the vine, unwatered, unplucked, untasted. Ideals we had as children—I will grow up to be a baker! A police officer! Do something meaningful with my life!—those rot on the ground, untended and untrue. What grows, what occupies that space, are other people's ideas and feelings, scripts from rom-coms and images of happiness from magazines. And so, we go through the motions of living, we smile for the cameras, but we know that inside us everything is fake, just a parody of life.

I know because I used to be like that, too. All Gardeners start this way, as normal people. But then some Incident happens. Sometimes, it's loss—a young person suffers catastrophic heartbreak; an athlete gets diagnosed with breast cancer. Sometimes it's an epiphany—a doctor learns she's not good at her job; a boy realises he's a bad friend. Always, it's a weight too crushing to bear. Usually, people break. But rarely, very rarely, instead of breaking, they find a way *inside* themselves, even as their world is collapsing around them, *because* their world is collapsing around them. And they stoop over the gravel of their souls and pound it to dust with their anger.

They water it with their tears, and in that newly fecund earth something of themselves grows. Roots draw bitter waters and transmute them into branches that hold up the sky. The space inside them that used to be a wasteland is now a Garden, and they are Gardeners.

Gardening is internal magic, so it's not particularly flashy. It is the skill to shape the elements and energies of your own soul, to cultivate what the Hasidic mystics call *sephirot* and the Daoists call *qi*. At the most fundamental level, it lets you conquer fear, grow virtues, and, through the nexus between the soul and the body, make yourself physically stronger, more resilient. Beyond this, each Gardener is different, choosing what they grow in themselves. I'd heard stories of Gardeners in history who grew monstrous trees of Faith or Charisma, the wars they started or ended, the lives they saved or destroyed.

There are cultural variations, the archives suggest, in what Gardeners grow. The Anglo-Saxon West makes a fetish of strength and size, tending towards solitary giants, single dominating redwoods or pines that represent a singular sort of personal excellence—Strength or Invincibility were common ones. The Chinese prefer to cultivate groves of willow and bamboo and peach blossom, supple trees with subtle alchemical resonances of more subtle virtues—Propriety, Fortune, Adaptability. Through their masonic lodges and secret societies, their *bang* and *pai*, these secrets of Gardening are passed down from each generation to the next.

But the white men never brought their most valuable high arts when they came to Singapore as colonisers, and the Chinese and Indians who came as migrants were poor, not privy to the secrets of soul cultivation. And so, the ways of soul-gardening in Southeast Asia, in the peninsulas and archipelagos, in the islands and the jungles, evolved as they always had—liminal, uncategorised, and from the perspective of the outside world, strange.

For all my English-language education and the media I consume, I'm a boy of the tropics. Here, beneath the equatorial sun, only dead things grow according to plan, and so what grew in my soul and held me together was nothing manicured, nothing pretty—not the curated monocultures and trimmed topiary that gave Gardeners our name, but instead the crazed diversity, the profusion of forms, that was familiar to me. Rainforest and mangrove.

I sank into myself, the locus of my attention shifting inside to my jungle, lit by a sky eternally noon, familiar and comforting—rattan, climbers, ferns, the soil muddy underfoot with the droppings of some unseen mousedeer, air heavy with brine and humidity and insects. It was vast, wild, more than I could explore in a lifetime, but every part I had ever seen had felt intimately familiar, and the techniques of cultivation and growth had come intuitively.

For a while, I tended to my soul. My will was water and sunlight, and I nudged additional growth from those parts of me that were important. That thicket of *Avicennia* at my borders, pencil roots rising, was an extension of my willpower, the first line of defence against darker impulses. There, that swarm of gnats, that was a collection of all the bits of information I had collected about Others and the supernatural world. In the forms of root and leaf and branch, I cultivated virtues I sought to grow, skills I was learning, recollections of things I wanted to keep, the garden of my soul.

Then my will was axe and fire, and I pruned back some of the wildness, some of the branches that threatened to spread out of control. I withered away weeds that had taken root, ideas from the outside that wanted a foothold, the collected detritus of stray distractions and intrusive thoughts. Here was one, leaves heavy and fleshy, a weed that was a spark of interest in an offer from a *ba jiao gui* for winning lottery numbers, no strings attached. Here was another, growing fast, a fragment of memory of a sob story we had heard from one of the Clementi residents, something about the guy's late wife. These things, greed and sentimentality, were not things I needed in my life, and so I passed the fires of my attention over them, and they shrivelled up and disintegrated. All except for one.

It was a familiar, stubborn plant, coarse and thorny, from the Incident. I didn't want to deal with it, but I knew it would grow if I didn't take care of it. It would return, in any case. I focused on it, and it started to smoke. Memories unfurled, unwelcome. The skitter of a small rock as I kick it along the sidewalk. The smell of my mother's medicine as she asks me a gentle question, and the shame that gags me.

Then the plant was burned away, and the memories were gone. For now.

A call from my father pulled me from my meditation. The proprietor, I noticed, had quietly cleared my cup of coffee.

"*Ba*," I said. "What's the matter?"

"You're very busy." It was a statement, establishing a fact to help us both avoid the shoals of a much more complicated conversation.

"Yes. Work, as usual."

An awkward silence followed, and I could feel the weight of his request before he even made it.

"I was thinking, if you're not too busy, maybe we could have dinner together tonight?" he finally asked, tentative.

I suppressed a surge of irritation. *I just said I was busy*, I thought to myself, but that wasn't fair to him. But I did have Adam's thing to go for.

"I don't know," I said, the resentment unfurling into guilt. "Sorry. I have a lot of work to do, and I'm going out afterwards. Maybe tomorrow?"

"Oh, I see. It's okay. I'll eat dinner myself. Don't work too hard."

"Okay."

I hung up first.

CHAPTER FOUR

I don't know what sort of magic they use, but bars are always dark. Even with all the lights blazing, even with all the mirrors on the walls reflecting neon signs, there's something about bars that collects shadows. Perhaps it's some connection between wine and secrets, or perhaps it's that darkness best gives us the freedom to be honest, and these seep into the foundations of such places. Stones remember.

My last meeting of the day was cancelled, so I arrived early—fashionably early, I call it. There was still a bit of daylight left in the sky, but even then, the bar managed to keep that out and remain cool and dim inside. It was my first time there, so I took a moment to take it in—everything was in shades of walnut and bronze and teal, and the tables and bar were solid wood rather than cheap aluminium or plastic. Something jazzy played from concealed speakers. From the ceiling hung small yellow bulbs, each enclosed in glass in the distinctive shapes of liquor bottles, the refracted light playing on the walls. In the air was a faint hint of wood smoke, perhaps from some pizza oven in the back, quite pleasant.

I had just assumed that Adam played at neighbourhood dive bars, but this was surprisingly classy. Even the bartenders looked like models—there was a tall woman with a glittering nose-stud piercing washing and drying glasses with fierce focus, and a girl, much younger, dividing limes into wedges with very professional cuts. They gave me identical scowls as I got a craft beer, then roundly ignored me as I parked myself at a table in the corner.

Say what you want, but there are benefits, like free tables, to being early.

I'm here, I texted Adam.

His reply was a string of hearts followed by several musical instrument emojis. Won't be there till the set, his message said. I'll come find you.

Well, I had time, then. I opened up my laptop, logged on to the office VPN, and worked on clearing emails while the bar slowly filled up.

And fill up it did, with a range of people. Near me was a table of middle-aged women, gorgeous and elegant, sipping on cocktails and eyeing all the younger men with predatory interest. At a different time of my life, I wouldn't have said no, but I was here for Adam, after all. When they sent a few looks my way, I kept my eyes on my beer until they eventually got the hint. There were also a few couples, and more than a few people who were there by themselves, some on their phones, some trying to chat up the bartenders. And of course, just as there would be anywhere else, there was a scattering of Others.

Some of us pass, as it's sometimes called—it's short for "pass for normal." I pass, for example, because you wouldn't know I was a Gardener if you looked at me. I look just like a regular guy.

But not everyone is so lucky to have their Otherness contained on the inside. A group of young men came in soon after I did, rowdy, all with the *botak* haircuts of Basic Military Training. Two of them had jutting fangs and a green tinge to their skin—minor tells, but enough to make people around them tense up without quite knowing why. Not long after, a woman showed up, no legs, no lower half of her torso, just entrails dangling loose. The DKP effect kept the crowd from realising what they were seeing, but it didn't erase the unease that followed her like a shadow. Conversations faltered as she passed, the brittle politeness of people trying not to notice.

I wondered, sometimes, what that must be like, to feel the world bristle against you, turn its face from you, reject you without even knowing you. I wondered what it was like to be a rogue comet, fierce and precious and beautiful but unwanted by any star system, drifting alone through a lifetime of darkness.

I glanced at the woman with the entrails as she hovered near the bar—*manananggal*, if I guessed right. For a moment, I thought about going over, saying something kind, not as DEUS, but just as myself. But what would I even say? She didn't need someone like me fumbling for the right words, trying to fix something I didn't understand.

So I stayed where I was, one more person pretending not to notice.

I turned my attention back to the room. Those who didn't pass were DEUS's most visible stakeholders, but those who did were in our care as well. And passing was never perfect—if you looked hard, you could catch the tells. The large lady with beautiful hair, for instance, before whom the queues to the bar or to the restrooms always mysteriously scattered. Someone in a hoodie, sneaking pretzel sticks to a muttering creature nestled in their backpack. A pale man sitting in the corner, sipping on a glass of red wine that seemed a little too viscous.

Him, I knew, actually. Senior Doctor at Tan Tock Seng Hospital, some sort of infectious diseases specialist, one of Mei's contacts. I'd read her reports, about how he'd helped us a few times to disseminate information on new policies relevant to his community, most recently around requirements to check on vaccination status before feeding. It was probably worth keeping that relationship warm, and I was morbidly curious as to how he ordered his drink.

I was about to get up, go over and introduce myself, when a flourish of chords bloomed from the piano and Adam sauntered onto the stage. Dark jeans, loose floral shirt, hair artfully tousled, he paused under the lights, head lowered as if gathering himself, then closed his eyes and let the first notes spill out. Adele. No preamble, no jokes, just his voice filling the space: masculine, gorgeous, nakedly vulnerable.

I sat back down. The senior doctor was forgotten. I was utterly transfixed.

As was the crowd, who hushed almost immediately. Adam was good—very good. The music held us, pierced us. For a long moment, then another, then another, all we could do was listen, hearts gored open, all of us entranced by a voice that seemed both intimate and keyed to the resonances of a world larger and deeper than our own. Then, he smiled, took a breath, and the spell broke. Light and sound returned to the room, and he was just a good-looking guy with nice vocals in a pretty fancy bar.

I noticed him scanning the room, so I raised my mug to catch his attention. When he spotted me, his face broke into the most idiotic grin, and to my complete mortification, he waved. I was saved from the horror of crowd attention only because he almost knocked his mic stand over.

Jimmy found me a few songs in. He had clearly come directly from the office, with his rumpled shirt and laptop bag, the latter of which he dropped heavily on the table.

"I can't do it," he groaned, slumping into the seat across from me. "These SMM notes, they are going to kill me."

He ranted for a while, treading over familiar ground. We'd all faced the misery of writing notes for senior management meetings, where our glorious leaders pronounced their opinions in turbulent, unfiltered streams of consciousness, and we, the Delphic sibyls of our age, had to translate them into meaningful records that showcased the sagacity of the speakers. A truly unreasonable amount of work went into finding ways to make them sound intelligent, all so they could read the notes, marvel at their own wisdom, and perhaps deign to exert a little more effort next time. Fingers crossed.

"Hey, hey," I interrupted mid-sentence. "Listen. Don't worry about finishing that tonight. Actually, you know what—just send me what you have, and I can deal with it and send it to Rebecca for clearance." It was the decent thing to do—after all, Jimmy had a wife and kids to spend time with.

Then I remembered that he'd said his family was in Bali, but it felt too late to retract the offer without being an asshole.

"Are you sure?"

I nodded, waving it away.

"Thanks, boss!" he said. "Let me go get you a drink!"

And he was gone before I could tell him there were wait staff around to take orders.

I flagged down a waitress and got a menu. I was pretty sure Jimmy had come here without eating dinner, so I figured I would get some finger food for him. And so it was that I was deciding between locally sourced char-siew nachos and artisanal duck sliders when I felt an arm drape around my shoulders, warm and unexpected.

"Hello, stranger," Adam said. His voice was low and a little husky from use, and he smelled nice. "Getting something to eat?"

"Hey, you."

He leaned his weight on me, beamed at the waitress, and pointed at the menu. "Let's do both. The nachos and sliders, and can you add a side of those mozzarella sticks? Put it on my tab, ya? He's with me."

"Oh, am I?"

"Stick with me. There are benefits," he said with a laugh. "Thanks for coming, by the way."

"No, thanks for the invite. I'm glad I came. This place is nice." I hesitated, knowing I needed to say more, wanting to say more. But there was a vine inside me, tangling up my thoughts, gripping my throat, and I just couldn't get the words out.

"You guys are... not bad," I finished, the words sounding flat and inadequate even to myself.

Adam's grin faltered slightly. "Just not bad?" he asked.

I hated this about myself, how I couldn't give compliments, especially to people close to me. It was, I knew, a knot of insecurity, a loop of worries that snagged and tangled in my brain. What if he thinks it's stupid? What if it sounded like pathetic flattery? *What if I came across needy?*

The vine swelled, tightened, and for a moment, I almost gave up and let it choke me. But then, with effort, I burned it down, the ashes still smouldering as I forced myself to speak.

"Sorry, I'm not good at this," I said, temporarily braver than usual. "It was amazing, actually. Just... wow. It's not even fair—how are you so talented at this, too?"

His smile returned. I wasn't sure, what with the dim light, but he might have blushed. It was adorable, and I was about to make fun of him for it when Jimmy returned, a beer in each hand.

"This is Jimmy," I said. "He's a colleague. Jimmy, Adam. Adam, Jimmy."

"Nice to meet you," Jimmy said. "Ben's told me a lot about you!"

I hadn't, but before I could protest, the piano started up again, a few experimental chords. Adam gave Jimmy a quick smile, then turned back to me, his hand squeezing my shoulder briefly. "I gotta get back for the next set. See you after the show?"

"Yeah," I said, and watched him walk away. It was a nice view.

"You know, you are the worst wingman," I said, turning to Jimmy. That was when I noticed that he was frozen, pale, his knuckles white around his beer.

"What's wrong with you?"

Jimmy didn't look at me. He didn't even blink. "Remember that moist feeling we talked about earlier?" His voice was tight, strangled. "From the Clementi stuff?"

I frowned, sitting up straighter. "Yeah, so?"

"Did you bring any of that with you?"

I rummaged through my bag and pulled out one of the pieces of evidence. This one was a few bits of bark from the broken tree in a Ziploc (well, off-brand, but close enough for government work) bag. I held it up to Jimmy.

He stared right at it, his nose wrinkling as if he were sniffing something just out of reach. Then, slowly, his eyes drifted past the bag, across the room. I followed his gaze as it moved, tracing an invisible thread that stretched farther, farther, until—

The stage.

Adam.

Jimmy's breath hitched. "Oh no."

"What?" I couldn't—

He swallowed hard. "I'm not sure. But it's him. I've been sniffing, like you told me to. The same ocean smell, but even stronger. More intense. It's coming from him, Ben."

"Wait. You're saying—what? Adam's connected to Clementi?"

Jimmy hesitated. "More than that. The strength of what I'm sensing . . . I don't think he's a victim. Or a bystander. He's Other." He took a shaky breath. "I think he's the *source*."

There was a roaring in my ears, and at some point a great hollow had opened in the pit of my stomach. This was absurd. Jimmy had to be wrong. There had to be another explanation. It was literally my job to tell when someone was Other. There were always signs, little inconsistencies that didn't add up. But Adam? Adam, who liked sushi and Disney songs, who cried at movies, could also erase reality? Why wasn't that last one on his Tinder profile?

I pushed down the beginnings of a manic laugh and forced myself to focus. Think. Breathe. OAR—Observe. Analyse. Respond. I clung to it like a lifeline.

Step one: Observe.

Observe had four components, again in a helpful government acronym. SPEED—Sensory, Precedents, Extrasensory, Engage, Distil. One step at a time. Procedures were made precisely for situations like this.

Sensory. Use your eyes, use your ears. I glanced back at

Adam, still onstage, his head tilted as he poured himself into song. He looked... normal. Just Adam.

But that didn't mean anything. Passing meant unseen, not harmless. I knew that better than most.

Precedents. What do we already know? I leaned on the table and lowered my voice. "You said the Clementi phenomenon wasn't in Binder Two, right?"

Jimmy nodded. "Nothing like this registered. Nothing like... him registered. He's... an unknown."

An unknown. Binder Two contained our valiant attempts to catalogue known Other types, assessed and tiered for public safety and socioeconomic contribution potential. Unregistered entities weren't just gaps in the system—they were blind spots, threats we couldn't measure, threats we didn't know how to counter.

The nachos and sliders arrived just then, but neither of us had much of an appetite.

Extrasensory. Jimmy had already picked up the scent. The question wasn't whether Adam was connected to the Clementi case, but how deep his involvement went.

Engage. Using a risk management approach, obtain further data points from the relevant entities through conversation. After that would come *Distil.* Extract the relevant pieces of key insights for analysis.

"Let me talk to him," I said once the waitress left. "Find out what's going on." Distantly, I felt like I was going to throw up, and had to focus to shut down the nausea. I had work to do.

"It'll be dangerous," Jimmy said. "He could be the sea ghost we've been looking for."

"He's not a sea ghost," I said. "Does he look like a sea ghost?"

"Well, no, but—"

"You go home. I'll handle this."

Jimmy valued family and being there for his wife and daughters, and I respected that a lot. We had an unspoken agreement that he never got put in risky situations.

He hesitated, his beer clutched tightly in his hand. Then he drained it in one long gulp. "Be careful," he said as he walked away, laptop bag slung over one shoulder.

I didn't watch him leave. My eyes were on Adam, still onstage, face half-turned to the light as he sang about lost love and not moving on. Somehow, the best guy I'd met in a long time had become the epicentre of an unreality wave that swallowed people and deleted architecture. I couldn't let myself forget that.

Every now and again, Adam would look my way and smile his stupidly beautiful smile at me, warm and unguarded. My stomach churned, and I was too uneasy to reciprocate. Instead, I counted fire extinguishers. Tallied the bystanders I might need to evac if things went south. Ranked them by mobility and distance from the exits. Catalogued lines of egress. That was the job—thinking three steps ahead, even when your heart was cracking.

And still, something else festered inside me, a plant I couldn't name. Not just confusion, not just exhaustion, but also fear, anger, resentment, all tangled together. Was it Adam? For doing whatever it was he was doing with Clementi, for not telling me?

Was it at myself? For the hypocrisy of expecting Adam to come clean about being Other, when I hadn't told him myself?

Adam must have caught the tension radiating off me like a heatwave. When his set was over, his bow to the crowd was half-hearted, and he hopped off the stage to come over, ignoring his exuberant bandmates' call for a celebratory drink.

"Hi," he said, unsure, trying to smile. "Is everything okay? Did... did I do something wrong?"

How could I answer that? My mouth was dry, and my chest hurt. For one aching moment, I wanted to reach out and say, *No, everything's fine. Your set was great.* But the words caught on something inside, jagged and unwelcome as duty.

"Can we talk?" I managed to choke out. "Outside?"

We stepped out into the back alley, lined with garbage cans and lit by harsh lamps. A few people milled around—mostly customers and employees, some smoking, some just taking a break and checking their phones. The only sounds came from the muted chatter from inside the bar and the rhythmic dripping of air-conditioning units.

A muscular woman in a tracksuit eyed us from where she was leaning against a wall, then took a pull from her cigarette and looked away, seemingly disinterested. My hackles rose, suddenly alert to danger. Was she shadowing us? Watching us? But no, that was absurd. I was just looking for an excuse, any excuse, to not have this conversation.

I put the woman out of my mind. Adam and I stood in silence for a while, not looking at each other. The weed inside was thick in my throat. I couldn't find the right way to start, and he seemed afraid to ask what was going on.

Finally, he spoke up, voice low and uncertain. "Look, Ben, if I did something to upset you, I'm sorry. I don't know what I did, but I want to make it right."

His vulnerability twisted a knife in my gut. It was hard to breathe, as if the unreality wave in Clementi had followed me here. I didn't want to know his answer. But people were at risk, and I couldn't afford the luxury of sentiment, so I had to be cold. Hard. Stating just the facts.

"Jimmy and I are investigating an incident. I want to know if you're involved."

He blinked once. Twice. "An incident?"

"Clementi. Things vanished there, yesterday. People too."

The words hung in the air, and Adam hesitated, confusion flickering across his face. "Like... someone stole things?"

"No."

"And you think I'm... involved."

"Yes. Are you?"

Adam stepped back slightly, searching my face for something he didn't find. "Wait, what? Are you talking about the ripple? You think I *caused* that? Ben, what are you even—"

I leaned forward, cutting him off. "We're not guessing," I said. No room for feeling. No room for anything but the facts. "Jimmy traced it back to you. What's your role in all this?"

"I— Ben, no. I didn't cause this. I—" His eyes narrowed, and the confusion began to shift, hardening into something more guarded. "How do you know about that? Is this your government job, that you're always so vague about? Is it work, or...?"

"Yes, it's work." I tried to stay professional, but my voice was tight. Sharper than I meant. So he *did* know. And then the totally unreasonable thought—why hadn't he just told me?

Adam turned away, dragging a hand through his hair. The silence pooled, rising like the tides, threatening to drown me. I wanted him to say something, anything, but the quiet settled, pressing against me.

When he finally turned back, his jaw was tight, and I was almost glad to see anger in his eyes. I didn't know how to deal with silence, but anger—anger I could fight. I marshalled my arguments, my evidence, my own anger a thick and thorny bramble sprouting inside.

"Is this why you came for the show?" he said, and my anger wilted, defeated. I was wrong. He wasn't angry. The edge in his tone, the set of his shoulders—that was hurt, right out there on the surface, raw. He didn't hide it like I would have.

"No, listen—"

"Are you so obsessed with work you can't even just, for one evening..." He swallowed hard, trailed off. Then, more softly, "Is that what I am to you? An investigation?"

"Adam," I said. The only thing keeping my voice steady was the strength of the trees I'd cultivated in my soul. "Jimmy felt it once he met you. We know you're involved." I knew I sounded colder than I meant to, but I had to know.

"Ben, I—" he said, looking away, down at the wet concrete.

Again the silence dragged. His guilt was obvious.

"Why?" My anger grew once more, irrational and unfair, this time intertwined with frustration, with betrayal. A few people turned to look at us, and I forced my voice back down. "What are you doing? What are you mixed up in? You know people could die."

He met my eyes, and I could see hurt and resolve in the set of his lips.

"I'll explain. It's not what you think, I promise. But can... can we not do it here?"

Every instinct I had told me that he wasn't the bad guy, but I shoved them away. Instincts were easily co-opted by irrelevant details, like how unhappy he looked right then or how I felt about him. I coldly parsed the pros and cons of various locations, evaluating risks and defensive options.

Most public places were out. Too risky. Too many people. A deserted beach? No, too much water—the sea or the water table might empower whatever ocean-based powers he had. The office? Not situated, as it was, on a node of dark resonance.

There was one other option. Where I lived—a new condo development I'd bought with my father, and most of my neighbours hadn't moved in yet. And it was my home, which gave me a powerful defence against certain sorts of sorcery. God, what if he hurt my father? What if I wasn't strong enough to subdue him, if it came to that? I shoved the spiralling thoughts aside. *Focus, Ben.* The condo—I could work with that.

"All right," I said. "My place."

CHAPTER FIVE

The ride home was torture. We couldn't do what we both wanted to do, which was to tease each other and laugh and argue about which of the ThunderCats was the best one, like we had always done. Instead, this thing hung between us, this mix of need and anger and not-quite-betrayal that made my chest tight and made him look out the window the whole way. I wanted to say something to make it better, to fix things, but the words just wouldn't come.

As a Gardener, I could tend my own soul and draw strength from within, but in moments like this, I wondered if that inward focus was a curse as much as a gift. Maybe it made me too self-reliant, too proud to ask for help, even when I was floundering. And when I floundered—like now—I did what I imagined every Gardener did best: I turned inward and overthought everything.

Lost in our own hurts, we sat in silence as the streetlights streamed by, each one lonely in the dark.

It was almost midnight when we arrived. The condo loomed over us, rows of identical balconies stretching up into the night sky. It was a new development, but not the most exclusive. My father and I had sold our HDB to afford the down payment, a decision I had made in the hopes of improving my father's health. As a young man, he loved swimming, and I had hoped the availability of the pool would encourage him to exercise again. Not that I would tell him that—he was even more stubborn than I am about taking advice.

There was another reason for moving out of the family home, one that I kept to myself. Our old home was a suffocating place, filled with memories even so many years after my mother had passed, old scripts I stumbled over with every action. My father seemed immune to this, happy to toss out her things, but I wasn't so heartless. This was a sore point between us, a bruise we'd fought over for a while and now just avoided talking about altogether. I'd hoped this fresh start here would help us both move on.

The car wound its way down several ramps to the car-park lift lobby. Our driver pulled away, leaving Adam and me standing in silence, the fluorescent lights harsh on the bare concrete. I couldn't bring myself to look at him, not with the awkwardness that had settled between us. Instead, I turned my gaze to the rear windshield of the departing car, where my reflection stared back at me, looking every bit as forlorn as I felt.

Then, in that reflection, a shudder of motion—incongruent.

I instinctively flinched, stepped back just as an edged blur whistled past my face with lethal speed. There was something in front of me that baffled the eye, something unknown, unseen, terrifying.

The vine of terror was all grasping roots and sweet-smelling sap as it coiled around my heart, up into my throat, up, up into my eyes, time compressing into a pinpoint. There are people who train to see and to think in such overwhelming situations—firefighters, soldiers, MMA fighters, Shaolin monks, kindergarten teachers. To not have their fear possess them, they train for a lifetime, practise *maraṇasati* meditation, ingest unusual chemical compounds, and a few manage to stunt the growth of these vines, to slow them down.

But I was a Gardener, master of my own soul. A flash of attention, fire like a lance reducing the vine to ash, and my head cleared. Another, an internal stroke of lightning, and the remaining alcohol from my drinks at the bar burned away. Where was Adam?

I darted behind a concrete pillar, pressing my back against it to close off one direction of attack. Adjusted my glasses. A rustle of movement from my left caught my attention and I spun around, sprinting for the next pillar. Behind me, I heard creaking metal as whatever it was slammed into a car, followed by the shrill retort of a car alarm.

At this point, I was buying time. My priority was to lead this thing away from civilians and from Adam. Whatever Jimmy had sensed from him, whatever cold suspicion my DEUS role demanded of me, that all felt merely academic now. There was no space here but for instinct, and my gut told me, without a doubt, that Adam was worth saving and I had to protect him from this monster. But how? I couldn't see it.

Even as that thought surfaced, I knew it was wrong, poorly rooted. I *could* see it, because I *had* seen it, at least for a moment in the reflection of the car windshield.

I peeked around the pillar, using the dark windows of the cars as makeshift mirrors. And there it was! Something monstrous and serpentine, bulky as a van, wings spread like the hood of a cobra, a suggestion of talons and iridescent scales. A wyvern.

A civil servant is most dangerous when he has a moment of calm, when he has time to access the knowledge and frameworks from the countless papers he's been forced to read. I took a breath to focus, clearing my head of everything but the task at hand.

I had read about wyverns years ago in a research paper by a previous DEUS officer, and now the knowledge opened to me like an annex in a sixty-slide PowerPoint deck: crammed with detailed research in twelve-point font, packed with acronyms, and ready for use. Wyverns were predators native to northern and eastern Europe, traditionally tamed and used by Flemish occultists (including, famously, Bartholomaeus of Bruges) to hunt and retrieve quarry. In the sixteenth century, the Portuguese navy brought a number of these *cobraladas*, flying snakes, over to Malacca, Malaysia, for use in controlling the indigenous supernatural population, but of course some escaped and bred, spreading to other parts of Southeast Asia. Since then, they had mostly died out, hunted down for their blood and bones—used by some *dukuns* for potions—and because they terrorised small villages, abducting chickens, infants, and sometimes even full-grown adults.

Wyverns were primarily ambush hunters, impossible to see, petrifying their prey with a venomed sting before they carried it off to their lair or master. Their invisibility hinged on an adaptation that shouldn't work but did—shivers in their body, scales, and wings. They matched the microsaccadic movements of the mammalian eye, allowing them to stay centred in the part of our eyes where the optic nerve connected to the eyeball, where our brains interpolated illusions to cover for our lack of photoreceptor cells. That is, wyverns stayed in our blind spot, and hunted us from where our brains told us nothing existed.

Supposedly, this sort of invisibility wasn't natural to wyverns at all. Some of the old Portuguese records suggested it was a result of crossbreeding of their *cobraladas* with *os baralhadores*, the "Scramblers," weird starfish they claim were extraterrestrials dredged up from the Azores.

It was nonsense. Probably.

In any case, the Portuguese discovered a way to overcome this camouflage, I recalled, by finding indirect ways to look at the creatures. They made extensive use of optical mechanisms in their training and control of their wyverns, creating cages and spectacles (blueprints from the paper flowered in my head) with elaborate arrangements of mirrors and prisms and lenses. I didn't have specialised equipment to hand, but mirrors and prisms and lenses, I knew, were how phones took pictures.

I slid my phone out, aimed it past the pillar, and peered through the screen. Just as I suspected, there it was, clear as day, stalking towards me. Much too close for comfort. Quickly, I slipped off my jacket, got my pen out of its pocket. Balled up the jacket, tossed it one way before dashing out again, sprinting in a wide circle back towards the lift lobby. Behind me, I heard cloth shredding. No big deal—I had two more jackets like it back home.

I found Adam, breathing raggedly, in a state of panic. I dragged him to a crouch behind a nearby car. "You have to get out of here."

He stared at me with wild eyes.

Okay, I had to calm him down first. I squeezed his shoulder, spoke slowly. "Stay here, okay? I'll handle this."

He closed his eyes and took a breath. Looked at me. "Let me help."

"It's not safe."

"I know! I can tell! What's going on?"

"It's called a wyvern. It's Dutch—well, European, not really native—"

"Like a dragon?"

"Not really . . . well, yeah. But invisible."

He thought about it for a long moment. "If we had

something to throw on it, maybe we could see it. Like paint, or a sheet. Something."

"Won't work," I said. "It hides in our visual blind spots. We have to use the camera to see it." I gestured with my phone.

"Got it," he said, pulling out his own phone. "You sure we can't just run?"

I shook my head, tightening my grip on my pen. "I have to take care of it. Kill it. The creature will be a danger to whoever else parks their car here tonight. But you should go. This is not your job. Not your fight."

He held his phone over the top of the car, and on the screen, I saw the wyvern getting closer, still padding towards us with the self-assurance of a predator used to invisibility. Adam glanced at the phone, then met my eyes. "After this, we'll talk about the Clementi thing, but we're also going to talk about why this is your job and your fight."

I must have made some sound of assent, because he smiled. "Let's kill this thing," he said. "You go left, I'll go right."

"Wait, what? I can't protect you if you—"

His grin widened. "Maybe I'll protect you," he replied. "Be careful, okay?"

"What, I—" But he was already gone, his own phone held in front of him like a warding talisman.

Who even was this guy?

I emerged from behind the car, phone in hand, just in time to witness the wyvern launch itself at Adam, its wings wide, its talons wicked and grasping.

I must have yelled something, but I knew that it was already too late. I couldn't look away as the talons came down.

And then Adam flickered and was gone.

What?

What he was doing was somehow deeply familiar, even though I was sure I'd never seen anything like it before. But there it was. Undeniable proof. Adam was Other.

Jimmy had been right.

I didn't have time to puzzle it out further. Adam reappeared on the other side of the creature, grappling with one of its wings. He braced against it, his body taut, twisting it with his full weight. The wing membrane stretched thin before tearing with a sickening sound.

What the hell? The thought wasn't fear, or even confusion. It was something electrifying, exciting. Erotic, like the charge in the air before a storm. He wasn't just Other—he was kind of *badass*.

The wyvern shrieked, drowning out the noise of the car alarm that was still going. It twisted its head around to attack, but Adam vanished again, so it darted at me instead, lightning quick, teeth like knives.

Fear should have overwhelmed me. I should have stood no chance against the monster. I wasn't even in the same weight class. But I was a Gardener. Fear was just another weed to incinerate, and my strength and reflexes were not rooted in the shallows of muscle or sinew or bone, but in depths of the soul.

The beast lunged, and I dipped right, twisting to give myself more space. A short step to the left, ducking low to avoid the scything tail. Duck again for the backswing. Claws snapped at me, fang and tail all razored, all deadly, all visible only on my cell phone screen. The beast was scaled murder, a blaze of animal fury.

I blazed brighter.

Flaring sunlight in my soul. The surge of wind and tree sap. I was stronger than it could be. Faster. Unafraid, looking for an opportunity to get in close, to stab it in the eye with the pen, this absurd weapon. It would be messy, but I didn't have much choice.

The beast shrieked again, its frustration palpable . . . not that I was an expert at wyvern emotions—those weren't covered in the DEUS paper, after all. It reared back, its massive wings flapping unevenly, eyes baleful with what looked like hate. Then it bull-rushed me.

The move should have worked, two tons of pure terror against seventy kilograms of skinny human—but it didn't know that I was Other. It didn't know about the trees I'd grown in the loam of my own soul, what I had cultivated over fifteen years to hold back my own inner demons. And compared to what I could level against myself, a wyvern was nothing.

It crashed against me as water against root, as wind against trunk, and I did not break. I shoved back, as a tree pushes against the sky, and the creature staggered one step, two, stunned.

Then Adam was there again, gripping the wyvern by the throat, dragging it in a direction somehow orthogonal to the world. The fluorescent lights overhead seemed to deepen for a moment, as though filtered through unseen currents. At the edges of my vision, I thought I glimpsed something—roots reaching out, fractured blocks. Adam's shadow splintering into many arms. The wyvern thrashed briefly, diminished, its motion frantic and then small, like it was drowning. And then it was gone. As if in sympathy, the car alarm fell quiet, and all was blessed silence.

Adam emerged again, and we looked at each other, both of us breathing hard. He smiled, and I must have, too.

"You okay?" I said.

He nodded. "We okay?"

I considered it. After that fight against the beast, our previous fight seemed, somehow, a little silly. Like I'd focused so much on doing my job I'd missed the obvious goodness of who Adam was. Like I'd been so busy looking into a camera and missed a wyvern.

"Yeah," I said. "We're okay."

He grinned and gestured upstairs, to my apartment.

"Drinks?"

"So, a wyvern, huh," Adam said contemplatively. We were on stools at the kitchen table, him with a glass of milk, me with some ice cubes in a glass. The air con was on full blast. My father had come out of his room briefly to tell us not to stay up too late and then gone back to bed. Adam and I were both working slowly up to what we actually wanted to talk about, and talking about monsters was one way to do it.

"They usually hide away in the jungle," I said. "Up north. Hasn't been a human abduction in decades."

"Then what was this one doing here?"

I shrugged. "I'll get the team to look into it tomorrow."

Adam sipped his milk thoughtfully. "This team... That's what you do for work? Fight monsters?"

That was a very Hollywood way to put it. "Rarely. Mostly it's paperwork and meetings. Sometimes we get to do the things that really matter, help people with their problems, but a lot of the time we're just poking our noses into places and convincing groups not to kill one another. You wouldn't believe how petty some of these *hantu* politics are, or how jealous spirit mediums... media? Mediums? Anyway, they're jealous of others borrowing their gods. And they are supposed to be more enlightened."

Adam leaned forward, resting his elbows on the counter. "And you? Are you more... enlightened?" His voice was casual, but the way he glanced at me, that look in his eye—it was anything but.

He was asking if I was like him. If I was Other.

"Yeah," I said. "I'm a Gardener."

I told him what that meant. About having rainforest and mangrove inside, how I could cultivate inner resources I didn't fully myself understand, courage and willpower and the energy to keep going. I told him how the trees gave me steadiness of mind and wholeness of body, and how I hadn't gotten sick since I was a teenager.

"Not to brag," I said, "but in uni I killed it at sports. I did judo, fenced, track and field—you name it, I nailed it."

"I bet you nailed everything," Adam said, laughter in his eyes. But there was also something else—a glimmer of awe, like he couldn't quite believe his luck at landing me. It made me uncomfortably warm.

It was such a different look from earlier, outside the bar, when I had accused him of drowning Clementi. I'd hurt him, but now here he was, sitting in my kitchen, looking at me like I was something special. Like the fight between us hadn't changed anything.

Like the fight with the wyvern had changed everything.

"So you're a superhero!" he said. "What happened? Why didn't you continue to the SEA Games? Or the Olympics?"

"Well, that's against the rules, first of all," I said. "But more importantly, it would feel . . . unfair."

He grinned. "You always follow the rules, do you?"

"You're mouthy for someone who hasn't explained himself."

Adam continued to smirk at me. Watching him, I realised how much of the tension from earlier had melted away with our easy banter. He wasn't a case to solve or a potential threat to manage. He was just Adam.

A sweep of the air con ruffled his hair, and it hit me that my father was probably freezing in his room. I had to go make sure he was properly under covers.

"I'll be right back," I said. "And then you're telling me what's going on."

When I returned, Adam was snacking on a block of cheddar he'd excavated from my fridge. I honestly didn't know how one person could consume as much dairy as he did and not be mooing.

"So," I said. "What's with you? Teleportation?"

"Not quite. You know, at this point of the relationship, most people would be content with small talk about their favourite pizza toppings."

"We're *obviously* not most people. Spill it."

Adam made a face. "Fine. I've just never had to explain this to someone before. You know how the sky looks—"

"Wait, hold on. You've never had to explain it? How's that possible? Hasn't anyone asked?"

"I haven't met that many people in the . . . community yet. I mean, I'm trying, I go to gatherings, but . . . I guess no one really cares about the metaphysics of how I do what I do. Or they're too busy showing off what they can do to ask questions. Not everyone is as . . . inquisitive as you."

"It's literally my job. When did it happen, anyway? When did you, you know . . . ?"

"Become Other?" Adam said. "A little over a year ago. It's still kind of new for me."

"A year?" I tried to wrap my head around it. He was a baby! "You seem so . . . confident."

He laughed. "I'm winging it. What about you? How long?"

"Secondary school," I said. "Ages ago."

Adam whistled. "That's a long time to get used to all this. What's it like, being part of the scene for so long?"

"I'm not really part of it. I'm not exactly a people person."

"Yeah, I can tell. You've got the whole Batman vibe."

"We've already discussed this. Batman beats Superman. Anyway, shut up."

"Do you want me to explain my powers or not?"

"Just get on with it."

"Okay then. As I was saying before being interrupted by Mr. Dark Knight, you know how the sky looks blue to us?" he said.

"Sure."

"But that's just an illusion, right? Space is actually black, not blue. It's like that. I can get past the blue we see into the darkness we don't see."

I frowned. "What the hell are you talking about?"

"I'm trying! Can't you just read about me in one of your government files or something, and save me the agony of trying to explain this?"

Binder Two had nothing on his abilities, as Jimmy had already ascertained. We had some spotty records of people who could project their consciousness and spy on other people, which in practice was mostly used for pornographic purposes. There were some spells such as the Seven League Stride (formally updated as the Thirty-Nine Kilometre Stride, but no one called it by the new name) that let practitioners move quickly from place to place, like a poor man's version of the spell Mei had on her shoes, but that was about speed, not actual teleportation. Magic was usually difficult and limited, requiring tools and rituals even for minor effects. Adam's ability to simply disappear and reappear put him in a category all his own.

Of course, this was true only for human Others with supernatural gifts—your shamans and witches and hermetic magicians. If we considered non-humans, though, there were rakshasa and pixies and fox spirits who could materialise and dematerialise at will, shadow monsters who would appear and disappear in darkness. Those weren't human and weren't subject to our limitations.

Adam was human. I'd seen enough of him—all the interesting parts—to be fairly sure.

"Why are you blushing?" he said.

"Shut up. There's nothing in the files on you. Can you just try again to explain, please?"

He took a deep breath, gathering his thoughts. "You see this glass of milk in my hand? What if I told you it's much more than you can see? That most of it exists in a deeper reality beyond it, which you can't see?"

"I got it from the supermarket downstairs," I said, deadpan.

He threw a kitchen towel at me. "I don't mean just the glass of milk, smartass. It's everything. The table, you, me. There's more to all of us than this. More than these slivers that we can see. There's something . . . deeper."

"I think I get it." I wasn't sure why, but what he was saying made sense. It felt familiar in the way a missing tooth was familiar. A memory unfurled in my head. "I had a professor—I think it was a class on Kant—who said to think of existence as an ocean, with little things bobbing on it. All that we see—all the chairs, people, and mountains—all that is just the surface. That's the *phenomena*, the surface appearances of things, but beneath it, there's so much more to these things that we don't see. Never see. That's the *noumena*, all under the water."

"That's it!" Adam said. "That's exactly it."

"Where are you going with this, Adam?"

He stilled for a moment, holding my gaze, and suddenly I could feel something massive present, some part of Adam that lay behind and beneath him like Shiva's many arms, but multiplied, ten thousand tendrils combing the currents of the deep.

"This ocean of existence you spoke of?" he said, looking me in the eye. "I can Dive."

CHAPTER SIX

"Wait, rewind that," Jimmy said, leaning forward in his seat. It was the next morning, and we were gathered in the only available meeting room, Adam as my invited guest. The room had a wall of glass, which was great for the curious but terrible for privacy, and it happened to be situated on the path the bigwigs took to and from their offices. The only thing worse than its location was its smell, a distinctive mix of mould, flatulence, and vanilla air freshener. It was not a popular room, you might imagine, and certainly not the ideal place to be talking about top-secret supernatural stuff. But at least it had a functioning projector. So there we were, watching footage I had managed to capture on my phone from the wyvern encounter.

"Right there," Jimmy said, pointing to the screen. I thumbed my phone back five seconds, pausing it at a full-frontal image of the beast.

"Incredible specimen!" Jimmy walked up to the screen to

take a closer look, bringing with him the packet of crispy fish skin he had been snacking on. He glanced over at Mei, who was, naturally, our resident historian and lore expert. Another great advantage to old age. "You ever seen one of these before?"

"Only when I was a child," she said. "This one looks very much like the *cobraladas* I remember—the trained lizards that the European witch hunters used to kidnap innocent women and put them through mockeries of trials. However, I am given to understand that these monsters have been in decline, because they do not compete well against the native predators. The modern ones are miserable creatures, filthy, malnourished, pathetic. This one…" She gestured at the screen. "It is as big as the ones I remember. Well fed. How curious."

Adam stared at Mei in open fascination. He was wearing one of my T-shirts, a little tight in the shoulders on him, and was leaning back in one of our rickety office chairs. It was slightly obnoxious how at ease he looked with a group of people he'd met just twenty minutes ago. To be fair, Jimmy had panicked when we first showed up, still convinced that Adam was some sort of malicious sea ghost, but had calmed down once he noticed no one was drowning. After taking a full five minutes to sniff cautiously at an amused Adam, Jimmy had declared him no threat, and we had all relaxed just a bit after that.

Adam, I realised with some envy, slipped into hearts and groups just as easily as he slipped in and out of reality. Maybe his real magic was charm.

"Europeans?" he asked Mei. "Childhood? How old are you?"

I shot Adam a look to warn him off this line of questioning. "Why would something like that be lurking in my condo's car park?" I asked.

"Definitely looking for a snack," Jimmy suggested.

"Maybe it's exploring," Adam said.

"Or seeking vengeance," Mei added.

I sighed. "So we have no idea. Did we just get lucky that it went for us—two guys who happen to be able to deal with it—instead of some small child—like her?" I gestured to Fizah to make a point, but she wasn't paying attention to me. She was peering very intently at the monster on the screen.

"I would've just burned it to death," Fizah said distractedly. "But do you see this, though? This shadow doesn't look right."

Once she pointed it out, it was obvious. In the shot, the wyvern had been in just the right place, at an angle to one of the car-park fluorescents, to cast a clear shadow across the concrete floor and onto a pillar. We could see the arch of its neck, the silhouette of a wing, and several thin threads radiating up and out of its back. Shadows of things that were not otherwise visible.

"Good job," I said.

"I'm an art major," Fizah said, semi-apologetically. "Like, we look at shadows *a lot* in class."

There were a few seconds of quiet as everyone tried to process all the weirdness, then we all turned to look at Mei. She stood, then took a single step, blurring from her seat to stand next to Jimmy. She was wearing the pair of heels she'd enchanted to, in her words, minimise walking while maximising fashion.

"Puppetry," she said, inspecting the shadow strings on the screen. "Old magic. Black magic. Not many of us left who know how to do it."

"Which means what, exactly?" Jimmy asked.

Mei was silent for a moment—I wondered if it was because she was hesitating, or if it was for dramatic effect. With her, it was hard to tell.

"Control," she said. "The most common kind is strings through flesh—the puppeteer can make you jump in front of a car. Go into fits. Strings through your eyes can make you see things that are not there. Drive you mad. This…this looks like *wayang* puppetry, strings through your shadow, to your heart. They can control what you fear, what you desire, what you want more than anything. They do not have to make you do anything, because you will want to."

Fizah looked horrified. "Can they do that to people?"

"Easily," Mei said. "Human hearts are soft, complicated, full of places to hook. A beast such as this, on the other hand—its passions and fears are simpler, its heart harder to find purchase on. Whoever it is behind this is frighteningly skilled."

So the wyvern wasn't a random wildlife encounter. It had shown up where I lived, just a few days after we started investigating Clementi, right as we linked up with Adam and were on the verge of getting some answers.

And of all the beasts it could have been, it was a *wyvern*. A creature with a paralytic, non-lethal sting, with a track record of kidnapping people on behalf of its handler. A handler who apparently was literally puppeteering it through shadow magic.

Someone wanted to stop us from uncovering what was going on, and they wanted to take us alive. Question was—why?

Just then, our Permanent Secretary walked by, her strides long, clearly on her way to something important. Jimmy dropped his snack packet, lunged to turn the screen off, but I was quicker. Wouldn't do to have senior leadership see what we had on there, get wind of this incident before we had a fully scrubbed and cleared report. It's just how the civil service works. You never show your bosses anything unedited, impromptu, raw, because you never know what they might want to do with it. You put everything into passive voice and flattering frameworks and you polish until your reports are smooth as a pebble, as empty of human complications as the heart of a wyvern. That's when the bosses get to see it, and you hope that the hooks of their attention slide right off.

This PS was one of the better ones, but she was still a normal, and wouldn't have been able to process this shit. Wouldn't have wanted to, either, presumably—that's what we were paid to do, after all. Outside the room, she slowed for a second when she saw us, smiled, and waved. We waved back, and she moved on.

I restarted the projector and there it was again—on screen, the wyvern leapt at Adam, and we all saw him vanish, reappear, tackle the wyvern. We were silent as the camera went wild while I had to avoid the monster's attacks, but once I had knocked it back and stunned it, the camera steadied again, and we could clearly see Adam grab the wyvern, grin at the camera, and drag it into some mind-bending other dimension.

"Tell them what you told me," I said.

So he did. We had rehearsed it over breakfast. Instead of talking about Kant's noumena and phenomena, he explained that everything had two parts—a small visible part in our reality and a larger part trailing in another dimension he called the Outside. He talked about how he could step Outside for a bit—what he called Diving—and how he could swim there, pulling things with him if he wanted, emerging back into our world somewhere else. How he Dived around the city the same way people took walks in parks, part recreation, part exercise, part exploration, and how he'd stumbled on the phenomenon at Clementi Block 375 just a few days before DEUS had. How, despite no official responsibility or authority, he'd done the same as we did, knocking on doors and talking to people to try to figure out what was going on.

A connection sparked in my brain. "Wait. When you were knocking on doors, do you remember speaking with an older lady—a *makcik*, tiny, wearing enormous glasses? She had a whole row of Hello Kitty slippers at her front door."

Adam squinted at me suspiciously. "I don't remember the slippers, but I remember the glasses. She asked if I wanted some kueh to go."

"That's her!" I said. "She told us someone had visited just before us, said he was—"

"Very handsome!" Fizah exclaimed, delighted. "Oh my god, she was talking about you!"

Adam's grin grew wide. "Handsome, huh?"

"Yes," I said, dryly. "Truly a gift to the township of Clementi, renowned the world over for its supermodels. Speaking of Clementi..."

"Yes, Clementi," Mei said grimly. "What is happening to that block?"

"It's sinking," Adam said. "Into the Outside."

"Why?" asked Mei.

Adam shook his head. "I don't know. Too much weight, maybe."

Mei furrowed her brow. "Weight?"

"Yeah. Sometimes there's too many people, too much stuff, too much history."

Jimmy sat up. "Too much history? That lines up with something I read in Binder Two. There was a white paper written back in the nineties—'Risk Assessment for Spatially Unstable Sites,' something like that. It talked about unexplained disappearances of places, like that market in Vuon Chuoi, or that one favela near Rio. Other places that vanished so completely even the memory of them is gone. The theory was that some places get sucked into a black hole because they accumulate too much... The paper called it *ontological and semantic mass.*"

"Right," I said. "Too many people, too much meaning, too much history. What happened with that white paper?"

Jimmy shrugged. "Nothing. I think the bosses decided it wasn't actionable."

"Of course," I muttered. "Nothing is actionable until it's too late. But this block in Clementi—we're saying that... somewhere in that block, there's too much...stuff? More stuff than a historical site in Vietnam?"

Adam leaned forward. "I don't know about Vietnam or Brazil, but this block? It's bad. Really bad. The whole place is barely keeping afloat. Those vanishings we saw—those were just ripples. The area has sunk so low in the water that the smallest waves wash over it, and it goes Outside for a while. And if we don't act fast, it'll drag everything else down with it. Dogs, people, buildings. All of it will be lost for good."

"Sorry," Fizah said. "But why *now*? It's not a new block, is it?"

Adam shrugged. "Maybe it's some kind of tipping point. Or maybe it's climate change."

Jimmy snorted.

Fizah turned to me, eyes wide. "Can't we evacuate everyone?"

I let out a bitter laugh. "Won't work," I said. "We don't have the authority. They won't leave their homes just because some random bureaucrats tell them to pack up and go. Even if we tried, the red tape would keep us busy for months before we could even start. And the Home Team won't be any help, either. They've got their own crap to deal with."

It was sad, but true. Almost everyone I've encountered in government has been a decent human being (or a reasonable facsimile thereof)—fairly bright, good heart, motivated to serve the country and the people. But somehow, put those decent human beings in their roles as Senior Manager or Assistant Director or Group Director of some team or whatever, give them a bit of power and a domain to watch over, and they become the most viciously territorial monsters I know. And in my line of work, where I've appeased Datuk Gongs and negotiated with stone chinthe, that's saying something.

And so, in theory, DEUS is supposed to have the support of a range of other agencies to do some of the work we are not equipped to do—sub-population health, social support, family reconciliation and mediation work, enforcement, rehabilitation, quarantine, even education, skills training, job placements. In actual practice, we do all this, under-resourced and under-trained, scraping by as best we can. It's totally unsustainable, but made better only because we know that every other team is going through the same thing. Solidarity in misery, and all that.

I stood, went over to the whiteboard. "We have a few things on our plate," I said. "First, and biggest, is that something is causing the Clementi site to sink." I wrote that on the board. *1) Figure out cause of Clementi Block 375 sinking (ghost? ontological/semantic weight?).*

"Second, we have some unknown person, or persons, highly skilled, able to control a wyvern." That was a second bullet point on the board—*2) Find wyvern puppeteer.*

"Add a third, boss," Jimmy said around a mouthful of fish

skin. Did he have a new packet? He really shouldn't have been eating in here. "We still need to find Mei's scarf."

I rolled my eyes and with a long-suffering sigh wrote *3) Ghost cat.*

Put so starkly in writing, it was clear what had to happen.

"Mei, Jimmy, Fizah," I said. "I'm taking you off the case."

"Why?" Jimmy and Fizah said simultaneously. Mei merely arched an eyebrow.

"It's too dangerous. Whoever is behind the wyvern, they're willing to use violence to interfere with our investigation. They could target you next. Jimmy, your family is still in Bali, yes?"

"Yes, but—"

"Good. Tell them to stay there for now. I want you all spending the next few nights here in the office, where we're protected. Just until we figure this out."

"No. You are being ridiculous," Mei said. "I have faced things far more dangerous than a wyvern and come out alive. I will not be sidelined like some fragile amateur. James's pre-cognitive powers will warn him of danger. Fizah's fire will be a deterrent for any adversary. We are not children, Benjamin, and you will not treat us as such."

I wasn't listening to her. My mind was already two steps ahead, trying to figure out where I could hide my father, how I could explain to Rebecca why DEUS was sleeping in the meeting rooms.

"I'm not going anywhere," Fizah said, breaking my train of

thought. Her face was set. "I want to help, and I'll do it with or without you."

"Come on, Ben," Jimmy said. "She's right. We're safer if we do this together. Just trust us."

Trust. That was a nice idea, but when it came down to it I was responsible for their lives and well-being. I wasn't naive, though—they weren't going to stop just because I said so. They would recklessly dig away and paint targets on themselves.

I'd just have to make myself a bigger target.

"All right," I said. "Compromise. We do this together, but you let me do all the legwork. You can help me with the investigation from behind the scenes."

"Deal," Jimmy said.

"What about me?" Adam asked.

"What *about* you?" I said. "Go home, stay safe. The professionals will handle it from here."

Silence.

"Wait," Jimmy said. "Do you mean us?"

I glared at him.

"Ben," Jimmy continued, with uncharacteristic firmness. "We need his help. He's the only one with any understanding of this *Outside*."

"C'mon, mister," Adam pleaded, looking hopefully at me. God, but he had beautiful eyes. "Let me do this with you. I can help."

I sighed, already knowing I was going to regret this. But... his powers *would* be useful. He had been a huge help already.

"I hate that I'm agreeing to this, but Jimmy's got a point. And you're not bad in a fight. Are you willing to work with me... with us, on this?"

"Hell yes! I want an official title and everything."

I sighed again. "Fine. By the power vested in me by the sovereign state of Singapore," I said, "by lion and orchid and sun, I hereby deputise you as a Knight Errant of DEUS, for as long as this quest may last. May you perform your duties with integrity, punctuality, and excellence."

"You can do that?" Fizah looked awed.

"No," Mei said.

"I don't care," Adam said. "This is awesome!"

"I feel like this whole ceremony is missing something," Jimmy said. "Bells and someone crying. Champagne and lots of cake. Can I be the best man?"

Adam and I ignored him. "Where do I start?" Adam said.

I gestured at the whiteboard. "We need to figure out the source of the Clementi sinking before another wave happens. Any ideas?"

We were all quiet for a while, even Jimmy, staring at the board in a thinking sort of silence broken only by the squeak of Adam's chair as he fidgeted, rocking it back and forth, back and forth.

Finally, he could take it no more. "Can't you guys just, like, find someone to magic up the information? Find out what's happening?"

"A Diviner," Mei said sharply, "is only for serious matters."

She softened at Adam's chagrined look, and continued in a gentler voice. "But perhaps these are serious matters."

Damn. It was indeed something worth considering, but there was a reason why we didn't go running to one every time we needed information and Google wasn't good enough. Well, three reasons, actually. One was that the good ones were very rare. Charlatans were as common as mosquitoes—there were, at any time, several dozen in Singapore alone who could guess the future in the way a coconut floats in the river, or cast dragon bones or channel farsighted minor deities, all to tell you, "March is a good month for your finances" or "You will meet the man of your dreams, and he will be wearing jeans." But only a very small fraction of those could read the currents of time and pick out something specific from them.

Of the small number of seers who had strength and skill, only a small fraction of them were sane. That was reason number two. Time and Fate were unkind to those who dealt with them, and so the majority of the stronger ones slid, after a few years, into babbling madness, unable to distinguish between the present and the future, the actual and the probable. Pre-TSD—Pre-Traumatic Stress Disorder—was a real issue. Sometimes, it was even worse—one of my first field assignments in DEUS was to deal with the body of a graduate student who had been able to see possibilities by inhabiting her own body in other possible worlds. She had stumbled on one version of herself that carried a transworld parasite, and unknowingly brought the parasite back to this world. When she learned about it, she immolated herself in her own flat, and I was the one who had to autopsy the charred cadaver, making sure that the dark-feathered things in her sinus cavities were fully dead.

The third reason why we didn't go to Diviners, upper-case *D*, for all our problems was that the few Diviners who *were* good enough and sane enough were targets for every supernatural community out there. The big organisations wanted to recruit them, brainwash them into serving their spiritual or temporal goals. The supernaturals who thrived on secrecy or anonymity—your shapeshifters, changelings, sectarians of the criminal *wulin*—they wanted to eliminate them to keep their own secrets. Everyone wanted to use them or kill them, but they were Diviners. They were impossible to find unless they wanted to be found.

Good, sane, available—as they say in the dating world, you get to pick only two out of three. I looked over at Adam, and he smiled back.

He'd told us that the place was sinking because of some metaphysical weight, but we didn't have a clue what was weighing it down. Ontological or semantic mass, the paper had said. Any stray knick-knack could be tethering a massive ghost, any jar of loose change could hold an old coin with the spiritual weight of a genocide. We could spend weeks wheedling our way into people's homes, examining every corner and every trinket for some sign of being supernaturally heavy, *or* we could ask a Diviner to point us directly to the cause of the sinking. With our time constraints, if we wanted to avoid a next wave, finding a Diviner was looking like the only viable option.

I stared at the list on the whiteboard, in my head running through the Diviners we knew of. "What about Kusu Island?" The turtle god there was old, and the prophecies he gave could be useful, if cryptic. He'd helped us before.

"Wrong year," Mei said. "He is still asleep."

Damn.

"What about the jinn?" I said, turning to Fizah. She shrank beneath my gaze, fluttering her hands in front of herself. "I'm sure they have one on retainer."

"No, no, no, bad idea. Baaaad," she said.

Adam tilted his head, looking puzzled. He looked at me, then at Fizah. "But Ben said your family is—"

"No!" Fizah said. "I mean, yes. But jinn families aren't quite like your . . . normal families. It's all contracts and deals. My father—he's human—he had to sign away the memories of his siblings to my mother so she would carry me, and when I was a child I had to, like, sign a contract giving her ten percent of my earnings in perpetuity, just so she would love me."

"Sounds like any old family, with extra steps," Jimmy said.

Fizah didn't dignify that with a response. "Take it from someone who grew up in that environment. Jinn drive hard bargains, with no discount for friends, for daughters, nothing. And anyway, you guys have, like, zero things to offer them."

Well, that was hurtful, even if it was true. Damn again.

But we kicked around a plan for calling the jinn anyway. A contingency plan for that last resort, just in case we ever needed it—even argued over what to call it. Didn't settle on a name, but the plan itself was ready. Just in case.

Jimmy cleared his throat. "If we're still scraping the bottom of the Diviner barrel, how about that Reverend...something, from that church? The one we spoke with last year?"

"It was two years ago," Mei said. "Reverend Peter has since returned to the peace of his god."

Well, god frickin' dammit. That left one option. The worst one.

I took a breath. "There is one more name, folks," I said.

"No," Mei said.

"No way," Jimmy said.

"Yes way," I said. "The Nagamuthu's daughter. She's our only choice. We have to go to the pasar bayang."

CHAPTER SEVEN

The shelves of NTUC FairPrice, the largest supermarket chain in Singapore, were the same no matter where you went. Milk powder, toilet paper, detergent all in immaculate rows, the orderliness perfect except where it had been disturbed by careless aunties reaching for products in the back. Some might have said that this tension between institutional order and individual disorder was the basis for all civilisation.

Adam was not impressed with my theory.

"That's..." he said, pausing for a second to consider his words, "the dumbest thing I've ever heard."

"It's basically Hobbes, you know," I said.

"The cartoon tiger?"

I narrowed my eyes at him, threatening violence, but then we reached the end of the baby food and cleaning products aisle, and I had to check the directions on my phone again. Another left, skip two aisles, then left again down cereal.

Almost there. The way the layout was the same at every

NTUC made it confusing to navigate, but it was precisely this that made the magic possible. When two places were close enough, similar enough, someone skilled could use the space between them to tunnel through to somewhere else, the same way that two identical stiles on either side of a doorway allowed a door to be installed. The Petronas Twin Towers in Kuala Lumpur, it was said, were constructed to be a portal of this sort, using their sheer scale to twist geometries into an opening. What the NTUC stores lacked in size, they made up for in number—over two hundred outlets allowed for a door to somewhere very far away.

"But doors can be locked, and locks need keys," I explained to Adam. "And the key in this case is the sigil we are tracing with our footsteps around the store."

We were following instructions from an online chat group on Telegram called OFFICIAL 24HRS MAKE RICH LTD, which Mei had shared with us at the end of the meeting the day before, warning us that, if we let it be known that she had told us about it, she would hunt us down. (She wasn't joking.) But the information was as good as she had promised—detailed instructions each month on the dates of the pasar bayang, which NTUCs led there, and what steps to take to unlock the passage. It was also full of vendors hawking their wares, advertising what goods and services they were selling. Just a few years ago, this would all have been passed by word of mouth, from trusted source to trusted source within the community. Now it was a Telegram group, hiding the pasar in plain sight.

"I need to tell you about this place before we get there," I said, trying to lead the way and talk at the same time. "The pasar isn't entirely safe."

Adam laughed. "I got that, yesterday, when everyone gasped and Jimmy almost fainted at your suggestion. And that's why you look like . . . this."

There was a glamour on me, from Mei. Though I didn't feel much beyond a slight pressure on my forehead, I knew I looked like a much older version of myself, which had resulted in a whole bunch of daddy jokes from Adam and Jimmy yesterday until I made them stop. Not like anyone was likely to recognise me as a DEUS officer anyway, but this was just in case. As a field agent, I couldn't take any chances.

Adam didn't have the same glamour on him, because he didn't need it. He was here partly because he was the only one who could describe to the Diviner how Clementi was sinking, and partly because, as someone not affiliated with the Singapore government, he was safer than any of the rest of us. And also because, last night, he had begged and pleaded to come with me, and eventually his eyelash batting and shoulder massage offerings had worn down my resistance.

"They don't like you government people, you said?"

"It's beyond dislike," I replied. "They hate us. Government in general, but DEUS in particular. They still blame us for . . . Wait, what do you know about the pasar bayangs? Anything?"

"Shadow markets?" he said. "It's where we are going, to find our Diviner, yes? I've seen *Aladdin*. I figured it's like a pasar malam—one of those night markets, some sort of open-air bazaar where you can buy and sell items strange and wonderful. Wishing rings, flying carpets, aphrodisiacs..." He winked at me in exaggerated fashion and groped for my butt, prompting a nearby auntie to make a disapproving sound.

I dodged and blinked. "That's... surprisingly accurate."

"So why do they hate you?"

I took us on a loop around the stacks of fruits, heaps of nectarines and guava and papaya. "Long story. Pasar bayangs started alongside pasar malams in the nineteen fifties, following the same weekly circuits. As more and more Others came to Singapore on migration waves, these pasar bayangs became places for them to trade goods and information, seek adjudication for disputes, find community. And you know how, in the nineteen seventies, we decided to shut down all the pasar malams because they were 'unhygienic'?"

Adam rolled his eyes. "*We* didn't decide to do that. The government decided."

He had a point. "Well, okay," I said. "They also decided that the pasar bayangs were too much of an enclave, too lawless, and so used the opportunity to try to shut them down as well. They set up a task force for this, because that's what government does."

"Of course."

"And that task force, that was the beginnings of DEUS."

"Oh shit, really? So you've been around since the seventies?"

I nodded. "It was a twelve-person team then. But once things settled down—"

"Once people forgot history, you mean."

"Yes. Once that happened, our bosses decided the resources were better spent elsewhere. The team was halved in the eighties, then halved again just before I came on board. It's just the three of us now, handling the work of a dozen officers."

We passed by some shelves of herbs, and Adam picked up some coriander to sniff at. He looked at me thoughtfully over the top of the frilly plant. "Those early clashes—they were bad?"

"They were bloody. A lot of desperate curses being flung around, weaponised ghosts, all of that. The cost was high on both sides, and it eventually became a game of chicken to see who would flinch first at the cost in lives and souls. And in those days, our government never backed down on anything. Never flinched first."

I grimaced, remembering what I had read, some of the pictures I'd seen in the archives. "After a while, the pasar bayang people stopped fighting and started running. You must remember that they were not a professional army, just people living their lives, trying to make a living."

"Yeah," Adam said, quietly.

"The DEUS task force eventually drove them into a corner, and would have rounded up and detained the remaining pasar bayang people, the remaining 'threats to public order and hygiene.' That's when this entity stepped up. They call him Nagamuthu, Snake-Born. He's some sort of deity-level power."

"He protected the place?"

"More than that. People say that he sacrificed a part of his own immortality to create a safe, secret space for the pasar bayang to exist. For them, he's quite literally the Creator."

Adam let out a low whistle. "And it's his daughter we're looking for? She's our Diviner? We're going to a place where everyone hates us, including literally the god, to find his daughter and ask her some questions?"

"Easy peasy," I said.

He laughed. "Thanks, by the way. I'm glad to have your government-issued super brain to sum up all this complicated history for me."

I snorted, but he was right. There was a lot of history here, complicating things. If we failed, if we didn't get our answer from the Diviner, if we didn't find out what the weight was on level six of Block 375, we could lose a lot of people. And it would be on me for failing them.

The thought sat heavy in my chest, and we both fell silent. Adam looked like he was processing the information, and I was caught up in what felt like shame, for something my government had done before I was born. I noticed the old moss spreading in a corner of my soul, and I let it stay. Sometimes it was good for lessons that hurt to grow slow and stay long. Sometimes it was important to not forget.

One final turn, if the Telegram instructions were accurate,

and there we were, at a nondescript door in the back marked EMPLOYEES ONLY. Right below eye level was a white U-shaped sigil, in what I assumed was *vibhuti* ash. "This is it," I said, checking to make sure no one was watching us. Then I opened the door, and we walked through.

CHAPTER EIGHT

I'd been with DEUS for a few years now, but I had never been stupid enough to set foot in a pasar bayang. I'm not sure what I had envisioned, but it sure as hell wasn't what I found.

Behind us was the door we had stepped through, one of many in what appeared to be a row of ancient shophouses, paint peeling, windows shuttered, curving to our left and right as far as the eye could see. The signboards were crazed, like the writing in a dream—the sign above the door we came through said CING JA PTE LTD, GODS AND SUNDRIES—and all the others were similarly nonsensical. Even as we watched, people entered and left through the other doors, presumably from the other NTUC connections.

The ground was dark dirt and dry grass, and the night sky was invisible, with no stars or moon in sight. But in front of us, the stalls were lit up like Christmas trees with a profusion of artificial light. A good number of bare sodium bulbs provided steady yellow illumination, but there were also clusters of candles and kerosene lamps and a few minimalist standing lights I recognised from IKEA. A collection of naked fires, some being used to roast food, some for god knows what, threw off light and smoke and shadow. It was humid, and it was hot.

And the people! I had expected this event, which happened once a month, to draw in the supernatural community, but I had not expected it to draw quite so many. The more common sorts of Others were there, of course. A group of kids in their school uniforms—khaki, white and blue, white and green—exposed as witches only by the way they consulted their unseen spirit allies (and their phones) before buying anything. Dozens of *jiangshi* with their signature stiff gaits, some selling Daoist charms, some purchasing unguents.

There were even a few exotic ones. Just from where we were, standing at the entrance gawking, we could see a multi-winged wheel of fire, paying for a plate of maggi goreng. Two haughty fae, or *orang bunian* as they're called in this part of the world, their perfect beauty marred only by the sweat stains on their fine dresses. A few *rukurokubi*, their elongated necks extending from middle-aged bodies. For all their unusual appearances, they were here for the completely mundane reasons of buying cheap things and eating good food.

I wish I had some framework they would all fit nicely into, so I could use this chance to pick up some data on which categories of Others were active now and here. But we had no such framework. Since as far back as I knew, categorising and better understanding the scene before us had been a to-do on the DEUS list of tasks—map out the types of Others, magical powers, holy and unholy places in Singapore and the region. Since as far back as I knew, the idea that we could have time to do this had always been a hilarious fantasy.

"It's all so...fantastic!" Adam said, grabbing my hand. "Let's go check things out."

We wandered among the stalls, immersed ourselves in the aromas of food, and tried to pretend to fit in. Adam was in his element, irrepressible, charming the uncles, bargaining with the best of them, having the time of his life. It would have been almost irritating if he hadn't been so earnestly, authentically happy. Within the first ten minutes, he had managed to get us some street food—a skewer of crispy squid heads for me, and for himself a bubble tea. I wondered what others thought we were, with me looking like an old man and Adam being, well, Adam. A sorcerer and his apprentice? A warlock and his familiar?

"They probably think you're an old cradle-snatching pervert, and I'm your fabulous toyboy," Adam said, drinking from his tea. "Should I ask someone?"

I grabbed his shoulder to stop him—I was only half-sure he was joking. "We can't play around," I said, keeping my voice low. "This place isn't safe. We have to get in, observe, analyse, respond, get our information, and get out."

"Oh, come on!" he protested. "This is your one time here. Also, there really is no better way to look like a government guy than coming in and asking a lot of questions about someone. What's your plan when you find her, anyway, this Nagamuthu's daughter?"

"We'll tell her about the sinking and ask her to tell us what the weight is. It'll save lives. She'll listen. She has to."

"Oh, right. Convince her of the righteousness of our cause. That usually works out well."

"Do you have a better plan, smartass?"

"No, but—"

"Is there a problem here?" A young lady interrupted us. She was dressed in some sort of draped robe and was a head shorter than either of us, but radiated confidence. The big staff she held by her side, which was as tall as she was, probably helped.

We had seen a few like her around the pasar. Naga Sangam, if I had to guess. Literally, it meant the Association of the Snake, but Tamil was a subtle language, and the files had mentioned that it carried many more layers of meaning. It implied the cultivation of learning and poetry, but also ideas of political resistance. The Naga Sangam were a volunteer militia that started as a way to fight back against DEUS, but had in the decades since solidified into a peacekeeping force for the pasar bayangs in general.

"No, no problem, officer," I said.

"My father here got some food on his shirt," Adam said, pointing to me and the greasy, empty packet I was holding that used to contain deep-fried cephalopod tentacles. "He was too embarrassed to ask where he can wash up, maybe get a new shirt. That's why we were arguing. I told him everyone here is friendly, no need to be embarrassed, am I right?"

She relaxed, mouth quirking into a crooked smile. "Toilets are that way, behind the generators, and there are some stalls that sell clothes over there. Make sure you throw that packet in the rubbish bins, okay?"

We watched her walk away.

I glared at Adam. "I'm going to murder you. Your *father*?"

"She didn't seem to care," Adam replied blithely. "Maybe I'm adopted."

"Hi, adopted," I said. "I'm Dad." Figured I might as well lean into it.

He snickered. "Come on. We need to get you some new clothes."

I begrudgingly went along with it, only because I was worried that the Naga Sangam lady was still watching us. Not getting a new shirt would have looked mighty suspicious. I let Adam pick out a T-shirt for me. And what did he pick out, you ask? A shirt with a damn yellow duck on it, with runes stitched into the seams, which the vendor promised would keep it wrinkle free. And, of course, it was oversize, like the kids all wore these days. I was absolutely sure he picked it purposely to make fun of me.

I found some cover behind a nearby stall to change into the ridiculous shirt. When I emerged, feeling like a complete clown, Adam was a few stalls away, talking animatedly with the shopkeeper about some silvery gadget on the table.

"Look at this!" he said. "This could be useful for your work, right? Oh, you look nice, by the way."

The shopkeeper, a young man with bad teeth, eyed us sourly. "Chi disruptor," he said. "From Japan, *kuji-kiri* style, new model."

Adam picked it up and waved it around, making happy

womm-womm-womm lightsabre sounds. It was the size of a thick pen, sleek wood and silver, and did look a little bit like the hilt of a lightsabre designed for a very small Jedi. At the tip, where the blade would have been, was a smooth disc of what looked like wood, intricately engraved with a single flower.

"What's it do, exactly?" I asked.

"Disrupts chi," repeated the shopkeeper. He turned away to tap at his phone, bored of us already.

I sighed and looked over at Adam.

"It's basically a Taser, I think," he said. "But next time you meet a wyv...uh, a big lizard thing, you can"—he jabbed at the air with the device—"pow! Take it out! Even if I'm not there to save you."

A weapon, then. This place definitely didn't have a licence to sell these things. But the world of us Others is a much more dangerous place than regular Singapore, and almost everyone already had some sort of device for self-defence, regulated or not. Anyway, I wasn't here to cause trouble.

"I don't know if—" I protested.

"Please. It would...it would make me feel better to know you have some way to protect yourself."

I hesitated, which was all the signal Adam needed. He happily paid for the thing, barely bothering to haggle, and shoved it at me. "Make sure you keep it with you all the time," he ordered. "Think of me when you zap things."

It was really annoying that he had the audacity to be sweet and funny at a time like this.

With Adam's shopping urges partially mollified, we could focus on finding our target. The Nagamuthu's daughter. There was no consensus out there about whether she was his actual daughter or just a protégé, but everyone agreed that she was a farseer of rare talent, with knowledge of secret and distant things. There were stories, too, of her fickleness and how she enjoyed thwarting her father, denying help to someone just because of the day of the week or because it would piss her father off. But I was a civil servant, with a lot of experience getting what I needed from capricious, spiteful people more powerful than me. I thought I could manage.

We did a couple of laps around the place, which was smaller than I had initially thought. Now that I was paying a bit more attention, it became apparent that the pasar bayang still bore scars from the government witch hunt (because that's what it was) two generations ago. All the stalls and structures were makeshift, constructed from wood and corrugated metal, with none of the clean engineering characteristic of modern Singapore. And, perhaps more shockingly, there was no running water or real trash disposal anywhere. Water for cooking and for washing dishes was stored in rusty metal drums, in jerrycans and open vats, most of which looked like breeding grounds for dysentery. Food scraps and plastic trash overflowed from the inadequate bins, and more waste was heaped in middens between the stalls and on the edges of the market.

Middens. A word I'd never expected to see or use outside of fantasy novels about the awful Dark Ages of Europe.

Again, I felt the creeping spread of something like guilt, something like shame, inside. This was government failure. What was worse, it was something we could realistically fix. I knew someone at the National Heritage Board, an ex-classmate, and maybe I could convince her to—

I stopped myself. This wasn't what we were here for. The Clementi issue was a pressing one, and we needed to locate the Nagamuthu's daughter. But what I had hoped to find—a young woman being treated like royalty, perhaps with some sharp-eyed bodyguards—was nowhere to be found.

"What do we do now? I'm bored," Adam asked after our second circuit. He had managed to find a handful of plastic straws, connected them to form a metre-long tube, and was waving it around. He didn't look bored at all.

"I don't know," I said.

"We could go home, come back another time."

"That'll be next month. The Clementi site might completely sink by then. Whoever is behind it might send more monsters at us... We can't afford to wait."

"But we've done everything short of directly asking someone. You're not thinking of doing that, are you?" Adam asked, jabbing me casually with his straw spear.

"No, but..." I eyed the contraption in his hands. One straw, to another, then to the next, individually small steps combining to reach a little farther. We had just passed by a fortune-teller, one of several we had seen. An older man, serious looking, a spread of tarot cards on the low table in front of him. The cards were ragged, and the coil of incense he had was mostly ash. He had no customers. "We don't have to *directly* ask..."

Adam didn't take much convincing to join me at the table. We sat down across from the fortune-teller, who it turned out was older than I thought. His hair was thick but grey, and his face a mass of wrinkles when he smiled.

"Hello, hello," he said. "Always new faces here. Very good, very good. New people, more people, is good. Today also very lucky day, very happy day. Can give you a discount, okay? Twenty-five dollars, you two, can ask anything, okay? Anything, anything also can ask."

"Uh," I said.

"You want to ask about work? About family? Love life? About women?" He winked a little grotesquely.

"Work, actually," I said, hoping to keep things focused. I had to do some quick thinking. I couldn't tell him too much and risk revealing who we were, but he needed enough to work with. My hope was that we could use him as one straw, to find the Diviner, who would be our next straw, to figure out Clementi.

"I'm having a little trouble with..." I hesitated, searching for the right words. "With reaching a target for my job. I was hoping the cards could guide me."

"Has trouble reaching the target in his love life, too," Adam muttered, deadpan. I shot him a dirty look.

The fortune-teller picked up his deck of cards and shuffled

it with practised ease, his fingers suddenly thick with strands of shadow. Something glinted in his eye, something whispered at his shoulder—he might have been merely a pasar bayang psychic, not in the big leagues, but he was no charlatan. There was real power here. "Can guide, can guide," he said, half to us and half to something else, a rhythm in his voice like an invocation. "The cards are very good, very good. Can help you reach your target, no problem, no problem. Can help you success at your job, get a promotion, anything also can! You work as what, ah?"

"I'm in sales," I said, grasping for the first lie to come to mind. "Nothing special."

He laid out two cards in the middle of the table, face-up, then another over those two, and then a few more face-down in a circle around them. It was a variant of the Celtic Cross, I supposed, but I had never really understood the tarot.

The man squinted at the cards, tilted his head to listen to unseen entities. He pointed to the two cards in the middle—the Knight of Cups and the Knight of Swords—then to Adam and me. "That's you, you," he said matter-of-factly. He tapped on another card with a shadow-stained finger. "Ace of Cups, here. You two are together."

Adam and I glanced at each other, uneasy. You would think that the Others communities would be welcoming of "deviants" and minorities of other sorts, but trampled people trample people, so that was rarely true in practice. But the fortune-teller was moving on, flipping over another card.

"This card is the path. What you need to go through to reach your work target. Five of Swords means you have an enemy. Wah, very unusual."

He paused. "You know who your enemy is?"

An enemy? The wyvern's puppeteer, perhaps? I shook my head.

"Then we can find out, we can find out," he said, voice again a rhythmic chant. He picked up the deck again and shuffled it, then drew a fresh card. The Nine of Pentacles. He frowned, puzzled, drew another card. The World. On the card, the snake enveloping the Earth seemed to glare at me with malice.

"The pasar bayang," he said. "Your enemy is us? Why?"

But he was looking for an answer from the cards, not from us, and he continued to draw fresh cards. "Seven of Cups. Lies, illusions. You're lying... but what are you lying about?"

I glanced at Adam, saw him looking back, worried.

The fortune-teller, not smiling now, was far from finished. He drew another card from the deck and studied it intently before flicking it onto the table.

"Emperor. You work for the government. DEUS." It was a declaration, not a question. With his cards, he had sliced through our disguise like fire through a forest.

Oh crap. It appeared I may have made it a bit too easy.

"Uncle, it's not... We—"

But his eyes had turned cold, and he was on his feet now, a slow and growing fury contorting his features as his finger rose to point at us like a loaded gun. Around us, people started to turn, drawn by the motion, by the intensity of the emotion pouring forth from the old fortune-teller.

I knew what you were supposed to do in situations like this. A two-day course on Aligning Difficult Stakeholders had taught me the FBI's Behavioural Change Stairway Model—active listening, show empathy, build rapport, defuse the situation.

"I understand you're angry, uncle, but if—"

He wasn't listening to me. He was forcing words out past his agitation, his voice quivering with heartbreaking ferocity.

"You FUCKERS," he spat. "Was what you did before not enough? Are you here to kill more of us?"

And then suddenly his fury turned cold and contemptuous. "This is not like last time anymore. Now you're here alone, and we have a protector. Naga Sangam!" He raised his voice, his finger still pointed at us. "They are DEUS. Take them."

I slid my chair back, reached for Adam, turned to run, but the guards were already there, behind us, and they asked no questions, gave us no chance to explain. As the fortune-teller watched with malicious satisfaction and the crowd backed away, the Naga Sangam wrenched our wrists behind our backs and forced us to our knees with their staves, bound us with strong ropes. In the fracas, the table tipped over and the cards scattered, one single card coming to land face-up against my foot. The Tower, struck by lightning and crumbling.

I looked helplessly at Adam, and he looked back, and we despaired.

CHAPTER NINE

Attention has a physical pressure. As the Naga Sangam escorted us through the pasar bayang, I could feel people looking at us, a few staring outright but most watching furtively out of the corners of their eyes. Their scrutiny was a prickling and palpable force, a weight that made me want to lower my head, hunch my shoulders, and cower like a beaten dog.

The silence, too, was a tangible thing. As we passed, conversations trailed off, haggling paused, even the most persistent vendors took respite from their sales pitch. It was, I thought, partly a recognition of our shared humanity, but also a sign of something more selfish. To speak in the presence of the condemned was to invite contamination, to risk being tainted by their sins.

We walked in a silence that was heavy with the weight of exile, flanked by four members of the Naga Sangam. I looked around, hoping for a glimpse of the guard who had stopped us before and pointed us to the clothing stalls, because there had been some kindness and humour in her eyes, but I couldn't find her. Our escorts were courteous but unyielding, absolutely certain of their righteousness.

Damn fanatics.

The thought came automatically, drilled into me from years in government, and I winced inwardly at how easily it'd surfaced. It was too glib, too cruel. Sure, the Naga Sangam followed the old formula—recruit young, offer people meaning, addict them to responsibilities, buy their loyalty with preset structures and the comfort of not having to make their own way in the world. Let work first offer meaning to life, then become *the* meaning to life. That's how you create a cohort of people who know, deep in their bones, that what they are doing is right.

Exactly like civil servants.

But maybe I was overthinking again. Right now, we had bigger problems.

They hadn't said where they were taking us, but we weren't getting any closer to the exits. This was a bad sign. If we couldn't talk our way out, we'd be detained for who knew how long. We couldn't let that happen. The fate of Clementi was hanging by a thread, and if we didn't act soon, it might very well topple into the deep. People might vanish, again, maybe this time for good, all because we were caught up in some stupid ancient feud. So, as we were marched through the stalls and the crowd, I forced myself to stay calm and racked my brain for a plan of escape.

We had three main problems. The first and most pressing: the guards themselves. They were young, but their spears looked ancient and enchanted, the pointy ends made of yellowed ivory and scrimshawed with the elegant curves of Dravidian writing. A sapling in my soul, the manifestation of the little bit of Tamil I knew, wanted tending, but even so I thought I could read the words for *keenness of blade*, for *accumulation of authority* and *puissance to pass down to the next generation of wielders*. These were formidable weapons, but I noted that the hands wielding them were soft and uncalloused. If it came down to it, I might be able to take them.

The second problem: the crowd, dense and unfriendly. In theory, they would pose a greater problem for our captors than for us. Spears were not a practical weapon for crowded streets, where you wanted something less lethal or more precise, like a club or a gun. But I couldn't be sure that these guards would hesitate over collateral damage to bystanders if it meant capturing a couple of fleeing captives. Justice was ever the goddess of fanatics, her blindfold as much for her as it was for them.

The third problem: Adam. I'd put him in danger by letting him come with me, but he hadn't fled, which meant either that his powers were unreliable in this weird pocket dimension or that he was staying back to protect *me*. That foolish man! I wasn't sure if I could protect him from a stray spear, and to be honest, just thinking of him getting hurt made me feel sick to my stomach in a way that might have been problematically heteronormative. I'd have to examine that later. For now, though, all I could do was look over at him, try to put on a brave face, and reassure him that things would be okay. But it was he who smiled weakly back, trying to reassure me in return.

If only I had come alone, things would have been different. I scrambled to come up with something clever, some way to get out of this mess, but before I could, we arrived at a small hill outside the main market area where the stalls were. The guards halted their march with a swift gesture, forcing us to come to a stop.

On the hill stood a makeshift structure that reminded me of a *getai* stage, with a striped awning laid over an aluminium frame and an elevated wooden floor covered with chintzy red velvet. A few floodlights lit the place harshly, but it was the absence of any audience or performers that made me feel naked and exposed. There was something desolate about this setup, a stage without a show. I couldn't help but wonder what kind of performances took place on it during festivals and celebrations, or why we'd been brought here.

The guards politely but firmly turned us around to face the direction we had come from, and the sight of the pasar blew away all the plans I had been formulating in my head.

With the benefit of our distant perspective, the shophouses around the stalls were now visible as a great perimeter, a curve of buildings cradling the pasar. Some trick of the light made the shadows on the buildings move, so the whole length of it seemed to be rippling, sinuous, animate. I could now clearly see that the creams and pastels of the flaking paint were reticulated patterns on scales. Those scales, echoed in the odd angles of windows and pillars, belonged to an enormous shape wrapped around the edges of where we had been, the whole market a glowing spot of noise and activity in its coils.

"Do you see that?" Adam whispered, his voice shaky.

I nodded, stealing a quick glance at the guards. "Are you okay?"

"Yeah," he said grimly. "Hate snakes, though."

"Don't worry," I said. "We'll figure something out."

Adam nodded, a small muscle twitching on his cheek.

We lapsed into silence as the bustling market continued to trade below us. Something was in the air, a hum of anticipation that made my unease grow stronger with each passing moment.

And then, suddenly, over the lights of the market, from the darkness of the sky, something colossal emerged. A monstrous, serpentine head swayed languidly near, its tongue flicking out to taste the air. The spicy, animal musk of it was overpowering. Closer and closer it came, its profile impossibly massive, eclipsing the world. An eye the size of a bus fixed on us, golden and slitted. There was cunning in it, sharp intelligence, but it was cold, caring nothing of mammalian instincts or the needs of warm blood.

In the space between one blink and the next, the image of a young man appeared in the eye of the snake. A boy, really, the oily dark of his hair the same colour as the pupil. He was bare-chested and slender, skin smooth as a lotus petal, his lungi a pale cream and gold. When he spoke, his voice was high but steady.

"Kneel," he said without preamble.

Someone struck my legs from behind, drove me to my knees. I heard a muffled grunt from Adam as the same thing happened to him.

"I see you met Mr. Woo," the boy said, a half-smile on his face. He had a hint of a British accent. "The fortune-teller. He was there at the beginning, you know. Many of us were. Do you know why he hates you? Why he would give his own left hand to end you?"

I kept quiet, my heart pounding in my chest. It seemed the safest option.

"He blames you for his losing his family, you see. Lost business when the pasar had to move, so his wife left, taking the children. He hasn't seen them in over three decades." The Nagamuthu (because that was surely who this was) smirked. "Of course, he's wrong. He would have lost them anyway, nasty man that he is. Used to beat his wife, you know, when the cards told him she was having disloyal thoughts.

"But still," he continued, voice dripping with venom and disdain, "it's convenient, having you to blame. You humans are all alike—you treasure mistreatment by the world as a distraction from your own inadequacies. You crave punishment to avoid reflection. Pathetic. And speaking of pathetic illusions..."

He gestured languidly, and I felt something slough off me. Mei's glamour was gone.

I swallowed. We had no other cards left to play. Just the truth.

"We need your help, Nagamuthu," I said. "Clementi is sinking. Into another dimension. We might lose everyone who lives there. Please, we just want to ask—"

His half-smile remained, and his eyes were mocking. "Ah, Mr. Toh, I can see your heart now. So earnest behind your mask, so eager to play the hero, yet so, so quick to ignore etiquette and history. But I'm curious—does your own organisation, your *government*, know you are here? Do they approve?"

I thought of the conniptions Rebecca would have if she knew I was speaking with the Nagamuthu without a script she'd thoroughly vetted. I shook my head. No use lying here.

"Then there's no one coming to rescue you, is there?" The snake's smile was sinister.

"You don't have to do this," I said to the Nagamuthu. Somewhere, in there, I knew there was goodness. He had given of himself to protect the community of the pasar bayang. Cold-blooded or not, he wasn't a monster. All I had to do was find the right words. "You can help the people of Clementi, the same way you—"

"The people of Clementi? Still so narrow a perspective, still so sure you know what's best. Tell me, why do you assume that saving your people is the right course of action?"

Adam made a frustrated sound. "We can't just stand by and

do nothing! How can you be such an asshole? Don't you care that people will die?"

The Nagamuthu's expression remained unchanged. "On the contrary, I care much more than you can imagine. Not just for your fleeting human lives, but the myriad organisms that inhabit the tapestry of the world. So your people die. So your town sinks." He shrugged a bare shoulder. "Then the worms and the children of the worms will feast. Or whatever creatures are in this other dimension, they will eat well of the bodies. Who are we to say that their lives and well-being are not as precious and worth considering as those of your human beings?"

"Why did you save the pasar, then?" I retorted. I had to make him see. He had to understand the stakes. "If you care so much about everything? You could have let all this collapse to feed the worms you're so fond of. The market, the people, your daughter—"

The image of the boy in the snake's eye leaned forward, and the monstrous head of the snake followed like the prow of a battleship. His voice was still relaxed, unreadable, but I was suddenly sure I had said the exact wrong thing. "Do you know why I hate you? Because you are rude. Because you reek, all the apes in your past, your present, your future, your whole network of stinking, grasping monkeys. And most of all, because you cost me my immortality," he said evenly. But there was an edge to his voice now, a thrumming undertone of anger that vibrated in the earth and in the sky, here in this strange realm. "Do you understand what it cost me to build this place, so you wouldn't exterminate us? Do you know what I had to sacrifice, how you have crippled me? Can your mortal mind even grasp what it is to lose eternity?"

He came nearer, his presence crushing. The force of who he was, a god who spanned the length of time itself, battered at me, threatening to erase my sense of who I was. His strength was a tsunami. But I was a Gardener, and the mangroves of my soul had held back greater storms than this. This close, exposed as he was, I could sense his soul was a vast but empty wilderness, wide basins in his secret heart holding stagnant water, the reserves of power he had cultivated for his immortality. But the earth in him was parched and hard, the flaws in his character fissures in the ground, and the water bled out steadily through these imperfections. I knew then, with certainty, that as he was, he would never have successfully gathered enough spiritual might to become truly undying anyway, whether or not he had created his sanctuary for the pasar bayang.

As he said, sometimes we treasure our mistreatment by others as a distraction from our inadequacies. We collect bruises so we don't have to look inside. We need the world to fail us so we don't fail ourselves.

"What do you want with us?" Adam said.

"With you? Nothing." The Nagamuthu's voice was casual now, dismissive. "Let him go."

The guards stepped forward, untied the knots restraining

Adam with practised ease. Adam scrambled to his feet and glared balefully around him. To my horror, he stayed where he was, face set in a stubborn look I'd seen before.

The Nagamuthu ignored him and turned his attention onto me. "What shall we do with you, then, agent of the government?"

I wanted to rise, to shake off the Naga Sangam, and explain that the government of before was not the government of now. I genuinely believed that. The task force of the seventies had been heavy-handed and cruel, but DEUS today was a skeleton crew of overworked officers trying our damned best to help people, even when the system made it hard. Mei, Jimmy, Fizah—we weren't the ones who had ordered the raids, we weren't the ones who had driven people like Mr. Woo the fortune-teller to ruin. We were the ones trying to make things better. Wasn't that worth something?

But there was no way I could make him see that. No way I could make a case without sounding like I was excusing the past. All I could do was grit my teeth and focus inward, burning away a snarl of weeds that was sprouting in my soul, useless anger and frustration and despair. When I looked back, my eyes must have mirrored the cold in his.

"I don't like the way you look at me," he said with a sneer. Time was frozen, nothing else moved in the world except for here on this platform. "Men were ever monkeys who thought themselves gods. Make him bow."

Without warning, I was struck from behind, the staff

forcing me down till my cheek was pressed against the platform. Someone kicked my arms until they were stretched before me, my palms splayed on the red velvet, a humiliating prostration.

"It would be quite entertaining to kill you and your friend here, and then hunt down your sad crew, for what you forced me to do, for crippling my power," he mused. "But alas, I would not want that karma on me! Do you know that one of your Ministers talked about what you did to the pasar malams as a public education campaign? Let me offer you some education in return."

He paused, and from a shift of the light I could sense the head of the snake moving away. From somewhere distant, I heard him give the command, voice still boyish and unconcerned.

"Break his hands."

I could hear Adam fighting against his captors. He was shouting something incoherent as the guards on either side of me raised their staves. And then the blows came down simultaneously, shattering agony exploding through my hands as my finger bones cracked and splintered. Another strike crushed my knuckles, and a third made a sickening wet sound against the mangled lumps that were all that remained of my hands.

The Nagamuthu's voice echoed like thunder from the dark sky. "You knew you were not welcome here, and yet you came, shameless, arrogant, self-righteous as your predecessors." Through the haze of pain, his voice had the finality of a god's.

"Let me make it very clear," he said. "If you ever dare to come here again, I will hunt down you and your families, and kill you."

They let us go, the guards stone-faced, the crowd staring openly. Adam had done his best to wrap my hands, now reduced to bloody ruins, with my old shirt. Pain and humiliation were weeds I extinguished without mercy. I'd like to think that it was with dignity, straight and tall, that Adam and I walked through the shophouse door that took us home.

On the other side, the beige floors, sterile lights, and cold air of NTUC FairPrice.

Leaning against rows of biscuits and shaving products was a young lady, dressed in a crop top that exposed a shoulder, her hair dyed a cheap brass already turning greenish at the roots. I supposed she might have been pretty beneath all that mascara, but it was a look ten years out of date. She put her phone away and regarded us with distaste.

"A Gardener and a Diver, straight out of the legends," she said in a hard, staccato rhythm. "I'd expected someone so OP to look less...pathetic."

Adam shifted uneasily beside me. Who was this person? I had a suspicion I had to test out.

"I'm Ben," I said, trying to keep my voice soothing, like she was a wild animal. "This is Adam. We've been searching for you. We need your help."

"No shit," she said, unimpressed. "I know. You met my father. He doesn't like you. I don't like you. But I'm bored, so you're in luck."

We had come looking for a Diviner, the Nagamuthu's daughter, and it seemed that we had found her. Or rather, she had found us.

"Listen," I said. "We are investigating this thing happening in Clementi, and we need—"

"Shut up," she interrupted. "I'm not interested in all your blah-blah-blah explanation. Piranhas are coming. A shoal. You need to stop it."

"We can't . . . I don't understand—"

"Forget it," she muttered, rolling her eyes. "I know you're not ready yet, that there are things you need to do before you're where you need to be. I don't even know why I try. Fine, we'll get to that in good time. For now, just because you pissed *appa* off, you get one question. I know what you're going to ask, and it's the wrong question, but I want to hear you ask it anyway."

I thought carefully about how to phrase it. We'd get just this one chance. "What entities, singularly or in plurality, constitute the factors contributing to the submersion of the public housing development at Clementi Avenue 4, Block 375, area code 120375, into the dimension identified by Adam bin Ahmad as the 'Outside,' specifically the submersion that occurred on Tues—"

She let out a sharp, mocking laugh. "Somehow you still

manage to surprise me with your stupidity. I'm not one of the *Aos Sí*. You don't need to play these language games. Your answer is fractals. Fractal memories and plural avatar hierarchies."

What? We couldn't afford more time to do research on arcane concepts. We needed information we could act on, now. But she didn't wait for me to speak.

"Anyway, I'm not interested in explaining everything to you," the Diviner said. "And definitely not interested in listening to you explain everything to me. I already gave you the keywords, go google it yourself. Now, excuse me, I've done my part. I'm out of here."

"Wait!" Adam pleaded, stepping between her and the door. "Please. I know we're strangers, and I know you have every reason to brush us off. But you can't— Look, people's lives are at stake. We've given a lot to try to find you. Can't you just... give us something? Anything that will help us understand what to do?"

I took a breath, steeling myself for what I was about to say. It was a low blow, but we had few options. "Your father doesn't care that people will die. Maybe you do."

For a moment, her façade cracked. Her eyes flickered with some mix of emotions—anger, longing, and an undercurrent I couldn't quite decipher. Her fingers spasmed, her shoulders tensing as if she was about to lash out.

"You don't know anything about my father," she spat. "You have no idea what it's like to be the daughter of a god."

With sudden clarity, I understood what she'd left unsaid. That she'd had to fight her whole life for his attention, against the needs of the pasar bayang, a whole dimension, an entire universe. Out of nowhere, a flash of a memory, a fragment of a ritual, my father saying to me, *It's okay, I'll eat dinner myself.*

"I'm sorry," I said softly, genuinely meaning it.

She sighed, the sound somewhere between annoyance and defeat. "Fine," she said, crossing her arms, "I'll spoon-feed you a little more. Talk. To. The. Man. With. The. Dead. Wife. Clear enough for you?"

It would have to be. "Thank you," I said.

She rolled her eyes again, shoving past Adam and me to get to the door, smelling like cigarettes and some surprisingly sophisticated perfume. When she looked back at us, her expression was inscrutable.

"Free advice, because you're so useless. Your next guide will be the ugly Indonesian clown. Trust him."

And with that, she passed through the door and she was gone.

CHAPTER TEN

Going home, to either Adam's or mine, was not an option. The last thing I wanted was for the neighbours to see me in this state. Going to Dr. Kamini was out of the question as well, since she was close with Jimmy's wife, and then news would get to him and he'd worry like he loved to do. We found ourselves back at the one place where being broken by the job was a badge of pride—the office.

It was Friday evening, and the whole building was deathly quiet: The cleaning aunties had completed their round of vacuuming and wiping and emptying wastebaskets, the maintenance crew had watered the plants and fixed the leaking air cons, and even the most work-crazed policy officer had gone home to pretend they weren't going to check their emails until Monday. There were no people to be found, only rows of monitors showing screensavers from IT on good password practices, gold-foil decorations for the upcoming Deepavali celebrations shimmering on the walls, and us.

Adam supported me as we stumbled past the rows of empty desks. Finally, we reached the DEUS section, and I sank heavily into my chair, Adam sitting across from me where Jimmy could usually be found. He reached for my hands, trembling.

"I need to see," he said.

Gingerly, he unwrapped the cloth over my hands. When the last layer of the shirt peeled off, his breath hitched. Then he turned away, pressing the back of his hand to his mouth, gagging audibly.

"Holy—" His eyes were wide, horrified. "Oh my god, Ben."

I looked down at the mangled wrecks of my hands. Broken bones, slender as those in chicken wings, splayed from my palms. My fingers were crooked, bent at unnatural angles, several attached to the hand only by bits of gore. There wasn't a lot of blood, but what there was, was very red. It didn't even look like it should belong to me.

"It's not as bad as it looks," I said, straining to keep my voice light. The truth was, the pain was excruciating, even with my Gardener skills tamping down the worst of it. I wanted to dig my nails into the armrests of my chair, until I realised I no longer had nails. My jaw was clenched so tight I thought my teeth would crack.

"Ben, this is—" Adam started, his voice choked. He reached for me again, hesitated, clearly unsure what he could do. "How are you even—how are you not screaming?"

I tried again to keep my face blank, to hold steady, to not

worry him, but my legs trembled suddenly and violently, betraying me. "Give me a few minutes."

I closed my eyes and went inside myself, seeking out the matted coils of pain and fear that had taken hold of me, invasive kudzu in my soul that threatened to overwhelm everything. Methodically, I started incinerating them, drawing on the same techniques that had worked for me in the past. They wouldn't do anything for my hands, I knew, but I could at least calm my mind.

But they weren't enough even for that. The lianas snaked through the brush—the agony of torn flesh, the horror of mutilation, the stomach-churning dread of permanent disfigurement and debilitation—crawling their way up my trees and strangling who I was. Where I struck them with fire, they smouldered but did not burn, new shoots twisting from the smoke like the heads of a hydra. My own soul, the one place in the world that I could control, would not obey me.

Frustration and desperation grew, more unwelcome weeds. I unleashed more fire, torrents of it, but the kudzu defeated my attempts, unstoppable. The smoke thickened, dense and choking, filling the rainforest of my soul. In my hands, the pain stabbed, sharp as knives, more serrated with each try.

I did not yield. People were counting on me.

I could not yield.

But it was too much. I drew on all I had, but I wasn't enough.

The agony ripped at my focus like blunt teeth, forced me to

pull back. The pain was a thicket of brambles dense with fear, smoke laced with horror, choking the space of my soul. I had to back out. I had to clear my head, to reorient, to push again, to push harder.

And that's when I saw it. A grove of trees, near the centre of my rainforest—something was wrong with them. The branches were discoloured and twisted, their bark cracked and splintered as if they had been struck by some great force. How had I not noticed it? It was my hyperfocus on the kudzu before, I knew, the tunnel vision I always had when there was something to fix. But recrimination was a luxury I didn't have now.

Ignoring the thorns, I dived, becoming an arrow of intent that tunnelled through the canopy, through smoke and leaf, circling the grove I'd found. I knew, with sudden, clear intuition, what the trees were. This one, cleft as if by lightning, was the tree of my bodily integrity. These two, trembling under the weight of their branches, were my hands, riven.

And from them leaked poison.

Sickness oozed from these broken trees, bled into the soil and fed the kudzu. Pale and bulbous growths carpeted the ground with unhealthy rot. The violent trauma to my hands, I immediately understood, had turned sap into sickness.

Violence corrupts.

And then it was whispering to me, the fungal growths and the infection-fed tendrils, poisonous loops that twisted, sinuated, telling me sweetly, kindly: *You're broken. You're useless now. You'll fail them. You're a burden.*

I tried to call fire, wind, storm, anything, but everything choked on the words.

More spore-born filaments drifted in, insistent. *You're not good enough. You're not enough.*

No. These were lies.

Weren't they?

I called fire again, reaching more deeply into the roots of myself than I'd ever done. I drew on the strength at the heart of me, what I'd made of myself over the years.

I drew on memories of my father, of my mother. How they never gave up. *Be strong,* their memories whispered. *Hold on.* It wasn't their voice, I knew—it was mine, twisting things to what I needed. Still, it was all I had. It had to be enough.

Fire erupted from within me, this time purer, hotter, the clean light of a midday sun. No finesse, no balance, just raw force. With such inelegance I scoured the infection from myself and turned the poisoned earth to cinders.

Then, on pure instinct, I pulled the soot from the ground and sky, gave it new life with fire and sunshine, and with it knitted together the ruptured trees. Broken branches I grafted back with radiant ash; cracks I filled with embers and light. As I did I felt a warmth in my hands, a tingling spreading through my fingers. The pain eased, replaced by a numb ache.

I opened my eyes, registered the gold and silver-grey scars on my hands where the torn flesh had been mended, echoes of sunlight and ash, iridescent tracks that gleamed against my skin. Perhaps I should have been more startled. After all, this was the first time I'd healed myself. I'd never needed to—between my Gardener reflexes and the authority of my position, I'd never on the job suffered anything worse than a bruised ego. I had no idea that healing myself was even possible. But somehow, now that I'd done it, it made sense, this aligning of my soul and my body. It felt right.

I flexed my fingers experimentally, feeling a slight ache but also a profound sense of relief. My hands appeared otherwise functional, if tender and a little weak.

Adam was staring at me, eyes narrowed.

"What?" I said.

"You have healing superpowers," he said accusingly.

That was news to me, too, but I wasn't about to reveal that.

"It still hurts, you know," I said.

"Could have at least told me."

"You didn't even tell me you could teleport."

"That's different," he said, reaching past me for a pack of wet wipes from my desk. "I'm going to clean you up while you... regenerate or whatever."

I watched as he wiped off the worst of the blood, tracing the metallic lines, his hands gentle on mine. I couldn't feel much yet, but I knew that my fingers, suffused with the heat of a distant sun, were warm in his.

"Why didn't you just leave when they set you free?" I asked.

"And miss all the fun?" he said with a little laugh.

"You could have just Dived out of there. I know you could have. You should have."

He looked up and met my eyes. "Someone has to take care of you," he said. "You're all plans and ideas and doing what's right, but mister, you're the dumbest smart person I've ever met.

"Besides," he said, returning his attention to my hands, "what kind of boyfriend would I be if I just left you behind?"

"Boyfriend?" I said, stupidly. We'd been on eleven dates, twelve if you counted the DEUS team meeting in the room that smelled like farts, lucky number thirteen if you counted the pasar bayang expedition. We'd survived a wyvern and a snake god. But did that make us *boyfriends*?

"Well," Adam said. "That was when I thought you'd have hooks for hands. I have a bit of a pirate fetish, I should tell you. But now that you have proper hands again, I'm reconsidering."

I was thinking about what to throw at him when, out of the darkness under my desk, something pale and clawed leapt on me.

It was just the ghost cat, plump and fluffy, but undeniably solid. I supposed it said volumes about my past few days that an attack by the supernatural creature that had been terrorising the office filled me with relief rather than horror. And I supposed it wasn't much of an attack. After the initial flexing of tiny claws to find purchase on my pants, the cat settled onto my lap. It gave me a slow blink with heterochromatic eyes, one blue and one yellow, then promptly fell asleep, snoring softly.

It takes a very bad person to move a sleeping cat, so I just sat there while Adam dabbed at my hands and the cat rumbled like a lorry.

"He likes you," Adam said with a grin.

"Don't let Mei know about this," I said. "Or she'll yell at us for not extracting some blood for her spells."

He reached over to scratch the cat's head. "We have to be unreasonably nice to him. Then he can come back to help us later, when we least expect it. That's how all the stories go."

"He's just a cat. Not Detective Pikachu. Anyway, the Clementi thing is our main focus, and we should keep an eye out for Indonesian clowns. Also, for avatar hierarchies and fractal memories."

"The stuff the Diviner was talking about? No idea what those are."

"I don't know, either. Haven't seen anything like them in our records. Could be that fractals are what's causing the sinking—if it's recursive, you could fold a lot of whatever it is into a small space. I've read a little about the Hausdorff dimension, but I don't understand any of that measure theory stuff."

Adam chuckled. "You lost me at 'Hausdorff,' but it's cute."

"This is why I'm in the market for a new... boyfriend." I considered the word, decided that I liked it. "Know anyone?"

Apparently done getting the gunk off my hands, Adam tossed a big wad of bloody wipes onto my desk and leaned back in his chair. "Not me. I only know guys who insist on wrestling with difficult mathematical concepts and lose sight of the straightforward stuff. Didn't the girl also say something about a man with a dead wife?"

"That's right," I said, using the chance to scritch the cat under his chin. "I think I know who she's talking about. Fizah and I ran into someone like that at the Clementi site. Sweet old man. Mr. Tan, I think it was. We should—"

My phone buzzed. It was my father.

"*Ba*," I said. "What's the matter?"

"You're very busy." Our own ritual.

"Yes, as usual."

He hesitated for a moment, cleared this throat. "It's almost nine. Dinner is getting cold."

A stab of guilt. With everything going on, I'd forgotten to tell him I would be home late. "You eat first," I replied, avoiding eye contact with Adam, who was watching me closely. "Got a lot of work going on."

"Oh, I see. I will cover it for you. You can eat it when you get back."

"Okay," I said. "I will."

There was silence on the other end of the line, and I shifted uncomfortably. My father and I had never been good at showing our feelings openly to each other. I couldn't share the details of my job or the dangers I faced—both because they were classified and because he would worry himself to death—and he couldn't understand why I was always so elusive about my life. He still blamed me for my mother's passing, I think, or maybe it was the other way around. We never talked about it, but this was the same story all parents and children got stuck in, wasn't it? Love and resentment, unclear boundaries of where guilt ended and blame began. Maybe I was projecting. Maybe he was. Either way, it was easier not to talk about it. Or anything, really.

He didn't even know I was a Gardener. He wouldn't understand, and so all that was left to us was small talk, something neither of us was good at.

"I'll eat by myself," my father said, responding to a question I hadn't asked. "It's okay. Work is important."

I felt a pang of shame as I hung up the phone and placed it on the desk. A ghost of a memory drifted by, something the Diviner had said about her father, but I shoved it away. We didn't have time.

"I should get going," I said to Adam, trying to return to shores I could navigate. "Time to find out what's going on with Mr. Tan."

Adam raised an eyebrow. "You don't seriously mean now, do you? Your plan was to rest, heal, reconvene everyone, and then go. Right? Right?"

"Well," I said. "We really don't know when the whole place will sink. I can't afford to wait."

He shook his head, clearly frustrated. "We also can't keep pushing forward," he argued. "You need to take care of yourself first, Ben. You're not invincible."

"People might die. I can't wait."

"All right," he said, after a while. "But at least let the team know what's going on. They deserve to know."

I hesitated, knowing he was right. "Fine. We'll tell the team, but they stay put. I'm just going to go talk to Mr. Tan, find out why the Diviner thinks an old widower has answers. No heroics."

He eyed my hands, scarred with faint radiance, and sighed. "You don't choose whether or not there are heroics."

"Neither would the team," I said quietly. "They aren't field agents. If there's danger, they could get hurt. I can take care of myself, and anyway, no heroics."

"Fine," he said. "Then I'm coming with you."

Hell if I was going to bring him along again, after almost getting him killed at the pasar. But he turned to me and he had that look in his eyes, that set to his jaw, and I knew he wouldn't back down. I realised then, with another surge of shame, that I selfishly didn't want him to back down. Anyway, we were just going to talk, and if the place sank while we were there, who better to survive it than Adam? Maybe it would be helpful, to have someone with me. "Okay," I finally said. "On one condition. You do exactly as I say."

The cat on my lap decided just then that it had enough of our drama and stretched out with a jaw-cracking yawn. It hopped off me and slinked under my desk, where it flopped on its side and hooked a paw around something in the narrow crevice between the desk and the wall. As it batted it out into the light, Adam and I both turned our attention to the thing the cat had recovered.

It was my phone, the lock screen displaying the sere

landscape of the Martian surface. I recognised the scratch on the screen from the time it had been knocked off its perch at the gym. But my confusion grew as I looked back at my desk, where my actual phone was still sitting, showing the same image of Mars and the same scratch.

Instinctively, I reached for my phone, the one on the desk, but my hands were still healing, my fingers still clumsy, and I knocked it away from me instead, the phone tumbling into the crack between the desk and the wall.

Into the same spot from where the cat had retrieved it, fifteen seconds ago.

Adam and I stared for what must have been a full minute, then I got it.

Mei was right that it wasn't a ghost cat. It was something far more astonishing—a cat that could reach through time, able to wriggle between the present and (at least) the past, interacting with objects and the world as they once were. Walking on air by stepping on shelves and cabinets that no longer exist, passing through walls with ease, vanishing without a trace. All cats were at least a little magical, but this one was extra special.

"How come it doesn't meet itself?" Adam asked when I explained my theory to him, the cat watching us calmly the whole time.

"I don't know."

"Can it go to before it was born?"

"I don't know."

"Can it eat one bit of cat food infinite times, by eating it and then going to the past before it ate it and then the past of that and then…"

"I don't know." These were great questions, actually. Pity we didn't have time to look into any of them right now.

"Are you actually any good at your job?"

"Shut up and help me get rid of all these bloody wipes. We are going to Clementi."

CHAPTER ELEVEN

Mr. Tan let us in without fuss, sat us down, and told us in no uncertain terms that we were having tea. It was late, far too late for tea, but we didn't object.

He had served us tea the first time, too, when Fizah and I met him. He was as I remembered him, an older man with greying hair and sad eyes, dressed neatly in a polo and slacks. His motions, as he made chrysanthemum tea, were refined and graceful.

Mr. Tan's living room was clean but a little dated, with terrazzo floor tiles and furniture that would count as retro in a more stylish apartment, but here was just old. A standing lamp lit the space from a corner near the window; a small pile of magazines was stacked neatly under the coffee table—*Discover*, *Popular Mechanics*, *Reader's Digest*. A piano stood against one wall, on it displayed the sorts of knickknacks and photographs one gathers over a lifetime. I recalled that Mr. Tan had told us about his adult children, moved overseas, and his late wife, recently passed. One of the larger frames contained a faded photo of a young couple, seated in the same room we were in, on what looked like the same sofa. It was presumably Mr. and Mrs. Tan. He was dressed in a denim shirt and flared jeans, she in a mustard polka-dotted dress, and she looked at him like she was the luckiest woman in the world.

Overhead, the ceiling fan clacked rhythmically, like the guru stone in a string of prayer beads, keeping count. The sound of the fan, the smell of the brewing chrysanthemums, the clink of cups being taken out of cupboards—it was all very peaceful, very domestic, no fractals or avatar hierarchies to be seen. It looked nothing at all like the locus of a sinkhole into unreality.

We were served tea in mismatched mugs. Mr. Tan sat down with us at the dining table, his hands loose and relaxed in front of him.

"You look a bit like my son, you know. Anyway, I knew you would be back," he said to me. His English was clipped and precise. "You grow things inside, like me."

Surprise coiled around my throat, a vine in shades of venomous orange. Was he a Gardener, too? How did he know about me? I burned the vine away immediately, but some of my surprise must have shown momentarily on my face.

"You just have to look and listen," he said, touching his chest. "With this. But you young people, you all think it is a waste of time to sit still and appreciate things. You want to rush, rush, do things. My children are the same, you know. They are so educated, so they don't listen to me—I'm just an old man, what do I know. They don't even listen to their own bodies, so their health is suffering, I tell them. But they won't listen."

He smiled wryly. "But you're not here to hear an old man ramble. How can I help you?"

I was still getting over the revelation he had so casually tossed at me. Gardeners were extremely rare, if the records are to be believed—rarer than Olympic gold medalists, rarer even than Nobel laureates—with no more than a hundred or so in the world at any one time. I'd never met one. I'd never even expected to meet one.

Could I have missed them all this time? Could *I* detect them if I just, as Mr. Tan said, looked and listened? I'd never heard of anyone being able to do that, but then again it wasn't like there were publicly available how-to guides for this. Gardeners, even relative to other already privacy-obsessed Others, were loath to write anything down. Something about what we did, our work with the intimate, growing parts of ourselves, made it feel like a violation to splash techniques out on paper as dead words. Even the most basic skills passed only through word of mouth, from mentor to apprentice, or not at all. But I hadn't had a mentor. There had been no one to guide me, no one to help me make sense of what was growing in my soul. Everything I learned, I'd learned on my own.

This—what Mr. Tan was suggesting could be done, that

you could sense another Gardener—was a revelation. A possibility. But I refused to be distracted. I was here to find out what was weighing this place down, and none of us knew how much time we had before the next wave. Before this whole place sank lower into the Outside, and the unreal water claimed more dogs and, eventually, people. I bludgeoned ahead.

"Do you know anything about fractal memories, Mr. Tan? Plural avatar hierarchies? Weighing things down, sinking them into another world?"

He blinked at me, genuinely confused. "I'm not sure what you're—"

This couldn't be a dead end. We needed something. Anything.

"Maybe you've seen something unusual around here lately? Something not normal?" I asked.

He laughed softly, this time with a hint of bitterness. "Nothing has been normal here for a while, not since my wife died. Ah Bee, she would give music lessons in the evenings, you know. I would have to turn the TV off, just like now, and the kids would come and sit over there and learn how to play."

He gestured to the piano. "There's no more music in the house anymore."

"I'm sorry about your wife," I said carefully, keeping the frustration from my voice. Something about the way he spoke made me think of my father, and I didn't want to go there. This wasn't the time to think about my mother or what I had left unresolved. We were here to solve a problem, and we needed clear and actionable answers about what was weighing this place down. Answers he wasn't giving.

"No, no, I'm sorry," Mr. Tan said. He folded his hands around his mug of tea, but didn't drink for a long, silent moment. "People say the pain goes away, but it hasn't. It still feels so near, you know. Sometimes, I call her name and it feels like she never left."

Adam leaned forward. His voice was soft, full of compassion. "In a way, for her, she never did, did she? Maybe she isn't there anymore when you call her name, but I have a feeling that you were always there when she called yours. She never lost you."

I glanced at Adam. This was a side of him I'd never seen.

"Yes," Mr. Tan said, blinking quickly. "She was everything. She was beautiful, you know, my Ah Bee. Everyone said so. I used to have to chase away other men all the time, because they would see her with me and think, *What's someone so pretty doing with this guy?* They knew she was out of my league. But she didn't. I tricked her into marrying me, staying with me for thirty-two years. And then just like that, she was gone."

He gave us a sad smile. "You probably think I'm a crazy old man. Have you lost anyone?"

Adam shook his head.

"My mother," I said. My hands ached. "A long time ago." A familiar clearing in my soul rustled as I said her name. Lilies, my mom's favourite, but these ones had never flowered despite me fussing over them daily. Even when I used to sit and watch them. This time, though, there was a foreign presence there, nestled like a maggot among the buds that had never yet bloomed. Green shoots pushed from the earth even as I watched—an invasion, unnaturally vital.

Then the first leaves of the alien plant opened, and they were mustard yellow, polka-dotted. Just like Mrs. Tan's dress, in the photo of her on the piano.

A shiver of fear whispered to the surface. I controlled the urge to scramble back, to grab Adam and flee this place. I reached for him under the table, grasping his leg. This was Mr. Tan's doing, I knew it without a doubt. With his words, he had somehow reached into my soul and sown something there, something related to his late wife. Something that had reached deep within me and made root.

"What do you grow, Mr. Tan?" I asked.

"Memories," he said softly. He had been expecting the question. "Just memories of her."

I heard the dull pain in his voice, so present, so close, and I felt a disconcerting moment of envy and anger. Why hadn't my father mourned this much when my mother passed? How could he have been so philosophical, so stoic? Didn't he feel anything?

Grief grew in me, but at least it was old and familiar. I turned my attention to it, to bury it with the same practised ease I had a thousand times before, but somehow, overtaxed as I was, here in this aging HDB flat so much like our old home, that old emotion was too much. It surged, dark and tidal, and it cracked me open, a wave sweeping over me, a momentary occluding of the sun of my soul. Just for a moment.

But in that point of stillness, with the steam of the chrysanthemum tea fogging up my glasses and with my hand still, somewhat awkwardly I was sure, gripping Adam's leg, I looked at Mr. Tan with my heart open, and I *saw*.

I saw not just what he was, an old man, a widower, a Gardener, but the truth of his soul. For him, his wife's death had broken the foundations of his universe, and he had become a Gardener out of necessity, grown something in the soil of his own self to keep his world from collapsing. Where I had cultivated a little bit of everything, he had cultivated Grief alone, and its fruits were memories. Specifically, memories of his late wife, made potent by his dedication and focus, a tree thick with flowers and heavy with fruits, its golden pollen hanging still in the quiet air. Each petal, each fruit, each mote was a memory—here was Mrs. Tan holding a newborn baby, looking tired but happy. Here was Mrs. Tan at some child's birthday party, in what must be her favourite mustard-coloured polka-dotted dress, half-crouched like a pretend monster, chasing a herd of giggling kids. Here was Mrs. Tan, drinking a beer, laughing so hard some of it came out of her nose. Here was Mrs. Tan, older, hair shorter, squatting on a void deck, feeding a cat.

But something had clearly gone wrong. The fruits I saw were overripe, skin split and leaking sticky juice. The edges of the flowers and leaves were swollen and fuzzy, the tips of the branches blurred, hard to see. I remembered what the Nagamuthu's daughter had said. Fractal memories? I thought also of the new plant growing in my soul, sown by Mr. Tan's words.

"Have you told other people about her?" I asked.

Mr. Tan met my eyes. He knew that I knew. "It wasn't just me who loved her, you know. Everyone loved her. The neighbours, the kids, even the cats. I tell them about her. I share my stories with them, my memories. This way, a small part of her can live on, you know? In me, in them."

Oh my god. Were these trees, these fruiting memories of Mrs. Tan, growing in all the neighbours? I remembered, suddenly, the women all wearing Love, Bonito outfits. The disproportionate number of ads on the noticeboard downstairs offering piano lessons. Was this a case of mass possession, not by ghosts but by memories? And if all the trees were sick like his were...

Fear stirred in me. Fear and excitement. I had almost the whole shape of the mystery. Mr. Tan was growing memories of his wife, in his own soul and in the souls of others, and these memories were sick. Something about the memories or the sickness was weighing Block 375 down, causing the whole place to sink, letting the wave we'd seen wash over and sweep things into the Outside. I just didn't know what it was, exactly.

But I knew what I was supposed to do—we'd done Observe and Analyse from OAR. Now it was time for Respond. The standard operating procedure at this point was to take Mr. Tan into custody, quarantine him to prevent further harm, and determine whether there was any need for further, more drastic measures.

But that was just the SOP handed down to us by previous DEUS officers. We did not actually have legitimate authority to arrest or quarantine anyone, much less anything more drastic. The police were the ones with the authority, but they didn't have the means to handle many of the issues around the Other communities—it's not like they could send a spirit to juvenile detention at Boys' Home, or hold a witch in prison. DEUS, on the other hand, had the means but not the authority. Over the years, we'd arrived at a workable arrangement. The police would quietly refer to us cases they couldn't or wouldn't handle, and then they would look the other way when DEUS had to take legally grey actions. One such action, developed early in DEUS's history for dealing with dangerous Others, was a procedure using the artefact we called Binder One.

Binder One was a stone roughly the shape and size of a slightly deflated basketball. A dull grey granite, the only indication that it was anything more than a mundane rock was a sentence scratched into it—*PROMISES ONE MAKES / BIND ONE*, it said. There were no records of how or when DEUS acquired it, because our records were Binder *Two*, and even the paper files didn't go back that far.

What Binder One did was enforce promises made when

touching it. A simple thing, really, but a powerful tool in our arsenal for managing the criminal or antisocial elements of the Others society. The earliest recorded oaths (dutifully logged in Binder Two by my DEUS predecessors) were simple ones—*I promise not to eat children anymore. I swear by my hope of rebirth that I will stop cursing Mrs. Soh.* But then, by the mid-nineties, some legalistically minded civil servant had gotten their hands on it and "standardised" and "streamlined" everything, so now what I had was eighteen different templates, each three to four pages of bullets and sub-bullets, which I was supposed to use each time we hauled in a dangerous Other.

Thing is, I never managed to get comfortable with it. The stone itself I understood the need for, and I even found it comforting that we had such an option. It was the boilerplate oaths I found troubling. Some of the common sub-clauses placed on the oath-swearer unreasonably onerous demands—abstaining from participating in unauthorised gatherings, submitting to unscheduled assessments for compliance, reporting on behaviour in their own communities "detrimental to social harmony." It had more than a whiff of dystopian fascism to it, and it didn't help that most of the Others I'd made make promises on Binder One had done so without understanding what they were reading out loud.

Here with Mr. Tan, I knew what was supposed to happen next, what the official protocol demanded. It was to get Mr. Tan in and coerce him into swearing upon Binder One our most stringent oath (that would be template 18B, including appendices A through C), just in case. But all this bureaucratic obsession with the correct process would do nothing to deal with the real threat, which was whatever was heavy enough to be dragging things into the Outside. I knew it would piss off Rebecca, but I couldn't in good conscience subject Mr. Tan to the whole ordeal of Binder One. He clearly didn't know what was going on, didn't mean to cause any trouble.

All the paperwork in the world wouldn't matter if Clementi got sucked into the weird ocean dimension.

"Mr. Tan," I said. "Can we take you to see a few friends of ours? Unofficially?"

We were so close to figuring this out. Mei would know what to do.

Mr. Tan stood and walked to the windows, looked out at the dark sky visible through his metal blinds. "I don't mind," he said, "but maybe tomorrow? It's late now."

"Tomorrow is okay. Don't talk to anyone else tonight, okay? In the morning, I'll come by and we can . . ."

Adam was elbowing me, urgently. He pointed to Mr. Tan's shadow, puddled at his feet, cast by the standing lamp next to him. From it radiated dark threads, the same sorcery we'd seen before.

I started to get up, and just then, something struck me. A dart was in my shoulder, pain and numb stiffness spreading from it. Then everything went black.

CHAPTER TWELVE

Why, hello, said a voice in my head. *Wakey, wakey, sleepyhead. Don't open your eyes yet, just listen. You should hear this.*

I was lying on the floor, my cheek pressed against what felt like concrete. And apparently, I was hearing voices. The air was cool and sterile, carrying the faintest hum of machinery. My body felt distant, disconnected, stiff, but inside, my soul rustled with activity. Whatever was in that dart had sunk deep, spreading its sedative through me. My rainforest was working steadily, trees transmuting the paralytic agent to new growth, hastening my recovery. At its edges, where the mangroves stood, storms lashed and currents raged. Something dark and barbed had been trying to find its way in, but even while I'd been unconscious, the defences of wind and tide that I'd cultivated had turned back the intrusion.

Where was Adam?

"It's not working," someone said. Low voice, nervous, standing perhaps a metre away. "He's more guarded than Asset

C-375, and his psychometrics are even less favourable. We'll need more time. If you could give us twenty-four hours—"

"You have six, *doctor.*" A new voice, this one deep, casually supercilious. "And don't waste them with whining. Wake him up. This one."

Footsteps. Someone jabbed me in the ribs with their shoe, hard. Then again.

I groaned, pretended to come to. A light, low on the floor and incredibly bright, forced me to squint, but I could see that I was in some sort of cramped room, empty of furniture. The walls were a clear plastic, thick enough to distort the view, and beyond them I could blurrily see steel surfaces, blinking screens, and wires. A laboratory, and I was in a cage.

Adam was on the ground next to me, a grey and crumpled heap. For a heart-stopping moment, I worried he was dead, then I saw his chest rising and falling and felt a flood of relief, followed abruptly by a spike of rage. These assholes, whoever they were—they got him, too.

Four people stood in front of us. The one in the middle was older, perhaps in his early fifties, dressed casually in a short-sleeved shirt and slacks. He had an expensive haircut and an understated Rolex, and there was a blurring about his face, a darkening in the air. A spell? The man on his left was in a lab coat, gangly and balding, tapping away on a tablet. Flanking them were two identical muscular women wearing some sort of dark uniform. They were the bruisers. The ones who'd kicked me awake.

I'd seen one of them before. She'd been at the bar where Adam performed, where she'd watched us in the back alley. In my head, pieces were falling into place.

Be careful of the twins, said the voice in my head. It was the same voice that had prodded me back to consciousness. The voice of someone? Something? *They're telekinetics. Dangerous.*

I decided the voice was the least of my worries.

Rolex spoke, his voice startlingly deep.

"I really must apologise for the way we are meeting, Benjamin. And for the precautions we must take." He gestured to the surroundings, then to the blurring spell in front of his face. "This is not ideal. I understand that you have expressed some interest in our Asset C-375. You have been to see him several times, haven't you? Once, we can accept. Twice makes us worry, just a little, that our interests are at odds."

He smiled, avuncular, and I disliked him immediately.

"So I'm afraid our Appropriations Team...misread the situation," he continued. "Especially when it looked like you were going to take C-375 away, perhaps to one of your DEUS facilities, and do something to him we'd all regret. They will be working overtime to review their processes so this doesn't happen again. But since you're here—"

"Who are you?" I asked, sitting up with some effort and ignoring the glare of the uniformed women. My body felt like it belonged to someone else. But my soul remained my own, and as I spoke I focused inside, scorching away the remaining traces of the sedative in my system, fortifying the mangrove trees against the barbed things trying to come in. Now that I was paying closer attention, I could see that these would-be intruders were threads and hooks of shadow, the same magic that we had observed with the wyvern and with Mr. Tan. They were trying to control me, too, but my defences were standing, at least for now.

Safe within my fortress, I catalogued what I knew.

First, these guys were formidable. They knew we were DEUS. Either they were powerful enough to be unconcerned about the consequences of kidnapping us, or they believed (correctly) that we were stretched too thin to offer much in the way of payback. Either way, powerful or knowledgeable, and mysterious. Too well funded to be academia, too much science and tech to be the Nagamuthu's people, too brazen to be the *wulin*, the clandestine criminal underworld of the Others. Some other faction, then, possibly someone we didn't yet know about. I'd have to keep my eyes open for more clues to their identity.

Second, Mr. Tan was somehow involved in this, an "asset" these guys wanted for themselves. Assuming their purpose was nothing so mundane as acquiring his flat or buying his late wife's piano, I thought it was safe to conclude that their interest was in his Gardener abilities. And judging by the lengths they were willing to go to, those powers were important to them. I'd have to find out why, and make sure to keep my own nature as a Gardener hidden from them.

Third, Adam. These *bastards* took him, too. I had to find

some leverage, some way to get Adam out of this mess I had brought him into. Until I found that, though, I had to be careful, play along and keep them talking. And the best way to get people to talk more, reveal more than they should, is to say something incorrect. People can't resist correcting others' mistakes—just look on the internet.

"The wyvern," I said, then gestured at the bruiser-telekinetics. "And them. You've been following us. Watching us. *Trying to kill us.* Why?"

"Kill you?" Rolex said. "No, no, no, I just want to have a little chat. I've been so curious. I wanted to meet you."

"You start all your meetings this way?" I couldn't help it. People like that, smug in their power, hiding brutality beneath a veneer of dishonest civility, they pissed me off.

"Well, you were getting close to very sensitive, very... expensive matters. Your friend over there, he was poking around for days on our site, and we just let him be. But then he linked up with you, and I knew DEUS wouldn't just leave things alone. So we tried to... invite you to talk, but you refused."

The wyvern. That was the first kidnapping attempt.

"Then I thought to myself," he continued, "maybe if we left you alone you'd leave us alone. But then you go and harass C-375, an asset we've put so much research time and funding into, and you want to take him away. That's when I thought, we really need to bring you guys in."

The poisoned darts. That was the second kidnapping attempt—the one that worked.

Rolex smiled with all the sincerity of an insurance agent trying to sell you another add-on plan. "We just want to talk."

The voice in my head laughed. *They want to talk because they can't make you a puppet*, the voice said. *Like they did with me. Otherwise they wouldn't bother.*

"Just want to talk?" I said. "You kidnapped us."

"I know we're starting off on the wrong foot. But you see, we are really on the same side."

I quirked an eyebrow. That was all this deserved.

"My scientists," he continued, somehow making the word sound contemptuous, "they tell me that the Clementi site, this Block 375, is... opening up to another dimension. The Void, they call it. Not one of the tiny, useless ones the physicists have found, but a large one, virtually a brand new universe. Surely, you already know that. But do you have any idea what this could mean? Do you have any idea of the possibilities? Clean energy, waste disposal, new materials, national security... My engineers already have prototypes for siphons. We could do something good for the world."

The Outside, and Clementi sinking—he was using different words, but that was what he was talking about. He wanted to exploit the Outside for... well, he had claimed it was to "do something good for the world," but I knew his type. He'd do something good, all right, but it'd be good for him, for his own advantage. That's all the world was to people like him—resources just waiting for his superior wisdom and vision to give it purpose.

I'd seen the way he treated his own scientists, his own employees, like they were idiots or tools. I've had bosses exactly like him, who thought inspiration meant delivering monologues that made them sound like movie villains. Confident in their power, they didn't care how nakedly they revealed their contempt, or how they came across to people beneath them. People like me.

"How's Mr. Tan fit into all this?" I asked.

"Why, he's the nexus of the opening, my door into the Void. His psychic overflow, as you know, is somehow tunnelling through the barrier between our dimensions."

Again, a different paradigm to explain the same thing we had been investigating. What we understood to be a weighing down and sinking, they saw as some sort of *tunnelling*. But it was fundamentally the same idea, and if these guys had been studying the phenomenon, they had to be aware of the same potential catastrophe we were—that this other dimension, the Outside, could come crashing in, engulfing Clementi. Did they just not care, or what?

"He will give us access," Rolex continued. He was still talking about Mr. Tan. "Just... a little slowly."

I remembered the strings extending from Mr. Tan's shadow, puppet magic that told him what to love or hate. What to obsess over.

"Too slowly," I said, realisation dawning. "You're forcing him to remember his wife. To speed up the process."

Rolex spread his hands in a gesture of helplessness. "Would

you hold us hostage to one man and the pace at which he works through his grief? But we're not monsters. When he finally breaks through, we'll be right there beside him to make sure he's safe."

Meaning, when Clementi sank completely, these vultures would be there to take advantage. Speaking of which, I had to find out if they were truly so callous, so utilitarian.

"What about Clementi? You know people will die when this door into the Void opens."

"We've learned that there is some risk, yes." Rolex's face was a mask of regret. "But I'm prepared to invite Mr. Tan to stay here, where we can manage the breach in a controlled environment. For his safety and the safety of the residents there. It will delay our timelines, since C-375 will have to start boring a new way through in this new location, but we can absorb the cost. As a gesture of good faith, to you."

"Why are you telling me all this?"

"Well, like I said, I just wanted to talk. Get you to see that we want the same thing—peace, prosperity, progress. Your job is to make sure our country's supernatural assets are properly utilised, and that's exactly what we're doing here. We are on the same side, Benjamin. All you need to do is back off, go back to doing what you do best. Handling your community cases and helping old *pontianaks* sign up for MediSave, all that meaningful stuff. Let us deal with the big, messy risks, make Clementi safe, and take Mr. Tan off your hands. Everyone wins."

Against the walls of my soul, against the mangroves and winds and currents that defended me, the hooked puppet strings flailed, lashed, failed to find purchase.

"And if I say no?"

He laughed. "Why would you say no? You—"

"And if I call the cops on you?"

He laughed again, this time derisive. "Don't be ridiculous. What are you going to tell them? Hello, *polis*, I was shot with wyvern poison and kidnapped? Good luck with that. Anyway," he said, his tone almost casual. "We've been working on some... cognitive realignment tools. You won't have to remember this whole... sordid episode."

With a chill, I realised that, even if they let us go, we would not leave with our memories intact. I looked over at Adam, thought about these guys rummaging inside his head, taking his music, his laughter, changing what he cared about. The exact person that he was.

Rage surged, sudden and uncontrollable. Vines straining upwards, thick with thorns. Blistering equatorial sun. Lightning against a clear sky.

Rolex squatted down on his haunches to my level, the spell hiding his face shimmering like heat waves. "Believe me, we are not the bad guys. Just think about what I said. Be reasonable, and leave this alone."

He must have seen something in my face just then, because he stood sharply, his performative charm discarded, and made a gesture behind him. The scientist with the tablet, whom I had almost forgotten, tapped frantically at the screen. There was a grunt of pain from the voice in my head, and the lashing shadow strings in my soul redoubled their efforts.

Rolex dusted nonexistent dust off his slacks and walked to the door. "Take a bit of time to consider your position, and our offer. We will be back in the morning for your answer."

CHAPTER THIRTEEN

Beside me, Adam's skin was still grey from the poison. Threads of darkness extended from his shadow, as they did from mine. I was sure, with absolute certainty, that my answer to Rolex was no. Hell no, and a middle finger.

The mistake they'd made was a familiar one. Like most of the movers and shakers in the technocratic utopia of Singapore, they made a fetish of Reason and called it pragmatism. They had put together an airtight case for letting them handle things—we could sit back, relax, and Clementi would be fine. We'd stop getting attacked by wyverns and strike teams. All our problems get solved. Who wouldn't want that? Whoever Rolex and his people were, they'd stacked the deck, set the stage, cooked the books until there was only one real choice for any reasonable person. The choice they wanted.

Problem was, I wasn't feeling reasonable.

They'd tracked Adam, listened in on our conversation in the back alley of the bar. They'd sent monsters at us. They were endangering hundreds of Clementi residents for some half-baked mad scientist shit, and they were forcing Mr. Tan to relive his grief, day after day. Mr. Tan, an Other and thus under my direct charge, but also just a poor old man who lost his wife. Mr. Tan, who never meant anyone any harm.

They wouldn't even say his name. To them, he was Asset C-375.

There was a time when, maybe, I would have burned away the plants of spite growing inside me, because they weren't productive. I would have uprooted my anger at the way they humiliated us and at their smug confidence, because it was irrational. I would have cauterised my emotions with the light of reason.

But then I'd grown up. I lost my mother. I fell in love, and made friends, and lost friends, and I learned. Pragmatism is no way to live a life. There are reasons beyond what is reasonable.

Also, this was the second time in as many days that I'd been captured by a paramilitary group and brought before their evil villain boss. It was frankly ridiculous, and I was sick of it.

So, now that our captors were gone, I let the vines, already straining to grow, sprout in my soul, shone the sun of my attention on them, anger bristling with thorns. They spread through the underbrush, twined up the trees, and in moments I was filled with the spikes of a focused and contained fury. At my bidding, sap surged in the trees representing strength, power, righteous vengeance.

We needed to get out.

Adam was breathing raggedly, and I couldn't get him to return to consciousness. I had to slam down hard on the heart-wrenching fear that Adam would not be okay, the panic that masqueraded as something prophetic, but even then I could taste some of that sour bile in my throat. I slung him across my shoulders in a fireman's carry and lifted my foot to kick down the door of the cage.

You'll set off every alarm in this place if you do that, the voice in my head said.

You! I thought, lowering my foot. *Who are you?*

More than a stranger, less than a friend. Already a branch, not yet a seed.

What?

What? the voice mimicked.

There was something about the timbre of the voice, the rhythm, the barbed mockery... It somehow reminded me of the puppet strings we'd seen on the wyvern, on Mr. Tan, on ourselves. And then there'd been that grunt of pain in my head just now, when the gangly henchman had pressed the offensive.

These shadow threads, I thought at the voice. *Those are from you, aren't they? Why are you helping them?*

I already told you. They control me. I'm a puppet, too. Weren't you listening? Do you have a reputation for not listening?

What? Wait. You know what, never mind. Can you unhook the strings?

There was a pause.

It'll cost me, the voice said. *But I like you, so... okay.*

I had no idea what he meant, but it wasn't like I could afford to be picky.

The puppet strings vanished from Adam's shadow. They withdrew from where they had lashed against my inner barriers. Adam coughed and subsided into what looked like a more natural sleep.

Thank you, I thought. *How do we get out of this place?*

Ooh, is this like a riddle? Let me guess, let me guess. Is the answer one asscheek clapping?

What? I don't understand—

You are so serious, it's honestly very funny. I can let you out, but they have guards outside. You'll have to deal with that yourself.

I felt the thorns in my soul, straining for blood. Those men had given us time to make a decision, as if it was free choice and not coercion. They had sent agents to Mr. Tan's flat, not to rescue anyone but to capture an asset.

Let me at them, I thought.

Your funeral.

A spike of shadow slid across the plastic walls, punctured what must have been a keypad on the other side of the door. A sizzle of electricity, a flare of sparks, and the door cracked open.

I shoved it the rest of the way with my foot.

On the other side was a laboratory, a large one. The plastic prison we were in was at one end of it, and at the far end, an exit. Dominating the centre of the room was a case of thick glass, brightly lit by spotlights and ringed with circles of lasers and laptops. Inside squatted a painted wooden effigy, bulky and crude.

And just in front of us, four guards, seated around a table cluttered with the remains of a meal. Their tactical gear looked more suited to commandos than corporate security. Beside their plastic plates, their white ceramic face masks—featureless, expressionless—lay like strange shells. They were turning now, their attention shifting from dinner to us, hands instinctively reaching for their masks, sliding them back into place.

All yours, the voice said. It seemed to come from the effigy in the glass case.

I set Adam down. Inside me, the sun blazed and wind howled through the vines and thorns and the leaves of the trees.

I charged.

They were trained combatants, and like most trained combatants, they were strong and fast and skilled. The speed of their reactions was top-notch. Two unholstered their batons with practised swiftness, whipped them towards me. The others stepped back, the ones with rifles raising their weapons in smooth arcs.

They had clearly drilled this a thousand times. They thought that strength came down to muscle and motion. They thought that skill was just a matter of repeating actions until they were bone-deep.

But the self lay deeper than actions. And essence lay deeper than bone.

I would show them their mistake.

Inside me, the roots of the rainforest plunged down, drawing up clear water. Gusts whipped through tangled canopies, the dull roar in my ears my battle hymn.

In three steps, I was among them, sidestepping the baton swingers to close with the more dangerous rifle squad. I ducked inside the reach of one of the guns and with one hand slapped the barrel of the other firearm upwards. It discharged with a hiss of air. More wyvern poison, I assumed. Pivoting, my elbow found a diaphragm. The heel of my hand slammed into a throat. Two guards dropped gasping to the ground.

The two with batons turned to strike together, synchronising their attacks in clearly practised motions. Shockingly disciplined—what was this place that could afford elite guys like these?

They came at me from opposite sides, trying to force me to split my focus. Professional, precise, yes, but loose and uncentred. Without depth. I wove between their weapons, turning from the attacks as a leaf turns in a breeze, as the seasons turn from monsoon to monsoon, unhurried, relentless. My palms found the centres of their Kevlar vests, and I pushed, a surge of wind, sun, thorn expelled with a released breath.

They were flung across the room like toys, their masks cracking against the walls, porcelain faces shattering on impact. The thuds echoed through the suddenly silent room.

Less than ten seconds. That was all it took.

Quite a show! the voice in my head said. This intrusion into my normally well-guarded thoughts was still jarring, but now I could sense its source. One of the spotlights had been knocked askew during the fight and now pointed at the statue, casting a long shadow across the room, and it was from that shadow that the voice came. There was something malformed and hideous about it, that patch of darkness, but I felt no sense of malice. I thought I could see the lips of the shadow move as it spoke. *No regrets about getting you out of there, though I wish you had made it last a bit longer.*

Then the shadow turned and winked at me. *I bet your man over there wishes the same thing, eh? Last a bit longer?*

I paid it no attention, instead did a quick OAR of the room until I found our belongings in a plastic box under a desk. Wallet, keys, phone, both mine and Adam's, check. Chi disruptor, check. I turned back to Adam, pressed my fingers to his neck. The pulse was there, already stronger than before.

"Come on," I said, brushing hair from his forehead. He really needed a haircut. The thought of arguing with him over barbers versus hairdressers versus cutting it yourself was infinitely more pleasant than other thoughts trying to creep in. Like whether the poison they shot him with would do any permanent damage, since he didn't have my Gardener defences. Or whether the shadow hooks that were in his mind were extracted too late. Whether they left scars. All the things that could go wrong. Irrational, stupid things.

I set aside the ache in my chest, the anger, and picked him up again, adjusting him across my shoulders.

"Ow," he said.

"Adam!" Relief flooded me, sudden and overwhelming. "How are you feeling?"

"Like the world's boniest shoulder is stabbing me in the ribs."

I set him down, magnanimously ignoring the jibe. "Can you walk?"

He stumbled to his feet, groggily. There was still a bit of grey to his skin, and his eyes had trouble focusing. But he was alive. I felt my jaw unlock, felt the tension drain from my neck. We were going to be fine.

"You need to Dive out of here," I said. "Please, just this once. Don't argue."

Adam's hand, trembling but resolute, found mine. "I can take us both. Let's blow this Popsicle stand."

"No one says that," I muttered. "Anyway, I can't. They have Mr. Tan. Probably. And I'm not leaving him."

His fingers tightened around mine. "Then neither am I."

"Adam, you can barely stand up straight. Please just—"

"That's homophobic," he said, with the ghost of a smirk. Then his expression hardened. "Get it through your cute little skull—I'm not going anywhere without you. Okay?"

His damn humour. His damn loyalty. There was warm and unfamiliar lightness in my chest, but I'd never wanted to strangle anyone more.

"Stay sharp, then," I said. "I don't think the guards had a

chance to radio for backup, so they don't know we're free. We have a bit of breathing space."

Even as I spoke, I was typing out an update to the team, giving them as much information as I could on what had happened to us, just in case we didn't make it out. And then, four words:

ACTIVATE JINN SUMMON JUTSU

Don't ask. I'd fought hard for *Contingency J.* Mei had suggested *the Suleiman Protocol.* But Fizah, the one with the jinn contacts, had veto power. Hence, here we were.

I pocketed my phone and tightened my grip on the chi disruptor. "Let's move. We're not going to find Mr. Tan if we just sit around."

Wait, wait, wait. Don't leave me here.

The effigy. Of course it wanted something from us.

I turned, finally, to study the setup that held it.

Two concentric circles surrounded the case. The inner one was a mandala of prisms and lasers, refracting light into patterns of sacred geometry. The outer was a ring of about thirty laptops on rolling desks, facing inward. Each screen cycled rapidly through images of holy iconography—calligraphy, prayer wheels, crucifixes. From the speakers came whispers of prayer, high-pitched and sped up to incomprehensibility.

Some sort of techno-shamanism, using modern equipment to supercharge age-old practices. The precision of the lasers and the speed of the ritual sequences were likely designed to amplify traditional containment rituals, using modern science to multiply their potency thousandfold. Ingenious, and exactly the sort of thing I would've spent hours geeking out over if I weren't, you know, otherwise occupied.

Such a cage was not meant for a minor spirit. Whatever entity the effigy was linked to was powerful and, by extension, dangerous. It had helped us, sure. And it didn't *sound* evil. But that didn't mean anything. It was a prisoner of the same people who'd imprisoned us, but that didn't mean anything, either.

Sometimes, the enemy of my enemy is also my enemy.

It wanted us to set it free, but I couldn't in good conscience unleash this creature without acquiring more information. And I just didn't have time.

"Sorry," I said out loud. "I can't."

You don't trust me. That's fair. You don't even trust your own people. It's obvious, you know. How closed off you are. This reminds me of a friend I had, from my troupe. He used to...

I stopped paying attention to his chatter and made for the exit.

The door whispered open, and I slipped into the corridor, Adam leaning heavily against me. The hallways stretched out ahead, sterile white walls punctuated at regular intervals by steel doors just like the one we had exited through, the air buzzing with the faint hum of unseen machinery.

And not ten metres from us were two guards.

Their backs were to us, thank whatever gods were listening. Their patrol must have carried them past our door just before we came out, and now they were stomping away in their boots. But it was what walked in front of them that truly gave me pause—four boars on leashes, two per guard. Not ordinary animals. *Stone boars*, lithic organisms native to the region—violent, impossible to hurt, notoriously untameable.

How had . . . ? And then I saw the threads of shadow hooked into them, the same strings that had made a puppet of the wyvern. The strings I had seen extending from the effigy.

You're still helping them? I asked in my head. *Are you controlling these things, or being controlled yourself?*

They are forcing me. But what's the difference? the voice said. *Every puppeteer is someone else's puppet.*

Or, as they say in leadership courses, everyone feels like middle management.

The door had shut behind us. Retreating back into the room wasn't an option. We were caught in the open, harshly lit by bright lights, nowhere to hide.

Adam and I edged back, eyes fixed on the guards' backs. One wrong move, one heavy step, and we'd be discovered. We inched backwards, closer to where the corridor turned a corner. If we could just get around it, we'd be out of sight. Safe.

Adam, still shaky from the poison, stumbled. His foot scuffed the floor. The softest scrape of sound, but it might as well have been a gunshot.

One of the guards paused, started to turn. A fraction of a second, and he would see us. I tensed, focused, got ready to drop Adam and fight. Not that I liked our odds against stone boars.

Then—

A vibration rumbled up through the floor. The lights flickered. From somewhere far below us, a boom like distant thunder. Glass shattered.

The guards froze, one raising his hand to his earpiece, the other fighting to control the agitated boars. Then, another explosion shook the building, and the first screams came from downstairs.

The guards hesitated just a moment longer, then turned and sprinted away, weapons ready, the boars stumbling after them.

I exhaled, slowed my hammering heart.

Fizah had come through.

The jinn were here.

CHAPTER FOURTEEN

"Are you fireproof?" Adam asked.

We were huddled in the stairwell, peering through the small rectangle of glass on the door that led to an office lounge area. On the other side was an inferno. Tables, vases, ferns all burned with a clean fire, the heat so intense we could feel it on this side of the door.

On one side of the room, a squad of guards—I counted eight—crouched behind black tower shields, their ceramic masks rendering them anonymous, instruments rather than men. They spoke into earpieces, and every few seconds, one would rise just enough to fire a dart-rifle towards the centre of the room.

Where the jinni sat.

She wore an elegant cream blouse and printed skirt, looking for all the world like a high-end consultant on her lunch break. Which, knowing the jinn, was probably accurate. Perched on a beanbag, she chewed her lower lip, feet tucked up under her, flipping through a folder of documents. One finger spun in lazy circles as she read, ribbons of colourless fire unspooling from her to burn the darts from the air, to twist in dazzling streamers and whip against the black shields with a dull roar, all while she kept her eyes on industrial secrets she was no doubt stealing. The guards cowered behind their barriers, unable to advance.

Naturally, the guards were cowering right in front of the door to the other wing, where Mr. Tan probably was. The door we needed to get through.

"Why would I be fireproof?" I hissed. "There's zero reason to think I'd be fireproof."

"Aren't some trees fireproof?" Adam said. "I saw this video about how their seeds need to go through a fire before sprouting." I was focused on the guards outside, and the fire, but I could hear the smile in his voice. This guy. We were literally in a life-or-death situation, and he was still making jokes. I was just about to yell at him when a familiar, irritating voice started singing in my head. I didn't know the language, but I caught my name. It sounded... vulgar.

"What?" I said, aloud.

"I mean, I heard that some trees are, so since you're basically—" Adam said.

"No, not you. I'm talking to... that voice I told you about. The statue."

We never got properly introduced, the voice said. *I'm Semar. You can call me Sem. I know you're dying to know what I was singing about, so let me tell you. It's about a boy with a big heart, a big soul, and a big cock, and how he doesn't know how to use any of them. It's a tragic story, really—*

I tuned him out again. Semar. I'd seen that name before, in a piece of folklore research I'd had to do for a case. A demigod of Javanese origin, a jester figure, sometimes a protector. The Nagamuthu's daughter, I remembered, had told us to trust the Indonesian clown. This had to be him.

Could you help us, Sem? I thought at it. *Talk to those guards out there and distract them?*

They can't hear me, sweet-cheeks. Their souls are too small, so they can't receive the frequency I'm on. Like radio antennae that are too short—but you wouldn't know about that, would you? Your antenna, if we are calling it that, it's a good fun size. That's what my song was about—did you get it? Is that what this boy likes about you?

You're disgusting.

Why yes, thank you. Like they say, one man's disgust is another man's delight. And right now you need to walk through some fire. But a fish isn't a monkey. Why walk when you can swim?

I glanced at Adam. "He's saying we can swim past the fire. Can you Dive with me?"

Adam made his thinking face. "I've never taken anyone before, but if you trust me, I can try. I'm just . . . No, you know what, it'll be fine. Let's do it!"

He held out a hand. I took it. A twinkle lit his eye as he took a breath—

I knew what he was doing. "If you start singing 'A Whole New World,' I *will* throw you into the fire."

He gave me a look of injured innocence. "I would never... Jasmine."

Then the world tilted.

Adam called it "Diving," but it was really just a shift of perspective rather than a physical plunge. We didn't go someplace else. We were in exactly the same place, but somehow deeper. The office, the fire, the guards—all of it receded, becoming distant, distorted fragments. It felt like I had slid beneath the surface of things, as if I had gone from paddling water to being fully submerged in a vast ocean.

Imagine, if you would, being deep underwater, plants and strange geometric rocks between you and the distant surface. Roots trail down towards you, weaving around and through the stone blocks. Ordinary things—the door, the stairwell, the fire on the other side of the door—are tiny and far away, like the sunlit tips of icebergs, merely the protruding edges of massive structures and the offshoots of gargantuan root systems.

That was how my overwhelmed mind interpreted what I saw. It was just as Adam had talked about. The *phenomena* in the ordinary world—tables, chairs, doors—were just one part of the reality of things. Everything was more than we could see, and the *noumena*, the greater part of their existence, was hidden beneath the surface, on the Outside of the narrow slice of the universe we knew.

Adam and I were, too, great masses of roots and blocks. The body I knew, with my two arms and two legs, was a fraction of who I was, just the one small part of me that the world sees. Then I looked over at Adam, and I saw the whole of who he was—not just the flesh, but the sprawling, impossible, many-armed *more* that made him *him*. I should have been horrified, but I wasn't. Somehow, it felt like I could finally see all of him, and he was exactly who I thought he was.

As alien as all this was, it somehow felt familiar. As if this was just like my Garden from a different angle, or perhaps just a different part. But before I could investigate this sense of similarity further, I was distracted by Adam doing something with the edges of me, unknotting the tendrils of my greater self still so alien to me, freeing me from attachments I didn't even know I had.

Then, he gripped me, and we were away. We shot under the hanging blocks that were the doors, wove through the roots of fire, dodged another great tangle that had to be the jinni. Small organisms darted fishlike around us. It was exhilarating. It was terrifying.

Then, ahead, the water turned cloudy. A heavy and dark mass loomed, warping the currents around it. Even from a distance, I could smell the stink of its foul gravity, the acrid smell of putrescence and death.

A tug, and we surfaced in the middle of a hallway, all white walls and harsh lights. We were past the fire, past the guards, in the other wing of labs. Just the small, visible parts of ourselves again.

I gasped for breath. "That was... really something. Almost a... new fantastic point of view."

Adam grinned the broadest grin I'd ever seen.

"That pollution. That was Mr. Tan?" I had to be sure.

Adam sobered, nodded. "It's got to be. Whatever they're doing to him, it's poisoning everything. Can't get too close from the Outside."

I thought about the juice dripping from the overripe fruits of Mr. Tan's soul, the fractal wrongness of the tree in his soul. It was all connected.

That is all very cute, the voice in my head said. *But danger's coming from your three o'clock.*

I yanked Adam round a corner, where we flattened ourselves against the wall. Guards again—two guards, four boars. Patrolling even with jinn in the building. They were admirably professional, I had to give them that.

Once they were past us, we padded out and crept down the main hallway in the direction we had sensed Mr. Tan. Signs on the locked doors hinted at arcane projects in progress: RED COURT/LIGHT COUNCIL LIAISON DESK. SIGIL DEVELOPMENT (NEW ATLANTIS SITE). FORMA DYNAMICS LAB. NIGHTMARE GREEN SIMULATION (RESTRICTED ACCESS).

I felt a flicker of resentment—so this was what private sector budgets could do for esoteric research. DEUS could do so much with this kind of funding, solve so many problems. But I turned inside and scorched away the weeds—envy, impractical dreams, righteous justice. Mr. Tan, first.

We pressed on, hyper-alert, Adam on the left, me on the right. The sounds of fighting were getting closer. Men shouting, dull booms, things breaking.

"Is this it?" Adam whispered. The nearest sign read VOID ENGINEERING GROUP. Beneath it was a printed sheet of paper that said *Experiment C-375 in progress. No entry.*

"Looks promising," I said, and broke the lock.

Another lab. Along the walls ran stacks of glass tanks, some filled with mice, some with fish, others with plants. Two rows of benches occupied the middle, supporting instruments, stacks of folders, bottles of colourless chemicals, and machines with winking lights. At the far end, there was a plastic prison cube like the one they had put us in.

A knife of shadow darted across the face of the cube, shorting out the keypad.

You're welcome, the voice said.

Inside, through the door now swinging open, I could see someone rising from a bed.

Mr. Tan!

Barefoot, wild-haired, dressed in a hospital gown, he blinked at us in bewilderment. A few Band-Aids covered the inside of his elbow where they must have drawn blood. I moved towards him, but Adam was there ahead of me, helping Mr. Tan to sit back down on the bed.

"Hello, Mr. Tan," Adam said, his voice soothing. "My name is Adam. Do you remember us?"

Mr. Tan looked from him to me, nodded, mumbled

something to himself. His pupils, I noticed, were very dilated. Had they drugged him?

Those bastards. "The men who brought you here. Did they hurt you?"

He blinked at me, searching my face. "Calvin? They don't tell me anything, but they tell me to do things, take their tests. They make me answer their questions... They keep asking me questions."

Calvin? Last time we spoke, he had thought I looked like his son.

"I'm not Calvin, uncle. Maybe we can—"

"They won't let me go home," he mumbled. "Why can't I go home?"

Because you might turn your neighbourhood into a sinkhole, change all your neighbours into zombies of your late wife. But how do you tell someone that?

"It's not safe back at your place, uncle." I didn't say for whom. "Those men who brought you here, they will still be looking for you. Can you walk? We can bring you somewhere else. We will... uh, take care of you."

He nodded mutely, took my hand. It was heartbreaking how frail and alone he looked, how confused he was in this new environment without his familiar things, without the armour of a polo shirt and the ritual of tea for guests that he'd favoured the two previous times we'd met. Without his shield of memories, he was just an old man, and I didn't know how we could help beyond just getting him away from these people who wanted to drug him and test him and use him.

Just an old man, but a dangerous one.

This close, the threat he posed was palpable; something foul and heavy radiated from him like ripples in a still pond. The tree he cultivated must have grown further, burgeoned here in this lab, nursed into greater monstrosity by these doctors under the guise of care. Space buckled noticeably around us, teetering on the edge of structural collapse. The air carried the same sweet rot we had smelled that first time at Clementi, when the wave had swallowed the sixth floor and that poor dog.

All this because of grief, a world-ending, all-crushing bereavement. Grief was in the lines of his face, the heaviness of his step, spilling from him in torrents and in tides. Grief enough to end all of this. To fall forever into darkness.

My father hadn't fallen. He'd barely staggered. Not when my mother was sick. Not when she passed.

A nameless and formless emotion blew through me, disturbed the leaves of my soul. It couldn't be jealousy—that made no sense. And this was not the time for it anyway.

I tightened my grip on the old man's hand, urged him forward. Somehow, he managed to be more than his sorrow. Step by shuffling step, we made our way towards the exit, Adam and I on either side of him. Slowly, so slowly, but it was progress.

We were almost there. The door a promise of escape.

Then it opened. Soundless.

Someone must have noticed it slightly ajar and come to investigate. A clatter of hooves on concrete, the soft step of boots, and a grey porcine head, low to the ground and snuffling, barged in. Behind them, a guard followed with his rifle raised, face mask expressionless.

And behind the guard, two figures entered.

They moved in eerie synchrony, two muscular women in dark uniforms. The twin telekinetics. One of them locked eyes with me, the faintest smirk showing on her face. *Got you now*, it seemed to say.

This wasn't a random encounter. They'd been looking for us.

(As a side note—learn from Star Wars. Once your paramilitary group starts wearing masks and employing sinister twins, you might want to think hard about whether you're in fact the bad guys.)

If I were alone, maybe I could have taken them all out right there and then—the twins, the boar, the guard. But Mr. Tan had my hand in a death grip, and if I pulled away he might decide he didn't want to come with us anymore. And Adam—Adam couldn't help. This close to the polluted waters of Mr. Tan, I knew he couldn't Dive.

This was bad.

The guard had frozen for a half second as he took us in, the boar beside him pawing at the ground. Then, all at once, the boar charged, and the guard fired even as he raised his other hand to his earpiece, ready to summon the rest of the horde.

A single instant to decide. I could take out the earpiece, keep reinforcements from coming, leave Mr. Tan to be taken out by boar or bullet. It wouldn't be our fault. The threat of his diseased, heavy soul would vanish, along with the infestation of memories and the poisoning of the waters Outside, all cleansed by violence we couldn't avoid. A neat, clean solution.

Or I could choose the messier path.

Mr. Tan barely made a sound as I spun him around his centre of gravity, twirled him like a lover, his hospital gown flaring like a flag. I lowered him and myself behind the solidity of a lab bench. Trusted Adam to fend for himself on the other side.

Then the boar was past us, razing the space of where we'd been, two tons of stone and tusks slamming into the tanks of animals behind us. Glass shattered. Mice scattered. Water sluiced over the floor, fish flopping and dying around us. A dart from the rifle whistled overhead.

I swiped a pen off the top of the lab bench, flung it blind where I could hear the guard speaking, reporting our positions. The arc of its flight was clear in my mind, the flight of a bird from treetop to treetop, the curve of a branch reaching from here to there, just so.

I heard the pen hit the earpiece I was aiming for. A crackle of static as the device broke, a curse from the guard, muffled by his mask. But it was already too late. More guards would be here any second.

I glanced at Adam. A gash on his forearm dripped red onto

his shirt. He was looking back at me, eyes wide, waiting for me to tell him how to get out of this.

Just past him, I saw the shards of glass from the broken tanks rise into the air. Glittering, deadly, turning as one to point like knives at us.

Shit. The telekinetic twins.

I didn't have a plan. Flinging pens wasn't going to be enough. I wasn't strong enough to protect Adam and Mr. Tan from a whole platoon of guards and boars and people who could fling things with their mind.

Help us! I thought, desperate. *Please!*

A moment of terrifying silence. The boar turned, readying for another charge.

Then—

All right, kid, the voice said, solemn.

Shadows swung down from all around the ceiling, thin threads detaching themselves from the hidden spaces behind the fluorescent lights and under the lips of the benches. They lashed the air, attached themselves to the shadows of the boar, the guard, the twins.

I remembered Mei explaining how the *wayang kulit* magic doesn't force you to do anything. How it tells you what to want and not want. How the human heart was soft, full of places to hook.

Just like that, the boar stilled. The guard's shoulders relaxed. The twins blinked, foreheads creasing in confusion, but then the glass shards fell tinkling to the floor, and their eyes unfocused. They all turned to one another, disoriented. Stepped closer. Closer still. Then mouths met in grotesque, clumsy kisses, ceramic mask to identical faces to porcine snout.

I've only got a minute of this in me, Sem said. He sounded strained. *Go. Now.*

We didn't look back. We hauled Mr. Tan with us, his feet barely scraping the ground.

Everywhere, devastation. The jinn were forces of nature, walking catastrophes, and whatever they didn't care for they had levelled with fire. We passed other guards, other guardian boars, some perhaps on their way to stop the jinn, some to root us out, but before they saw us they were all momentarily pierced by strings of shadow, their desires not their own. Some scratched at itches they couldn't reach; some moaned in hunger, rummaging in bins for food; many turned to the walls in some desperate instinct for privacy, pleasuring themselves in obscene ways. All caught in a fragile web spun for our escape.

We fled down flights of stairs, Adam and I half-carrying Mr. Tan. Then we were at the door, out the door, and were free.

Again, a whisper in my head, fainter now. Frayed.

That took a lot out of me. The jinn will take me soon—this sliver of me, at least, is going to be stuck with them for a while. The voice sounded almost sad.

I'd be honest, I felt bad about putting him into the hands of the jinn. I was probably going to regret this, but I had to offer. He had helped us, and he was... almost a friend.

Stay put, I thought. *I'll come get you.*

I appreciate the offer, but if you come back in now they'd get you. All my effort would be wasted. A pause. *But I can send over a small part...Maybe if you could host just a tiny fragment of me?*

Just do it, I said, gritting my teeth. The Diviner had told me to trust him.

Okay, the voice said, shy. And then there was something in my soul, a seed in the soil, new but somehow very, very old. At the edges of my vision, the shadows twitched, linked to me now.

Take care, kid, Sem said, and there was a strange resonance, like his voice came from outside and inside at the same time. *I won't be able to talk to you for a while, because the small piece you have will need time before it can speak. But I'll be rooting for you, especially against the piranhas that are coming.*

A pause. Then, wryly—

And if you remember nothing else, remember this: Floss more regularly.

CHAPTER FIFTEEN

There's a report from our American counterparts that suggests that over 70 percent of supernaturals are physical in nature. But as always, despite their best attempts, their focus had a bit of a Western lens. Here in Southeast Asia, we like our supernaturals even more present. Our spirits don't drift so much as hop, scurry, loom. Our demons are confronted not with religious symbols but with nails and strings on banana trees. Our gods can be tricked with sticky rice cake, gumming up their mouths so they can't speak poorly of us.

I'd say the number is closer to 90 percent over here. And that means there are a lot of us who could have physical problems—sprains and splinters, sometimes, but also indigestion, eczema, the common cold. But you can't just go to the doctor for these if your diet is bad dreams or your skin is made of sticky tar, at least not without causing an incident. So, naturally, a few places have popped up that provide medical services to those of us who are a bit more unusual.

Dr. Kamini was my favourite. Technically a vet, she was insatiably curious about the supernatural world, and would trade advice, medicine, and even minor surgical procedures for tidbits of news. Given how frustrating the system was for claiming medical expenses—especially for some of DEUS's more unusual activities—this bartering of medical help for stories was very welcome. Also, she was one of those rare non-Others who weren't subject to the DKP—the *don't kaypoh* effect that makes regular humans ignore the weird things happening around them. It might have had something to do with how Dr. Kamini was, in fact, extraordinarily *kaypoh*.

Her medical practice was in Singapore's heartlands, nestled in a row of shophouses in Bedok. She lived right where she worked, and so she was ready (and eager) to receive us when we called in the wee hours of Saturday morning. The rest of the team was already there by the time Adam, Mr. Tan, and I arrived.

Fizah sprang to her feet the moment we stepped through the door, her expression frantic, hands twisting the notebook she carried with her everywhere. "I'm so sorry, I didn't have—"

"You shouldn't be here. It's"—I checked my watch—"two in the morning. You should be asleep."

She shook her head, words tumbling out. "I didn't have a choice. You and Adam were in danger, so I just told the jinn we'd give them whatever, they had to help. I promised them a meeting. I'm sorry, I'm sorry!"

From the other side of the room came the soft tinkle of

cups—Dr. Kamini offering water, no, tea, to Mr. Tan. She was checking up on him, her movements steady, reassuring. He seemed tired but calm, now that he was safe. A rare thing that'd gone right tonight.

"It's fine, Fizah," I said. We'd agreed on Contingency J—no, *Jinn Summon Jutsu*—as a last resort, and Fizah had executed it perfectly under pressure, even if it hadn't been ideal. None of this was ideal. "You did the right thing. We wouldn't have made it without them. Without you."

I took off my glasses to rub my eyes. Man, I was exhausted. "What do the jinn want?"

"They didn't say. Just that they expected us to show up soon to . . . discuss payment." Her voice wavered. "I really messed up, didn't I?"

Mei sniffed. "Of course they did not say. They hold the cards."

I forced a smile, feeling the tension in my neck, in my temples. "You didn't mess up. You saved us. Can you set up the meeting, first thing in the morning? The sooner we know what we owe, the better."

Jimmy looked up from his laptop, perched on a crate meant for large dogs. "You sure about this, boss? Rebecca will kill us if we talk to a major stakeholder group like the jinn without clearance."

"I'll manage Rebecca," I said. Meaning, I wouldn't tell her about this until it was done. We didn't have time for her bureaucratic nitpicking.

Fizah nodded, resolute. "I'll arrange it."

"Good," I said. "Now go home. You've done enough tonight."

She protested, of course, but I wouldn't budge. The danger was real, and this was no place for an intern. For a kid.

The moment she was gone, I turned to Jimmy. "Any luck identifying the bastards who attacked us?"

"Yeah," Jimmy said, fingers clattering on the keyboard. "I dug through the company registration records, triangulating those with the building where the lab was. Layers of shell companies, and it wasn't easy, but...I found the name." He tapped the screen. "Vanguard. Vanguard Dynamics."

The word hung in the air, bland and meaningless.

"That's who took us?" Adam said, voice low, angrier than I'd ever heard him.

Jimmy nodded. "But that's really all I got. It's a labyrinth of fake proxy directors and dead ends. Whoever they are, they know how to play the system. Cover their tracks."

And they had money. Power. No hesitation in crushing any opposition to their goals.

If I didn't know better, I would've guessed they were government. Us.

"What now, boss?" Jimmy asked. "What if they come after us again?"

"Can't you get the police to help? The army?" Adam asked.

I shook my head. "I wish. If we start right now and write the papers proposing an inter-Ministry task force, it would take months at the minimum before we could move. And by that point we could all be in cages."

Adam grimaced at the absurdity. “Call the jinn again? Ask for their protection?”

“We cannot afford to call the jinn again,” Mei said. “We could not afford it the first time, either, but what is done is done.”

“But,” I said. “Vanguard doesn’t know that.”

Mei’s eyes narrowed. Then she nodded. “The appearance of power. They will not risk another confrontation with us, now that they think the jinn are on our side.”

“And we did torch their labs,” Jimmy said. “That shit’s got to be expensive. They’re a business, and it can’t be good for their what-do-you-call-it bottom line to keep coming after us.”

“True,” I said. “We just need—”

A rustle of movement as Dr. Kamini stood. “Everything looks fine,” she said, sliding the blood pressure cuff off Mr. Tan’s skinny arm with a soft rip of Velcro. “I think you just need some rest. We have a guest bedroom upstairs. My wife won’t mind if you—”

She never got a chance to finish her offer. Mr. Tan shot out, slapped her hand away with Gardener strength. He was shaking, his movements uncoordinated, jerky and wild. Eyes wide, Dr. Kamini stumbled back. Mr. Tan opened his mouth to speak—and the danger snapped into focus.

How could I be so stupid? I lunged, clamped one hand over his mouth, pinned his thin wrists with the other. He was gnarled and strong as old branches.

“Do you have a sedative?” I asked the doctor, trying to keep my voice calm. “Something strong.”

She nodded, left to rummage through some shelves. By the time she returned with a syringe, Mr. Tan had stilled, once again a quiet, scared-looking old man. We sedated him, placed him on the couch in the waiting room, covered him with a blanket.

Mr. Tan's memories were contagious—we knew this. I had first noticed the intrusion of memory-seeds when he told me about the late Mrs. Tan. So, *words*. Words could be the vector. That's why I had to stop him from speaking, from spreading his poison. But I had to know for sure.

I relaxed into myself, tried to use my soul's sight in the way that Mr. Tan had suggested I could. My exhaustion, I thought, would make this a challenge, but it was oddly easy, like falling asleep. I opened up my inner eye, and I looked.

Everyone here was clean, I saw to my relief, their souls their own. Even Adam, who'd been with me in Clementi. With that same inner sight, I turned to look into Mr. Tan, unconscious on the couch, and I finally understood what was dragging us down into the Outside.

Memories are like water. They soak you, sometimes they drown you, but then they dribble away, evaporate, and are gone. Sometimes, you might bring back an old memory, but it is never the same recollection. No matter how similar it may look, it's a different water. It's fresher, from a river we can't step into twice.

But Mr. Tan had trapped his old memories of his wife, snared them with grief in leaf and sap. Captured, these versions of her had grown more and more potent, fermented on the vine, and developed their own memories. Memories of her own life, memories of him. And those memories of him, in turn, had memories of her, which had their own memories of him, and so on, a recursive swelling that was becoming too much for him to hold. And so the tree of his soul suffered. It bowed under the weight of fruit turning purulent, the bark bleeding, leaf and flower drooping with growth.

His memories were a cancer.

The memory-tumours were dragging Mr. Tan, and everything around him, into the Outside. And worse, now one of them had ruptured, its swollen fruit bursting like an abscess. More could follow. His condition might get increasingly unstable as more fractal poison poured into his soul, leaking out to pollute the waters Outside.

When I told the team this, Mei let out a sharp breath, her lips thinning to a hard line.

"What was the point of retrieving him, then?" she snapped. "We have accomplished nothing."

"We saved him from being an experiment," I said. "We got the shadow hooks out of him and slowed down the sinking. Bought ourselves some time. And we hit Vanguard hard enough they won't have the resources to come after us for a while. That's worth it."

But she wasn't wrong. Vanguard was, to be sure, the big bad evil guy behind this mess—they had sent the wyvern and a SWAT team at us, accelerated Mr. Tan's condition to sate their own curiosity, and endangered hundreds of Clementi residents. We had smacked them down with the help of the jinn, *literally* set the villain of this story on fire, but that hadn't solved everything. Or much of anything, really.

We were no closer to a solution. All we'd managed to do was move the danger from Clementi to…here. Where our friend, Dr. Kamini, lived her life.

Things were still sinking.

Speaking of the Outside…

"Adam, have you noticed anything…out *there*…that might be coming at us? The shadow man, Sem, said something concerning. The Diviner had mentioned it, too—something about piranhas. A shoal of them."

"No, but I've been a little busy. I can go look."

"Let's get that cut on your arm cleaned up first."

"It's fine, it's nothing."

"We are literally at a doctor. It will take one minute," I said.

Adam sighed, went over to Dr. Kamini, and offered his arm. She started wiping it down with a swab. "You didn't even want to go to the doctor when you broke your hands," he said.

"That's different. You don't heal like I do."

"You don't know that."

I looked at him levelly. "Well, do you?"

"No. But you didn't know that."

"Once you get that looked at, can you check Outside?"

"Yes, Dad," Adam said. A few moments later, with a Band-Aid printed with dinosaurs on his arm, he got up and sauntered out of the clinic, presumably to get some distance from Mr. Tan before he did his Dive.

"We need to kill him," Mei said.

"What?" we all said, turning to her, aghast.

She rolled her eyes theatrically. "Not him—*him*." Her gaze flicked to Mr. Tan, her eyes dark as polished stone. She rose to her feet in a fluid motion, took a step. With her enchanted heels, she blurred across the room in that single step, until she was standing over Mr. Tan. There was no hesitation in her stance, no guilt or doubt. Only the ruthless calculus of survival.

I sometimes forgot how old she really was, how far removed from modern ideas of civilised ethics.

"If you are right," she said, "we risk infection every time he opens his mouth to talk about his wife. His memories are dragging us down into an abyss. The solution is obvious."

"We can't do that!" Jimmy said.

"Why not?" Mei said. "We are in a veterinarian's office. We could just put him down like we do to dogs and cats."

Dr. Kamini gaped at her in horror.

"He's not an animal," I said. "He's Other. Our responsibility. We'll find another way."

"What is your plan, then?" Mei pressed, relentless. "Tell us."

I didn't have an answer, but I was saved by Adam returning. His face was pale.

"The shadow man was right," he said, collapsing into a chair next to me. "The Diviner, too. There's something coming."

"What is it?" I asked.

"I'm not sure. I saw a few predators sniffing around, creatures that reminded me of piranhas or barracudas. I didn't want to get too close, but I know the behaviour. They were investigating, confirming the presence of food, swimming back and forth from someplace much deeper. These are scouts, leading the way for the main shoal."

"Leading them . . . here?"

Adam nodded. "Here. To Mr. Tan. The stuff he's leaking into the Outside, what you said are his memories—that's drawing the creatures. Could be that it tastes like many, many lives being released into the water all at once."

"We kill this man now," Mei said.

"No," I said, fiercer than I meant to be. Out of nowhere, from the darkness beyond the shores of my soul, came a tendril of a memory—my father at my mother's funeral, patting my shoulder awkwardly as I wept. His own eyes were dry, his face stoic and emotionless as ever. I remembered him just a month after she passed, and how he returned to his old routines, as if nothing had happened. How I resented him for it, for letting go so easily.

Mr. Tan hadn't let go.

"No killing," I said. "He's not guilty of anything. Holding on isn't a crime."

Adam reached over and squeezed my hand. "Ben's right. Killing Mr. Tan won't stop the creatures. It's like when someone bleeds in the water and attracts a shark—once it scents the blood, the shark keeps coming even if you get rid of the bleeder. It knows that it still has all those other swimmers it could munch on."

"Wait," Jimmy said, voice thick with dread. "This sounds bad. Is it bad? Is this as bad as the waves at Clementi washing people away? Or the town sinking?"

"Worse," Adam said, sombre. "We're talking about the whole city, maybe Malaysia, too. And this isn't a one-and-done type of deal. If those monsters get here, they'll stay and breed and feast off all of us. It'll be impossible to root them out. We're talking years of predation, generations of people becoming snacks."

Jimmy shuddered visibly. "How about Binder One? Can we use it on Mr. Tan to stop this?"

"Won't work," I said. "Even if we set aside the moral issues of that stone, while we could make him promise to stop using his powers, Mr. Tan isn't really *doing* anything anymore. The memory-cancer is metastasising all on its own, a black hole, and it's the weight of that that's dragging everything around it into the Outside."

"Why isn't he sinking alone? You two don't pull things with you when you Dive."

We all turned to Adam.

"Uh," he said. "It's complicated. There's a whole process of disentangling ourselves from things we were connected to. It's the difference between diving and drowning. We are going in voluntarily. Mr. Tan is not. As he sinks he's instinctively grabbing on to everything he can, and dragging it down with him."

Jimmy scratched his nose. "If we could convince him to release his grip on things, or if we could go detach him from—"

"No," I said. In theory, I knew Jimmy was onto something. In theory, it could work. If we could free Mr. Tan from his attachments, if we could make him stop holding on, we could have him slip into the Outside and drift away. The incoming predators might then follow his scent instead and be drawn off. But someone would have to talk him into forgetting his wife. Someone would have to go into the Outside, into the cloud of cancerous poison around Mr. Tan, and unhook his connections to things around him. Only Adam could do that, and I would not accept putting him into more danger. More fundamentally, this option of letting Mr. Tan sink—it was giving up. It was saying that it was okay to let go.

"That's too risky," I said, as confidently as I could. "We have no guarantee that will work."

Mei blurred back to her chair. Her expression was steel and fury when she turned to me. "You refuse to kill him. You will not let any of us do what is needed. Do you have a better plan?"

I really didn't, but I had to make something up.

"The shoal," I said with more certainty than I felt. "That must be our priority right now. We have to stop the monsters in the shoal from getting here, find a way to drive them back to the deep water where they came from. Then we can find a way to cure Mr. Tan." A chance my mother never had.

"And if you don't find one?" Mei was relentless.

I didn't know. She must have seen something in my expression, because she let out a breath, pressed her mouth into a tight line, and gave me a curt nod. She was willing to trust my judgement on this even if she disagreed, thank god.

"How much time do we have?" Dr. Kamini asked, morbid fascination in her voice.

"Time gets weird out there," Adam said. "It gets sticky. And luckily, the creatures are slow, cautious, circling. I think they're not used to being in water this shallow. I'd say a week, maximum, before the shoal gets here."

A week? How could we possibly stop this in a week? We would need every second of it, and even then—

Our phones buzzed, simultaneously. We all glanced down. Nothing good could come at this time of night.

It was a message from Rebecca to the group chat—the official one. The one that included her. Of course, like any self-respecting team, we had a chat that included the boss and a safer, much more active one that didn't. Rebecca had messaged to remind us it was MOC Sports Day this afternoon and that we'd better show up and participate.

Of course she was still awake. Of course she'd send messages like that in the dead of the night. And of course Sports Day was today—mandatory, unavoidable. God dammit.

I rubbed my face, feeling the exhaustion in my bones. I

started to set research tasks for the team, who to look into which part of the threat, but Adam was shaking his head at me. Then I saw how haggard Jimmy looked, how even Mei was clearly tired beneath make-up, the weight dragging at us all.

We were done. For tonight, at least.

"All right, folks," I sighed. "Pack it up. Get some rest, and later, we can figure out how to balance team spirit and making sure people don't get eaten. See you all at the Sports Hall."

But as the team shuffled out, my mind kept spinning. There was work I'd been putting off. Mdm. Annapurna, the lady who'd been having trouble with her racist landlord, had sent another email begging for help. Once dawn broke, I was going to go down there and have a *word* with that jackass.

Or so I thought. Adam had other ideas.

He dragged me home, shoved me into the shower, and threw me onto my own bed. It was a little sexy, to be honest, but I was suddenly too tired to do much about it. He must have drawn the curtains and turned down the lights after that, but I didn't notice.

CHAPTER SIXTEEN

I got four hours of sleep before my phone rang.

It was my work phone for secure communications, the one we swore we wouldn't use except in dire emergencies. I had set the ringtone to an old-school fire-engine siren, to make sure I wouldn't miss it. I had some minor regrets as it dragged me from sleep.

Fumbling for the phone, I had to shove Adam off me—he was snoring gently, having fallen asleep with one arm draped protectively around my head. He had, as usual, managed to kick all the blankets off himself.

I managed to answer the phone on the fourth shrill *wee-woo*. "Hello?"

It was Rebecca, my absentee boss. "Ben, why aren't you online?" she asked, sounding annoyed. She must have tried messaging me on my laptop and noticed I wasn't signed on.

I blinked away the sleep, trying to focus. "I'm...just getting ready." Also, it was seven in the morning on a Saturday, but I didn't say anything about that. The weekend wasn't considered a valid excuse.

"Well, we have a situation. One of your *friends*, one Nadia, called Minister to offer a sponsorship for this year's Heritage Fest. Her niece is one of your interns or something, and apparently you have a little chat with her scheduled for today?"

Do these people ever sleep? And shit. Rebecca wasn't supposed to find out about the meeting with the jinn.

"Anyway," she continued, sweet with venom. "Your friend mentioned that she wished her meeting with you could be a bit earlier than usual, because she was so excited to explore potential collaborations. Minister *called me to make it happen*."

"Earlier?" I said, still groggy from waking up.

"Seven thirty. You have twenty minutes to get there, plenty of time. I want to clear your planned talking points, and send me the stakeholder engagement report by end of day, understood?" Impossible tasks, Rebecca's passive-aggressive way of letting me know she wasn't happy. I'd just have to accept a scolding for this later.

"I'll handle it," I said, already getting out of bed. Through my bedroom window, I saw that it was drizzling outside, the rain softening the white glow of the rising sun.

"Good. And while I have you, have you gotten the team banner and cheer ready for MOC Sports Day yet?"

I hesitated for a moment. "No, not yet." *Because we've all been kind of busy, Rebecca.*

"This is important. We need to demonstrate the three *C*'s—collaboration, remember?"

I rolled my eyes. "Got it. Collaboration. Rah, rah."

"And Ben?"

"Yeah?"

"Try to sound more awake next time I call you."

I hung up and went to splash some water on my face. My head still felt stuffed full of grass and my hands still hurt, but between the short nap and having something concrete to do, I already felt better. Adam stayed asleep as I dressed, and I got the chance to admire the angled edge of his jaw, the smooth taper of his shoulders into the small of his back, the way he mumbled and smiled to himself in the throes of some dream. The morning light, lucid as clear water, highlighted the lines and the curves of him, made him look like a photograph, too beautiful to be real, and for a moment I felt my heart wrench at the thought that he was here, with me.

I felt also a stirring of the familiar heat of attraction, but now was no time to fool around. I scribbled him a quick apology note and rushed out into the rain shielded only by an inadequate umbrella, fending off my father's questions about work and whether I would be home for dinner. I didn't know, and didn't really have time to think about it.

In the cab, I fired off a group message about the new meeting timing, then emailed IT with new arrangements I had decided to make about Fizah. My brain felt like sludge, but I forced it into gear and logged in to the Binder Two database.

I needed intel—any intel—that would help me survive this negotiation.

~

The meeting was at a construction site on the west side of Singapore—mud and men and machines in the damp heat that always followed a morning drizzle. Fizah texted me the updated details and apologised for the change in plans (not her fault), apologised that she couldn't join in (also not her fault). Apparently, her presence would have involved her family in the deal, and debts and obligations between jinn families were even thornier than those between jinn and non-jinn. As usual, we demand the most of those closest to us.

Relieved that she would be out of the action, I thanked her and took the chance to let her know that I'd made IT revoke her security pass to the office. For her own safety, of course. I ordered her to stay home for the next few days, just until this thing with Vanguard and Mr. Tan was resolved. As expected, she did not appreciate my concern, and I had to mute the chat after it degenerated into upper-case shouting.

There wasn't any other choice. She was just a kid.

The foreman at the construction site was waiting for me. He'd clearly been told I was coming, but not to bother with being friendly or welcoming. He showed me to a patch of shade—a tin-roofed shed stacked with a hundred traffic cones and a faded, laminated poster of an improbably busty woman, declaring *Hydration begins with me!* Then he walked off to yell at his workers.

All of this was theatre. The casual call to my Minister, the absurdly early meeting time, the snub by a low-ranking employee—it was all carefully designed to tilt the balance of power in these negotiations.

Not that the jinn *needed* to. We already owed them, and really didn't have a choice in whatever they demanded. For them, this was just habit. Or maybe it was fun.

Four minutes after I got there, three of the jinn showed up. I knew, from Fizah's brief, who they were. One was a small woman in a grey blouse and skirt, jewellery flashy and expensive, curly hair in a tight bun. She must have been Fizah's aunt on her mother's side, the chair of the board for the construction company that worked on this site. Behind her trailed a familiar figure—the woman I'd seen at the Vanguard offices, the one who'd so casually hurled fire at the guards. Today, she was just an assistant, her power sheathed.

The last one was a stout young man with a scraggly beard. He, I knew, was the crown prince of the family who owned the second-largest trading company in Singapore.

Together, they represented the two major jinn factions in the city, rivals for power and wealth. One faction had helped us take down Vanguard, but settling debts was a balancing act. If one side was collecting significant payment, the other needed to make sure the scales of power didn't tip too far.

Thus, this meeting between the four of us.

"Mr. Toh," the older woman said, friendly and extending a hand. "I'm Nadia, and this is Zikri. It's a pleasure to meet you. We've heard so much about you." Her smile was the kind I recognised from high-stakes interagency meetings—pleasant, practised, entirely unreadable. There was a blade in there, just waiting for the right moment.

"Likewise," I said, making sure to shake Nadia's hand first, then Zikri's, as Fizah had told me to. The assistant remained in the background, silent and watchful. The rules of etiquette here required split-second calculations based on seniority, gender, how close we were standing, plus a dozen other variables, but a decade in the civil service had made me very good at identifying these nuances, and at understanding what was left unsaid, especially by people who thought of themselves as more powerful than me.

"Your office does very interesting work, Mr. Toh," Zikri said. "So different from what we do."

This was code for *We don't share your interests, so our help will cost you*. We were barely thirty seconds in, and the negotiations had already begun.

I gave him an easy smile. "Oh, I wouldn't say that, Mr. Zikri. We are all on earth for the same reason, aren't we? To do good to our parents, kinsfolk, orphans, those in need, neighbours who are near, neighbours who are strangers...?" I quoted this last part, in a moment of inspiration, from a memory of the Qur'an.

Zikri inclined his head, conceding the point to me.

Nadia swatted me playfully on my shoulder. "Oh, you're not a stranger. You're keeping my niece out of trouble. But come, let's talk somewhere with a breeze. You can tell me about how Fizah is doing."

She led us into the skeleton of the building, motioned us onto a tiny lift platform. Pulleys activated and we went up slowly and steadily, one storey, then five, then ten, until we were at the top of what had been built, thirty storeys off the ground. She stepped out onto the elevator landing, then strolled out onto the girders, heels clacking on the steel.

"Walk with me, darling," she said. She looked tiny against the stark backdrop of blue sky.

This was another move to intimidate, to gain an advantage. Cheap, but I could see why it would have been effective on other people—their only choices were to say no and look like cowards, stay on the lift platform and shout their proposal like brutes, or walk out with her and discuss business while staring at a hundred-metre fall, *l'appel du vide* turning their insides to jelly. Unfortunately for her, fear is just a weed, and I'm a Gardener. I stepped out onto the beams, noticing that Zikri and Nadia's assistant hung back a few metres, where the lift platform gave surer footing. She looked bored. His face was a thundercloud.

The wind rose, shrieked through the empty space beneath us, tugged at my blazer, teased a few strands of hair from Nadia's bun. I hopped onto an adjacent girder, channelling Adam to give her my best, most charming smile.

She measured me with a glance, then gazed off into the distance. This high up, we could see a lot of the city spread out before us, glinting in the sun.

"I used to babysit Fizah, when she was little, you know," Nadia said. "Her and her cousin, Izzy. Such precocious children! They were just a few years apart in age, but inseparable, the two of them. Always getting into trouble. Does she get in trouble now that she's working for you?"

"Not at all," I said. I had no idea where she was going with this. "Fizah's great, actually. She's been a big help to the team."

But Nadia wasn't really paying attention to me. She gestured below us, through the latticework skeleton of the construction to the sand below where a few bulldozers churned up rocks. "One thing I remember. She used to love playing with sand. At the beach, at the playground, anywhere she could find it, tracking that around the house. I always said that was her father's influence, the human half of her. After all, man is just mud and soil, isn't he?"

And jinn were purer—which she left unspoken. They were smokeless fire, semi-divine, while we were made from common clay, less worthy by virtue of our provenance. The implication was that I should have been grateful to even get this audience. But there's a lesson every civil servant knows, that to claim power is also to claim responsibility.

"Your kind are indeed our elders and our superior," I said, inclining my head. "And deserve our respect. After all, mud is worthless. But fire—fire gives light and warmth. Selflessly, with generosity and grace. We have much to learn from you."

She gave me another long look, pursing her mouth.

"Enough of this," she said, finally. "I appreciate your willingness to fence with me, to set aside your kind's barbaric ways for the more... idiosyncratic courtesies we prefer. Let us talk business. About what you owe us."

At last.

I cleared my throat. "We are grateful for the assistance you rendered us, in our ongoing... misalignment with this other organisation."

"Vanguard," she said. Of course they'd done their research, too.

"Vanguard," I agreed. "We thought that, with your concurrence, we could count as payment the value of the information we have shared with you—the existence of this... Vanguard, the location of their laboratories, their security measures. Even the information—and goods—that you and your team no doubt extracted."

I glanced at her assistant, remembered her coolly flipping through Vanguard's classified files. Remembered also the statue of Sem—it was very unlikely that that was the only priceless artefact Vanguard was experimenting on. The jinn did not leave those facilities empty-handed, I was sure.

Nadia laughed in my face.

"That," she said with a patient smile, "was by DEUS's own lips freely given. And, by our own hand, deftly taken. You will need to do better."

I swallowed. "What do you want?"

She traced a finger along the railing at the edge of the lift platform, tucked a stray hair behind her ear, and leaned back against the railing. Casual. Confident.

"Your oath-stone. A loan to us, for one single day. No more."

Binder One.

A thousand oaths were bound to it, decades of fragile social order maintained by its magic. We barely understood how it worked, but the jinn had resources we didn't. If they should unravel the bindings, subvert the threads of grudging cooperation that held us together...

And even if they didn't. Word would get out. People would whisper that Binder One had been compromised. That the oaths were no longer secure. That one particularly rich, particularly powerful faction had gotten to tamper with what we'd all thought was inviolable.

Chaos would follow. Chaos where someone sufficiently motivated could gather a lot more money. A lot more power.

"Nadia," I said slowly. "You know I can't do that."

From the platform, Zikri cleared his throat. He was listening, and in his eyes was a hint of irritation. "Perhaps Nadia sets too high a price." This wasn't just a negotiation with me—it was a balancing act between them.

Nadia's smile sharpened. "I know. I just wanted you to know it, too, how much your work rests on one small thing. But no matter. Keep your rock. How about something simpler? Access to your databases. The ones on artefacts."

I kept my expression neutral. She was aiming high, and she

knew it. Giving her faction access to our records would set a precedent, open the door for every faction, every wizard, every grudge-bearing spirit to demand the same.

"If we gave you access, the other factions will see it as betrayal. DEUS is supposed to be neutral, and neutrality is the only thing holding this house of cards together. One whisper of favouritism, and we'd lose what little trust we had left."

Again, she laughed at me. "You're the only one who still believes that, Ben." Then her eyes narrowed, all pleasantness and coquettishness gone. "You do realise you don't have a choice, do you not? We saved your lives, and you owe us. You are in no position to bargain."

Hardball, then.

"As much as we appreciate your aid," I said, keeping my voice level, "your assistance was by your hand freely given. We pay not out of obligation, but out of courtesy. Respect."

Her smile curled into something more dangerous. "Well, you are a tricky one, aren't you? Perhaps something...even simpler, then."

I waited, my breath tight in my chest.

"A favour. When we call, your team answers, just once."

"What will we need to do?"

She chuckled. "Information isn't free. We will tell you when you need to know. But I can promise that your task will not be illegal or immoral, and will violate neither the laws of the land nor the laws of God. You might even enjoy it."

She must have given some signal, because the lift arrived with a grinding sound. "Time is up," she said. "Yes or no?"

Zikri stared stonily, but he said nothing. His silence was agreement, or maybe just reluctant acceptance that this was the best they were going to get.

"I can't agree for the team," I said. But I really had no other choice. We had to pay back what we owed. "You can have me."

"Deal," Nadia said, extending a hand. Her eyes gleamed with predatory fire, and I was suddenly certain I was exactly where she had planned to manoeuvre me to from the beginning.

We shook, her fingers cool against mine.

"We will be in touch with arrangements," she added as we took the lift all the long way down to the ground. "For now, consider your debt... postponed."

CHAPTER SEVENTEEN

I get Sports Days. They're good for camaraderie, for building those relationships so essential to getting things done in any large organisation. They get people to feel positively about themselves and their work, all while making them a bit healthier for having got away from their desks to kick a ball around, or whatever. And they have the great power of humanising your bosses, by letting you see them in all their fumbling, sweaty glory, giving you that flash of recognition that they are just like you and me.

I get it, I really do. But this one could not have come at a worse time. We had maybe a week, if we were lucky, to deal with this shoal from the Outside, and here I was, stuck hiding for the last two hours in the Armoury.

After that early morning fiasco with the jinn, I had popped by Dr. Kamini's to check on the still-sedated Mr. Tan, then come to the office early. My plan was simple: leave some food out for the cat and grab some weapons, counting on everyone else taking advantage of the weekend to sleep in before Sports Day kicked off in the afternoon. But, of course, the organising team had other ideas.

They arrived just after I did, promptly setting up shop right outside the Armoury door to meticulously sort through several hundred collar pins. I heard the clink of each pin as they dropped them into separate bags, and their heated discussions over logos printed a millimetre off centre and whether those were acceptable. They were being good bureaucrats and being very prudent regarding the use of our tax dollars, but it was supremely inconvenient for someone trying to avoid getting drafted into Sports Day prep. Or answering questions about what they were doing in the Armoury.

It had a fancy name, but it was just a room in the Ministry office, nondescript, labelled STORAGE. It was locked—physically, of course, but also with stranger wards, both to keep people out and to keep things in. Because, you see, the Armoury was where we kept all the weird stuff DEUS encountered in its work where the owners either weren't responsible enough to handle it, had passed on without specifying an inheritor, or in one notable case, had lost a bet with a previous DEUS officer.

The movies might have you believe that a place like this would be full of, I don't know, weapons and statues of dragons. But, contrary to popular belief, most people who made magic stuff didn't produce swords and guns, nor did they put spells into sculptural decorations. Instead, they made things more fitting for the age we lived in, like eyeglasses or jewellery or stickers for cell phones. What else were you going to have with you all the time? The majority of these were basic enchantments, falling into the categories of *Fu*, *Lu*, or *Shou*, the three-star Daoist gods of fortune, prosperity, and longevity. These charms tended to be quite safe, and so we had entire shelves for the things enchanted to grant exceptional luck, success in your career, or good health. Then there were a couple of shelves for all the items that dealt with romantic love—pheromones from rare cryptids for attraction. Mirrors that let you spy on your spouse. Jars of spirits that could mimic companionship. Next to these shelves, unsorted in a big tub because no one wanted to touch them more than necessary, were all the magical sex things. So, so many magical sex things.

Tucked in the back was a single rack for weapons. It was what I was there for—though, thanks to the overeager Sports Day organising committee, I instead spent two hours cleaning the place up and redoing some of the labels on the *Shou* shelves. It was calming, I admit, and needed doing. I also got to experiment a little with using the tiny black seed in my soul—the fragment of Sem. I couldn't do much with it, just make the shadows shift a bit. It was a fun little party trick, sure, but nothing like what Sem could do.

Finally, the noises beyond the door died down. I peeked outside and, seeing no one, picked up what I'd come for and hurried to the Civil Service Club to watch some three-legged races, play some Ultimate Frisbee, and maybe save the world.

The team was already there (sans Fizah), dressed in their bright yellow microfiber MOC T-shirts and huddled on the bleachers, one cluster among many. Even Adam was there, pretending to fit in with the civil servants. Rebecca was out presenting something to one of the Stat Boards, and wouldn't make it till the afternoon.

"What is *that*?" Jimmy asked as he spotted me, his face shifting from confusion to scandalised horror.

I glanced at the harpoon in my hand, all pale wood and black metal. "From the Armoury. It's from that incident at the docks in '98. If we want to do anything about this... piranha swarm, we'll need to be prepared."

"Are you serious? Give it here," Jimmy said, snatching it out of my hands. Muttering imprecations about carrying weapons in public and over-reliance on the DKP effect, he started wrapping a large piece of fabric around the curved head, disguising it as a flagpole.

"The *Dapur Nala Wahi*," Mei said. Did I detect a hint of approval in her tone? "Draws power from dreams and the sea. If this Outside dimension is as you have described, this may be a suitable weapon for this confrontation."

That was the same line of thinking I'd followed, but it was good to have it validated by someone who actually knew what they were doing.

"Do we have a place we can talk? Somewhere a little more

private?" I asked. The place was buzzing with activity. Two emcees we couldn't see, only hear, were bantering, trying to get the energy up. On the bleachers, where we were, the various divisions had staked out their fiefdoms, and every group was busy either painting banners, dressing up their mascots, or practising cheers. Invariably, though, in every group, one or two people were hunched over their laptops, answering apparently urgent emails. Whether they were heroes tanking all the work for the team so others could have fun, or overachievers who couldn't put down their work and who were killing everyone's buzz, that was between them and God.

On the court, a few stations had been set up, and there were already teams practising, tossing balls, sprinting circuits around traffic cones, kicking *chaptehs* to one another in a circle. I felt a twinge of anxiety that the DEUS team hadn't practised at all and wasn't even warming up, but quickly stamped down on that competitiveness. We had more important things to focus on. Like where to Dive.

"I did a quick recce," Jimmy said, handing me the harpoon-flag. "People literally everywhere. But I have a good feeling about the toilets."

So that's how we found ourselves, Adam and I, squeezed together in a toilet cubicle. Thankfully, it was mostly clean and smelled of disinfectant and that yellow urinal cake they always seemed to have. Mei stood guard outside, while Jimmy manned the sinks. Two lines of defence to keep people away, but I was pretty sure Mei's regal glare would be enough to frighten people into seeking out another restroom.

"I love our dates," Adam said, edging around a puddle of unidentifiable liquid on the floor. "You take me to the nicest places."

"Oh, congratulations on graduation from sarcasm school. Are we ready to go?"

He grinned, took my hand, and we Dived.

This time, I was a little more ready for it. Behind us (or above us? Again, the perspectives were weird) rose a vast vertical wall of grasping roots, tendrils, and massive polyhedra, stretching away to every horizon. Again, I felt like we'd plunged under some drifting island of old seaweed, and that we were looking up through the matted plant matter. Far off, through the roots, I could see that what poked above the surface of the water were the things we had left behind, back in the real world. People, walls, urinal cakes, each thing the small and bright tip of a plant that was vast underwater. I could even see Jimmy, looking bored, unaware of the vast mass of his greater self lying just Outside. Below the surface.

All this—the roots, the blocks of stone—these were what lay behind people, beneath ordinary objects, not the mere fractions we normally saw but the whole darn thing. And Adam was floating there with me, his physical, biological body once more a splinter of something larger, and from his back or from his feet—I couldn't grasp the directions and perspectives here—again sprang innumerable filaments ten thousand times his regular mass, a tangled arrangement of blocks and roots and radiant nodes that were his full person. I was the same, though perhaps a little smaller, a little dimmer, definitely much clumsier. He was an Olympian here, athletic and godlike, and I was a toddler learning to crawl.

The harpoon had come with us, translated into a massive spike of stone and wood. Even as I looked at it, it creaked and grew, sucking greedily from the strange not-waters that surrounded us to grow in puissance and murderous lethality. Good to see that my hypothesis worked out.

Just like before, Adam had to extricate me from the surrounding morass, disentangle the roots of my being from the tendrils around us. Once done, he tugged at my arm, or whatever the equivalent was in our new form, and gestured forward, presumably in the direction he'd seen the approaching monster. He darted off, and like a jellyfish, I followed.

We swam for an indeterminate length of time, Adam scouting ahead and returning to guide me, me doggedly paddling forward. We had no company but for the endless dark water illuminated by our own light, and when I turned back I saw that we had put some distance between us and the world we'd left behind, which was now revealed to be a great bubble, drifting in this noumenal ocean. Did we live our whole lives inside such a bubble, not realising how tiny a portion of reality it made up, unaware that there were greater parts of ourselves alive in a vaster, grander universe?

Far off, I thought I sometimes caught glimpses of what might have been other bubbles, perhaps other realities, but they were too far away to tell. My own form was a tangled mess, my ungainly limbs dragging me forward, the strands of my being flailing like roots yanked from the earth and tossed into a river, every motion a clumsy struggle to keep up with Adam's fluid grace.

Finally, Adam returned and pointed vigorously at something ahead. I squinted my not-eyes, noticed lights. Distant, but steady. A city, perhaps. Some Atlantean civilisation from whom we could seek aid? Perhaps another Diver? After the kilometres of darkness, the light meant...something. So we altered our course, started towards the promise of warmth, of welcome.

Then, a disturbance in the water. A change in the pressure, a shifting current.

Adam yanked me sharply aside, and a dark shape sliced lethally past where I had been. It was enormous, the size of a car, a fridge, finned and toothed and ravenous, lunging from the gloom just beyond our sphere of light, vanishing back into the murk.

It came again, and Adam pulled me aside once more, but I was a liability and we both knew it. I just didn't have the coordination to avoid the creature, here in its native habitat. A moment of communication, agreement, consent, and Adam pulled me into him, wrapped his self around me, wove the fibres and fronds of his being through mine so I would dodge where he dodged, move when he moved.

Have you ever been so close to someone you had trouble distinguishing you from them? It was like that, more than I'd ever felt before, a connection beyond skin-on-skin, beyond sharing secrets with inadequate words. It was exhilarating, and it was almost too much, almost overwhelming.

I saw him (us?) whip at the creature as it passed, an exquisite choreography of appendages, and I (we?) felt the water shudder with the strike. When I had fought alongside Adam against the wyvern, he had been agile, impossible to hit, impossible to avoid. Here, in his element, he was all that and more, a juggernaut with strength that could break mountains.

He hammered at the beast again and again with shattering force, slamming at its armoured scales until the water turned jellied and strange from the percussion. But he was just setting it up, I knew from my intimate position at his core. The monster came at us faster now, hungry, enraged, and I heard Adam whisper in my heart of hearts. *The harpoon.*

I held it out, steadied myself (ourselves), braced for impact. And when the creature came again Adam spun us, the weapon drawing out a single curving brushstroke in the inky darkness. A lethal calligraphy. The behemoth slowed, paused at the edge of our globe of light, and something gushed out of the opening we had just created in its side, coppery and ichorous. It tilted over, pale eyes pleading, then dimming into what passed for death in this place.

We fled. Adam released me, and we were two individuals again.

Is that part of the shoal? I asked, the remaining connection between us carrying the message.

One of the scouts, Adam said. *Stay alert.*

We had barely beaten a single fish. A swarm of them was coming? My god.

The lights were closer now. Maybe the fight had moved us more than we thought? I had a horrible feeling, though, that the lights were moving towards us.

Wait, I called out. Only, our connection had faded, and Adam had already started towards the lights. I hurried after him, but he was far ahead of me, not turning back, drifting towards that not-so-distant light.

And then, like one of those magic eye images popular in the nineties, the ebb and flow of water, the patches of shadow, the spots of light resolved themselves into a school of alien fish, some as large as warehouses, some the size of butcher knives, a heterogeneous collection of nightmare shapes. Some were sinuous and ugly as eels, some had the antediluvian silhouettes of sharks. A number, their forms blunt and improbable, had pustules or illicia that glowed like lantern lures to bring in prey.

Prey like Adam, who didn't have the defences I did as a Gardener, whose sense of adventure was snagged by the seductive radiance, reeling him helplessly towards hungry mouths and sharp teeth. He should have been immune—this was his domain. But protecting me, guiding me through the dark, watching my every clumsy move must have distracted him, left him vulnerable. The lights pulsed, whispering promises.

I let the mangroves of my soul weave a barrier against the luring light, and focused on wrestling with Adam. My frenzied clumsiness fought his dazed, half-hearted resistance, his form straining to go towards the shoal. I threw away the harpoon, weapon of foolish hope, which would have been like using a toothpick to fight a hurricane.

As we struggled, the fish hung motionless, radiating a dreadful patience. They knew how to wait. Their bodies bore the evidence of it—barnacles formed from the consumed fragments of other realities. Here, jutting from a gill, was a splintered beam of wood that might have been a ship's mast. There, a curved pane of manufactured glass, reflecting the clouded sky from some world. Rusted gears trailed from their flesh, and dragging roots, and eyeballs with odd irises, and arms with too many joints, all fused to these predators who silently, patiently watched us. They had no need to rush.

Metre by metre, I dragged Adam away, twining my self through his to lend him strength, to keep him with me, until we were outside the influence of the light and he was himself again.

Again we fled, this time towards home.

We emerged back in the cubicle, mere fragments of

ourselves again, panting, terrified, overmatched. We were alive, but we had failed. Jimmy was pounding on the door to the cubicle, yelling, and from the hoarseness of his voice I guessed he'd been at it for a while.

"Are you guys there? Guys? You have to hurry. They're calling for you, and Rebecca will throw a fit if you don't go. The Ultimate Frisbee game is starting!"

CHAPTER EIGHTEEN

So here we were, the four of us, huddled up on one side of the court, in our own end zone. Mei, for once, was wearing sneakers rather than her signature enchanted heels. Jimmy looked pumped. Adam was there, too, and not one person had thought to ask him whether he'd registered or even who he was. He had clearly mastered the art of what the Italians call *sprezzatura*, a studied carelessness that suggested he belonged right here. That, and here was yet more evidence that the DKP effect could apply to non-supernatural things.

Across from us were our opponents, the formidable IT department, who you'd have thought would be nerds but were actually surprisingly athletic. They talked animatedly and loudly, presumably about their plans for the game. Even from my distance and over the background buzz of the crowd, I could catch a few words, something about a horizontal stack and chrome walls. Were they talking about work? But then why did they keep looking over at us?

"They are taking this really seriously," I said.

Jimmy nodded. "They've been practising for months. I see them sometimes at the field outside the office. They're good."

"We will crush them anyway," said Mei. "We are Others."

"What? No!" I said. "Okay, first of all, that wouldn't be fair. And if we win we'll have to play the semifinals and the finals. We don't have time for that."

"Okay, boss," Jimmy said. "We will lose quickly and get on with things, then."

Mei looked horrified, and I sighed. "We can't do that, either. If we don't even pretend to try, Rebecca will kill us. Or at least give us a long lecture about the importance of teamwork and collaboration." She'd already sent a message to the group, wishing us luck and telling us u better win lol. "Do you want that?"

"I've never heard that lecture before," Adam said brightly. "I don't mind!"

We all stared daggers at him until he wilted.

"We need to lose," I said. "But let's put on a good show while we're at it, ya?"

Jimmy's eyes gleamed with sudden excitement. "Can we use our powers? Just a little, promise."

I sighed again. "Sure. Just a little."

And then the whistle blew, the crowd roared, and the game began. The IT team was genuinely good. They had all these formations, strategies around who marked whom, code words for who to isolate, where they were going to throw the

Frisbee. And on our side...we barely knew what was happening. Adam was in good shape, but Jimmy's enthusiasm could make up for only so much lack of fitness. Mei refused to sweat, on principle. If this were a normal game, and we were normal people, it would have been a total wipeout.

But we weren't normal people.

Adam seemed to be everywhere at once, but I couldn't tell how much of that was because he was slipping through the Outside and how much was because he was a heck of a physical specimen. Jimmy didn't move as much, but he was always coincidentally in the right place to catch the disc, even after Mei's half-hearted throws. Being a precog had its advantages.

Ten minutes in, we were down 3 to 5. Respectable, I thought—not too wide a margin. We could relax a little, keep playing at this tempo.

I jumped for the disc, plucked it out of the air over an attacker, flicked it forehand to Adam, and found myself next to Mei. "We saw them," I said, taking a breather. "The fish. They—"

"Not *they*," she corrected. "*It.* Your mistake is that you think of our adversary as many individual creatures. But it is not. It is singular. A god. Even noncontiguous, it will take a significant level of power to overcome."

"What do you mean by 'overcome'? Do we need to kill it, drive it off, or what?"

Mei hesitated. "I do not know," she admitted. "We have never faced anything like this before. It is not of our world and is not bound by our rules. Destroying it might be impossible. Forcing it to retreat may be our only option."

I nodded, my mind racing. "And we need power for that. Serious power."

She crooked two fingers in a mystic gesture, and across the field, one of the IT guys who had been running towards Adam stumbled inexplicably, allowing him to pass the Frisbee to Jimmy. He scored effortlessly.

Reset back to the end zone. Everyone except Mei was breathing hard.

"Can you rustle up enough?" I asked. I knew she had pacts with innumerable minor spirits and deities. "Power, I mean. If we add up all your allies..."

"It will not be enough," she replied. "My pacts are with beings of this world, and their power is attenuated out there. All our magics will be, except perhaps yours and Adam's. To fight a god, we will need the power of a goddess... or god. If I could draw down the full moon, with all her ethereal grace, it would be possible, but it is not the right time."

The full moon had happened over a week ago, so Mei wouldn't be able to pull enough power from there for at least a few more weeks. Dammit.

I lobbed the Frisbee across the court, sprinting for the other side. We played more, but my mind was elsewhere. What other sources of power did we have available?

I intercepted a throw from the other team, sent the disc to Jimmy. Perhaps something in the Armoury? No, the *Dapur*

Nala Wahi was our best bet, and that had already proved insufficient. If Mei was right, even the jinn didn't have enough spiritual clout to be the answer here.

With a twist of shadow to fake out the guy marking me, I flung the Frisbee backhanded. Scored. Perhaps we could ask some of the major religions, the distant and solitary God of Abraham, the Hindu pantheon, some bodhisattva? No, that wouldn't work, either. Those beings certainly had the power, but they had too many worshipers to take care of, too many prayers to answer, and they were surrounded by bureaucracies both terrestrial and celestial. A lone petitioner might have had a chance of getting through, but we'd have to do this government to government, as it were, and I knew bureaucracies. No way we were getting the help we needed in the time we had left.

I jumped, flung the disc back before it went out of bounds. Adam made the catch, Jimmy went on to score.

The timekeeper called halftime, and as we huddled on our side of the court, the score stood at an alarming 10–5 in our favour. We had too wide a lead, and it was time to put on the brakes.

"We have to stop scoring, folks," I said.

"Sorry, boss," Jimmy said sheepishly. "Got carried away."

"Me too," I admitted. "But we have to give them this win. We—"

One of the IT folks was storming over, face flushed with exertion and anger. I recalled that her name was Sandra, and she'd been very friendly when she helped me with some pass card problems months ago. But she didn't look at all friendly now.

"You're cheating," she declared, her voice low and controlled.

"No, we're not," Jimmy said. "You are."

But Sandra wasn't backing down. "I don't know how you're doing it, but I know what I know. People don't move like that. You didn't even train. You . . . you don't even know the rules!"

"We know the rules," Jimmy retorted.

"Oh really? Then how come you asked the timekeeper which side you were supposed to throw the disc to? We heard you!"

I had to step in before this blew up any further.

"Okay, look, Sandra," I said, trying to project calm. "We may be a bit unconventional, but that doesn't mean we're cheating. We're just having fun and got some lucky shots. If you have any concerns, we can call for a . . . what's it called, spirit timeout. We don't want any bad blood here."

Her expression wavered for a moment, torn between her suspicions and the very civil service reflex not to escalate the problem further. Finally, she took a breath. "Fine." Her voice was a mixture of frustration and reluctance. "Let's finish the game. But remember, I've got my eyes on you."

As she walked away, Jimmy leaned in, his voice lowered. "Boss, we need a plan. We can't use our powers anymore, not if we want to avoid further suspicion."

"We cannot afford to play too poorly, either," Mei said. "If our performance drops too much in the second half, it would only raise more suspicions."

"Right," I said. "From this moment on, we play like any other team. No powers, no extraordinary moves, no funny business. I know they're better trained, but we can still give them a good run for their money. You know why?"

"Why?" Mei said suspiciously.

"Because we've got heart. And because we've got"—I looked over at Adam—"him."

Adam's look of astonishment drew out cackles from Jimmy. Even Mei broke a smile.

"But seriously," I said. "Adam could run circles around those clowns, even without Diving. Mei, I bet you know strategies of play they haven't even heard about. And Jimmy, oh Jimmy. You know some of the rules now! But the point is, we got this."

I was quite proud of my pep talk. We even did a *hoo-ah* thing where we all put our hands together in the centre of the circle and then broke at the same time. We were motivated, and we were ready!

The second half started, and to put it mildly, it was a disaster.

Despite our determination and heart, the IT team's actual training and skill became quickly evident. With us holding back our supernatural abilities, we stumbled, tripped, and fumbled the Frisbee with embarrassing frequency. Even Adam, so fast and agile, found himself struggling to keep up with our opponents' relentless pace. His attempts to outrun them were met with swift interceptions and deftly executed defensive manoeuvres, and his precise passes faltered without adequate support from the rest of us.

But DEUS, I'm proud to say, doesn't give up. We kept playing, sweat-drenched and gasping, as the other side scored point after point.

Then, I spotted it, a gap in their defences, just a moment where their players were out of position. I caught the disc from Mei, one-handed in a magical moment of confidence, flicked it into the space between two defending players towards Adam. He leapt, caught it, and scored!

The crowd erupted in cheers for us, the clear underdogs of the second half of the match.

But the clock ticked down. In the last moments of the game, our opponents sealed their triumph with one final spectacular play, securing the winning point. The score read 13–11 in their favour. We had scored exactly one point in the second half.

But it was good enough. We hadn't shamed ourselves, and it had been an exciting and close enough match that the crowd didn't think too hard about the differences in our performances between the first and second halves. The IT team was ecstatic with the victory, and came over to shake all our hands with no signs of rancour. Rebecca even sent a message to congratulate us on a good game. Catastrophe averted.

We still didn't know how we might drive away the

monstrous fish swarm we saw, or save Mr. Tan from dragging wherever he was with him into the Outside. At best, we had a week. But all this physical exertion had given my mind time to work through the possibilities.

I had an idea of where we could get the power we needed.

I had a plan, but it was appalling.

I sent the team home, and I went back to the office. Emails didn't stop coming in just because the world was ending.

I was multitasking, toggling between one final round of revisions for that update to Minister and fielding questions from Rebecca about our performance at Sports Day. I was definitely *not* thinking about the fact that there were monster fish coming to eat us all. Or the fact that I now owed extremely powerful jinn a mysterious favour. Or that Dr. Kamini's clinic might sink anytime. Or that there were a bunch of Clementi residents slowly being possessed by rotten seeds. Or that I had a weird seed from a Javanese deity lodged in my soul.

I was very busy not thinking about these when I had a sudden disorienting moment—was there something I needed to be thinking about?

I checked the time: past seven p.m.

My father hadn't called. He always called to ask if I was home for dinner. His stubborn refusal to quit was the only stable point in most of my days.

Dread opened a pit beneath my ribs. Had something happened? He was old, older than I wanted to think about sometimes. Did he have a fall? He was relatively healthy for his age, but accidents happened. Or was it Vanguard? I had been worried they'd come after our family and friends, and this could be it. They'd sent the wyvern to the car park of my apartment, which meant they knew where I lived. Where my father was.

I took a breath, called my father on his cell phone.

One ring.

Two rings.

Ten. No answer.

I tried again. It rang until the automatic disconnect.

The pit gaped wider. I was sweeping my things into my bag and getting ready to rush home when my father called.

"*Ba*," I said, my voice tight. "Everything okay?"

"Yes, everything is okay. You're at work still?"

"Yes," I said, relief like cool water pouring through me, draining out of me. I sank back into my chair, suddenly exhausted.

Silence on the line.

"Why didn't you call?" The words came out sharper than I intended, edged with sullenness, anger, guilt.

"About dinner?" He sounded bewildered. "I know you're busy these few days. You're a big boy, you have your work. So I don't want to always disturb you. I can eat by myself, it's no problem."

More words than we had said to each other in a long time.

"Are you sure you're okay?" I demanded. I didn't know what else to say.

"I'm okay, I'm okay. I'll cover up some food, you can eat later if you're hungry, okay?"

There was a stone in my chest, heavy but too soft, too little like the perfect heart of a wyvern, too full of complications. I swallowed, nodded even though he couldn't see me.

"Yes, *Ba*. Get some rest."

CHAPTER NINETEEN

How do you set up a meeting with a Diviner? The one we wanted wasn't on social media at @nagamuthusdaughter or @ahlianprophet (we tried). We didn't have her number, her email, or any clue where she lived.

So we convinced Jimmy to stop morbidly looking up pictures of shark attack victims and to make a list—every home in Singapore, along with a schedule for visiting each one. The plan? We'd knock on every door until we found her. Our message was short and sweet—Burger King, Funan shopping mall, today, eleven a.m.

This wasn't a *realistic* plan. Singapore had close to two million households. At a measly five minutes per visit, it would have taken Jimmy a good nineteen years to complete the task. But I was banking on the fact that it wouldn't matter. The Diviner could see futures. As long as there was even one single future where the message got to her, she would get it—and hopefully, she'd decide to show up.

And show up she did, to my immense relief. I found her already there, dressed in what appeared to be pyjamas, clutching some sort of enormous plush animal. Was it an anthropomorphic egg? I supposed I'd seen weirder things.

We smiled, we talked, and we waited until no one was watching.

And then, having lured her out, we took her. I'm not proud of what we did.

But desperate times, desperate measures.

Standing at the door of the meeting room, I spoke the words we'd gotten from the Diviner, the passphrase that obviated the need to go through the NTUC portals. Then once more, more carefully, I fixed in my imagination the correct ritual pose, legs held just so, my left index finger grasped in my right hand. A mudra held in the mind rather than the body, the invisible other part of the key.

The doorway twisted, a sinuous wormhole. Jimmy was pale with fear but gave me the thumbs up anyway, and I stepped through into the pasar for the second time.

Again, that explosion of colour and humidity and heat, the coils of the Nagamuthu disguised as shophouses curving around the central square. It was quieter this time, off-cycle from the brief window each month when it was open to the public. Just a few stall-keepers organising inventory, a few of the Naga Sangam cleaning up.

The last time we'd gone to the pasar bayang, I had been in disguise, masking who I was and what I did. But that wasn't the right approach this time. This time, I was a representative of the duly elected government of Singapore, the sharp point of the spear of DEUS, and I had to show them I meant business. No more hiding.

I stood there, with the pasar spread out before me, and I made myself think of my mother and my father.

There was a time, when my mother first started getting sick, when things were good. She was still vital, still so full of life, philosophical about her illness. *Sheng ming wu chang*, she used to say, smiling. Life is change, impermanence, death nothing to be afraid of.

But she got sicker, and things got worse. The guiding principle of her life had always been to pull one's own weight, to not be a burden to others, so when the illness took that away from her, she broke. As her throat and lungs degenerated and the pain became constant, she couldn't hold on to her equanimity, and turned bitter and spiteful.

My father bore it all, stoic as a stone lion. I never saw him show any feelings. Until one day, when I came home from work, a young man angry at everything, and had said something to him about my mother. I didn't remember what it was I said, but it was something self-righteous and certain.

But I remembered the feelings behind my words. Spite, the need to hurt someone, the closer the better. Not lashing out, but lashing *in*.

I remembered my father slapping me across the face, the only time he had ever struck me.

I didn't know why I remembered that slap as love, as the clearest way my silent father had ever expressed it.

In the years since, I had returned to that incident now and again, worried at it like you do a scab. And each time, a surge rose in my chest, massive and nameless like the crashing of unknown waves in some hidden ocean, the unseen presence of some tree I hadn't found.

This time, I raised a fist as the emotion filled me, a good hurt, and as the vast, inchoate feeling swelled, the scars on my hand flared incandescent. I became a miniature sun in this midnight realm. Light the colour of gold and ashes threw stark shadows across the dirt floor, illuminating even the shophouses on the far side of the stalls, stripping the place of a layer of mystery and revealing it to be smaller and dingier than it first appeared.

Across the pasar, people turned to me like moths to fire. They gaped, squinting against the glare, and a profound silence settled.

"Hello," I said into the empty air. "Nagamuthu, we need to talk."

Without warning, without transition, I was in a void, the only light coming from my hands. From the depths of that darkness, a voice emerged, bass deep enough to feel in my bones. The Nagamuthu had dispensed with his boy-avatar this time.

"You have the balls of a bull, little man," he said. "Coming back here. But monkeys ever confuse cowardice for pragmatism, foolishness for courage. I will admit to some curiosity, though. So, before I obliterate you, tell me: What could you and I possibly have to talk about?"

No point delaying it. I held out the scrap of paper the Diviner had given us, a sketch of a few mice playing, a pathetic paper shield.

"Your daughter," I said. "We have her."

For a few moments, the Nagamuthu made no sound, no movement. I braced myself. The balance here was precarious—if my read was wrong, if he wasn't a cold-blooded snake through and through, if he let his emotions move him, the smallest revealed flash of his anger would crush me.

When the Nagamuthu spoke again, his voice was black silk wrapped around a knife.

"You think to threaten me?" he said. "To manipulate my heart for your own gain?"

"Not *my* own gain, no. We need to avert disaster, so I'm begging you. Help us to—"

"No," he said, final as the grave. "You forwent that option decades ago when you murdered my people, when you came sneaking in here like a rat last week. And now, you have taken my daughter, once more treating our lives as currency. Did you think I can forgive this? No. There will be no alliance between us, Benjamin Toh. No peace."

We'd expected something like this, but I had thought the proposal was worth a shot.

"Then we trade," I said.

"Oh?"

"For her safe return, a portion of your power."

"You would take more of my immortality?" There was venom there, warnings of danger.

I ignored it. Had to keep him focused on the present, not the past.

"Not all. Just enough to turn the tide," I said. "Enough to drive away a god."

Silence descended again, suffocating.

"You overestimate my love," he said finally.

"Do I?" Weeds of fear, born of self-preservation, growing in my soul, burned away. "Then we have nothing further to discuss. Kill me now, and my colleagues will do the same to her."

He hissed then, the first animal sound I'd heard him make.

"You won't hurt her. You would not dare. She would not allow you to hurt her."

"Try us," I said. The government had a reputation for having secret and esoteric resources, for being authoritarian, cruel, with no qualms about sacrificing lives and morality for the greater good. It was exactly what had happened to the earlier versions of the pasar bayang, stalls razed to the ground and livelihoods destroyed so more hygienic markets could take their place. We made hard choices and didn't always count the human cost.

The Singapore of today was different. The government of today was different. Kinder. Better. I had to believe that. But memories lingered. There was power to that reputation of ruthlessness, and I was banking on the Nagamuthu, wrapped in his ancient rage, still fighting the ghosts of history.

Another fraught moment, dragging.

Then, out of the void, a stone drifted towards me, illuminated from some inner source. It was the size of an egg, black rock flecked with mica, humming with immense power.

"Take it," the Nagamuthu whispered, defeated. "My chintamani stone. Take it and be damned."

I swallowed. There would be unpleasant consequences for this play, I was sure. But, for now, this was victory. I took the stone and bowed to the darkness. It felt... appropriate.

"We will release your daughter unharmed," I said. "You have my word."

I left through the pasar, where everything felt just a little less vibrant, less real. But I was unmolested as I made it back to the office. The whole team was there, waiting.

"It worked," I declared, holding up the stone, unable to contain a tinge of triumph in my voice. A smile crept across my face. "We've got the power we need."

Palpable relief all around. Adam wrapped me up in a big hug that was entirely inappropriate for the office, and it was really nice. We'd earned this, I supposed. This small victory carried a glimmer of hope. This was a flicker of possibility in the face of impending disaster. We might pull this off yet.

Midway through my debrief, the Diviner wandered out of the meeting room, stretching and yawning, eyes still heavy with sleep. She was still wearing her pyjamas, and clutching that same plush egg. The ghost cat, that traitorous little ingrate, twined around her legs before vanishing off to… wherever.

"Well," she said, eyeing the chintamani stone on my desk. "You guys finally did something right."

"Thank you," I said, meaning it.

Jimmy raised his hand. "I still don't get it. Not that I'm not grateful, but why are you helping us against your own father?"

The Diviner arched an eyebrow and flopped into a chair. "Why did I let you *kidnap* me? Oh, you know, the thrill of being held hostage by the government. It's the hottest new trend."

Jimmy blinked. "So…you just did it for fun?"

Her sneer was a cover, I saw. Her fingers worried at her plush egg, and there was something underneath her contempt. Something…younger and kinder.

"You wouldn't be here if you didn't care," I said.

She rolled her eyes so hard I worried for her ocular health. "God. You guys are such clichés. Useless bleeding hearts. Why should *I* even care about any of this?"

"I don't know why you *should*," I said. "But I know you *do*. You're not your father."

"You don't know shit," she retorted, her tone aiming for caustic, but it was half-hearted. Then, her mask came back up, and she pointed to me. "You had a reason prepared, didn't you? This morning at Burger King, in case I didn't agree to come with you. A backup in case appealing to my sense of moral duty didn't work."

"No...?"

"Say it. Say it or I will not agree to anything."

Damn it all. I took a deep breath, searching for the right words, knowing there was no gentle way to put it. "We thought this could be an opportunity," I finally managed. "A chance to make your father prove how much he loves you."

She stared at me, and I saw anger, bitterness, and longing cross her face, but when she spoke again her voice was emotionless. "As much as he loves his pasar?"

"More," I said. "I know it. We all need a reminder now and then, that's all."

I hesitated for just a second, then reached into my pocket and pulled out the scrap of paper—the one with the drawing of the mice.

"Here," I said. "Maybe you want this back."

For a heartbeat, she didn't move. Then, carefully casual, she plucked it from my fingers, started smoothing out the creases in the yellowing paper.

"When I was a child," she said, her tone light, "he would draw pictures of mice to cheer me up. Silly, right? Little mice doing dumb things—building houses. Baking cakes. Going to school. This was before the pasar." Her fingers traced the edges of the paper gently. "I kept them, you know. Every one. I wasn't sure he'd remember. Wasn't sure this would work."

The silence stretched between us, fragile as the paper she held. Fragile as love we couldn't speak.

"Whatever," she muttered. "Anyway, you guys better get moving. You don't have much time."

"Less than a week," I said, relieved to be back on firmer ground.

"Three days," she said, suddenly solemn. A shimmer unfolded from her brow, iridescent and delicate as the scales on a sea serpent. It spun, grazed all of us. The world exploded.

Apokalypsis. A lifting of the veil of time.

I saw Mr. Tan in his flat, on his recliner, mouth locked open in agony as something half-seen tore at him. He raised an arm to defend himself, but it was useless. He stood and flailed at the air around him, but that, too, was useless. Then something pushed against the underside of reality, stretching the terrazzo floors and piano and coffee table magazines until they split and it came through, alien and ichthyic. Savagely it dragged Mr. Tan down, down into dark water where more of the swarm waited, hungry.

I watched the predation spread beyond the initial breach. The monsters were here, in the shallows, and prey was plentiful. They feasted, gorged themselves not on flesh but on the greater part of things, the part under the surface, which could not defend itself. Shapes swam through the streets, through offices, through people's homes, half-seen, only the sliver of a fin, the edge of razored teeth.

I saw people, just living their lives, suddenly dragged into an ocean they couldn't understand, then erased, forgotten. They wept, terrified and confused as to why they felt diminished, like they'd lost something as essential as an arm or an eye. I saw adults holding children's schoolbags, pushing baby carriages, bewildered and aching from a bereavement that made no sense.

The veil fell again, and I gasped, back in the present. Mei, Jimmy, Adam, all looked stunned. They'd seen, too. The Diviner was watching us, inscrutable.

"Don't screw this up," she said, getting up without ceremony and making for the exit. "I'm going home."

No one stopped her. We were glad to be done with that ugly hostage-taking business, even if it was pretend-hostage-taking.

"What do we do now? What about Mr. Tan?" Jimmy asked, letting out a shaky breath. His eyes landed on the glimmering chintamani stone sitting innocuously next to my laptop. So much power in such a small thing.

"I will prepare," said Mei. "At midnight, I will forge of this stone a weapon to drive away this alien god, and what a sting it shall have! We will pit snake against fish, at the turning of the day, and—"

Something changed, the pulses of light from the stone quickening. In that instant, I sensed danger, some unseen snare set to activate now that the Diviner was safe.

"Get back!" I shouted, my Gardener reflexes kicking in. I shoved Jimmy away, lunged to put myself between the stone and Adam and Mei. But Adam had the same idea, and we collided, our bodies entangling as we both tried to protect the other.

The stone flared with an ominous, obsidian radiance. Everything seemed to slow as the dark light enveloped us, a tsunami of corrosive magic. Full of malice, the curse insinuated itself into Adam and me, corrupting our flesh and turning our blood to poison. My veins lit up like molten razors, then went numb.

Nerve damage, I realised with horror.

I fought to absorb the toxin, to contain it, but even as I tried, I realised the curse was overflowing in a thousand venomous streams, seeking targets beyond us.

In desperation, without understanding quite how, my soul expanded, branching to follow the streams of poison. My attention, too, forked, and I sent my focus racing ahead of the curse, trying to block off the spiritual channels that led from me before my brain shut down.

One channel led to my father, cutting vegetables in our kitchen, then to my late mother, my deceased grandparents, my cousins. I drew from the soil of my soul a stand of new trees to take the brunt of the poison, deflected it from my family, but confusion slowed me. How was this magic affecting even the dead?

Another channel led to the DEUS team, to Mei and Jimmy in the room with me, to Fizah at home watching a movie on her laptop, and I raised a wall of earth and braided mangrove to protect them. The corruption snaked outwards into a dozen new tracks, towards MOC colleagues, towards Others, towards exes and old friends.

It was following lines of connection—those of blood or love or friendship or affinity—backwards into the past and forward into the future, paying no attention to the arrow of regular time. It sought to contaminate our friends, parents, ancestors long dead—everyone.

It was too much, this venom of a snake god, too much for me to transmute and neutralise before it overflowed the banks of my soul. I had to give it somewhere to go. I had to choose who to direct the poison towards, who to sacrifice. I had no choice.

I had to choose.

The poison brimmed, lapped at my hasty dams, starting to trickle through. Then I spotted it, highlighted by the runnels of poison—the threads of faint connection between me and all the other Gardeners in the world, across history, a network of paths between our souls I hadn't known existed.

Sorry, I thought, an arrow of a message sent into the space between us. *At least you can take care of yourselves. At least you have a chance.*

I threw the last of my strength into directing the curse to this network, even as my lungs seized up, as my eyes burned with tears and poison, as the trees inside me withered in the corruption, as my fortitude failed. The pollution flowed out from me, a hundred thousand rivulets into the past, and then the curse overcame me and dragged me under, into darkness.

CHAPTER TWENTY

1057, Duanzhou, Wen manor. Sixteen guards surround me. I am the precious first daughter of a wealthy merchant family, but I have been accused of the practice of heterodox arts in seduction and witchcraft, as well as the castration of my betrothed, a renowned philanderer. I am defiant and unrepentant, spitting curses at the guards and shaming the family name of my late fiancé. The guards move in to apprehend me, but I move first. I am among them, using the skills I have learned from my secret association sisters, my elbows crushing windpipes, fingers jabbing nerve clusters, my yellow dress flaring like the petals of a chrysanthemum. But I fight also with other weapons, with the greater part of myself they cannot see. I pierce them with unseen whips, against which their lamellar armour is no defence. I grip them by their souls, under the water of the human realm, and sweep them away on invisible tides. I fight like a whirlwind, like a warrior, like a woman.

But out of nowhere a diluted poison clouds my head, still

potent enough to make me stumble. I die on the end of a spear, bleeding onto the flagstones of my family home. But I know all sixteen guards who were there have been amputated in spirit, and will not long outlive me. Six take their lives within the year, and others die from internal injuries. No other woman will be accused of witchcraft in Duanzhou ever again.

What? Who? These were not Gardeners. I struggled to find myself, but the Nagamuthu's poison gnawed at who I was, and I was sucked away again.

1916, outskirts of Gorizia. The town had been evacuated earlier in the year, caught between two armies and their artillery shells. The ground is mud and rubble and ice, and the stars cold and merciless. I walk across the town, down the main thoroughfare, picking my unhurried way through broken glass, and yet I am not quite there. I walk a straight line, but my steps turn me at an angle to the world, and my path leaves behind long stretches of unbroken snow. I slip back and forth between here and somewhere deeper. An observer would see just the curve of an ear, the edge of a knife, a scrap of shadow. I am making my way to the enemy's camp to do what has to be done.

The next day, I know, a dozen Austro-Hungarian commanders will be found murdered in their sleep. The sentries will have seen nothing. I know they will find my body there, too, out of place, tongue and eyes blackened by some unknown toxin. But my mission will be done. A few weeks later, in August, the Italians will take the town in the Sixth Battle of the Isonzo.

These were Divers—I was seeing the lives of Divers like Adam. The connection between us must have duplicated what I did, spreading the poison out not just among people like me but also among people like him. I had to find him, see if he—

2023, Ar-Rabitah Mosque, Redhill. I approach the ustaz, my mouth dry with fear. I have something to ask him, and even though my parents have told me to keep it to myself, I have to know. And Ustaz Iqbal has always been kind to me. If he declares me a witch, that what I can do is sihir, *I will accept the consequences bravely.*

"Ustaz," I say. "I need guidance."

"Adam, my dear child," he says, a soft breeze on a troubled sea. "Speak your mind."

Taking a breath, I tell him my deepest secret—my discovery of another world under our own, how I can go into it, swim in its currents, play among the roots and the colossal blocks of stone. The words spill out, and I cannot call them back.

I can see from his eyes that he doesn't understand. I am sure, as he reaches out his hand, that he will cast me out.

"There's no need to be scared," he says, using his thumb to wipe

tears from my eyes. His voice is gentle. "Are you using this… discovery… to harm others? To do what you know to be haram?"

I shake my head, and he smiles, warm and unafraid.

"Our faith teaches us that Allah is Al-Khaliq, the ultimate creator, and His works are vast and wondrous. The world we know is but a glimpse of His divine masterpiece. Perhaps what you speak of is a part of that grand tapestry—a realm known to only you and God. Are you not glad?"

I am! I am! I feel something lift from me, a weight I hadn't even realised was there. I open my mouth to thank him, but something is in me, a pain in my throat and eyes from a terrible poison. I feel myself start to fade, sinking into the Outside as I panic, and I'm thinking I must not vanish now, I must not Dive, for if I do he will see it and call my parents and this moment would be lost and he would never understand again.

Adam! I reached out—I didn't know how—across the years, drew the poison into myself, and as I did I pivoted and flung Adam out of the mindscape, out of history. And then I was falling again into the past.

Seventeenth century BCE, Nineveh. I sit by the light of the oil lamps, letting the shadows dance across my bare arms, making sure to angle myself to show the line of my neck. Old habits. My customer is speaking, as others have a thousand times before him, tongue loosened now that the knot in his groin is released. He speaks of a wife, unfaithful; children, ungrateful; business ventures, failed. He avoids looking at me, but he talks, this release no less important than the earlier, physical one.

I feel inside myself, past the bruises of the last rough client, past the physical aches of my trade, and I find the tamarisk tree, delicate pink flowers in full bloom, each blossom a promise of a better tomorrow. I release a breath and they drift out, a shower of tiny petals, filling the room with their subtle fragrance. Some find their way to him, this little boy in the body of a man, and I smile as I watch as his eyes soften, as he turns to talk of fresh possibilities, renewed effort with his family. Hope, I have given him, planting my seeds in him even as he spilled his on me.

Then something intrudes, some trace of blight seeping into my soul. But it is just a trace, like watered-down Babylonian wine, like the dribblings of an old man, nothing to me. I handle worse every day. And so I ignore it, let time transform it, as it does everything, to something better and more beautiful.

It worked! Spreading the poison out diluted it, and Gardeners could handle it, as I'd hoped. Hope—that's what the woman did. Not only did she cultivate it in herself, she gave parts of her soul to others. She could share the hope in her soul with them, just like Mr. Tan could share the grief in his soul. Maybe that was true for all of us. Mr. Tan wasn't an anomaly—maybe we could all do this, give pieces of ourselves to help others survive.

Before I could think more about it, once again the Nagamuthu's trap frayed the thread of my self, unravelling my mind further. But I could still smell that tamarisk perfume, and it gave me something to follow, a path back to my own soul. Against the overwhelming malevolence of the curse, I fought to return to my rainforest and mangroves, led only by a scattering of pink petals and the faint scent of desert flowers. Almost, I made it back to myself, almost I could see the edges of myself, but once more I was swept away.

2003, Raffles Institution. The sun dips low. Seng and I are walking home from school, kicking a small rock back and forth between us.

"I don't know," I say.

"You don't have to do anything, Ben. Just . . . stand next to me. That's all. They won't force me if you're there. Friends against the world, right?"

Those Secondary 4 boys. That's who he was talking about. They're confident, loud, bigger. Mean. Always looking to press-gang the younger students into being their errand boys. Their pets, someone to boss around. They haven't picked on me since my growth spurt, but Seng is still small, wiry. Easy prey.

I look away, look down. Focus on the skittering stone we're kicking. I want to help, I really do. But finals are coming up, and I shouldn't be getting distracted. What if things escalate? What if me being there makes things worse?

And I already help Seng with every other thing, big or small. And I have my own problems. My mother is sick, and I can't disappoint her with bad grades. With getting in trouble at school. I have to be perfect, so she can focus on getting better.

"I don't know," I repeat. "You should say no. Maybe you can just tell them no."

Seng turns away, kicks the stone into the bushes by the side of the street. "Yeah, okay. It's fine. Whatever."

Blink. This was me. My memories. I'd played this a thousand times to myself in the years since then. There was more coming up, I knew.

Blink.

The next day. Recess. Seng is sitting with the Sec 4 boys. They laugh, clap him on the shoulder, a little too hard. Seng's smile is brittle.

He sees me. He looks away.

Blink.

After school. We're walking home again. I don't like this feeling in my chest, whatever it is.

"Seng," I say.

"It doesn't matter," he mutters.

"I—"

He rounds on me. His eyes are blazing. "Shut up. It's not about you. I decided, okay? I made my own choices. It's nothing to do with you."

I flinch. I have nothing else to say.

Blink.

That night, I'm telling my mother about my day. She's taking her medicine, the one that always gives her nausea. Her hand trembles. I want to tell her about Seng, but I stumble. I don't know how.

Shame gags me, and inside, I shatter.

Inside us all, there is a Garden. Sometimes, when we face too much, our Gardens collapse, the roots torn up, the soil turned to dust. That day, confronted with the kind of person I am, my soul crumbles. But I can't. Not in front of my mother. I can't give her something else to worry about.

And so, inside me, from the ashes of the broken illusion that I was a decent person, I force a fresh shoot to grow. That first plant in my Garden, it takes my broken self and transforms it, takes the pieces of shame and grief, the bits of some foreign poison, and transmutes them into growth. A new tree.

It was strength. Responsibility. I won't let anyone down ever again.

I gasped for breath, back in the present, closer than ever to myself. The last of the venom clawed at me, but I was a Wen girl, spitting my defiance of the patriarchy. I was an Italian soldier, my loyalty to my people stronger than any fear of death. I was a Mesopotamian woman in a dark room, holding on to hope. There were new saplings in my soul, the wisdom of an ustaz, the resolve of a boy who won't let others down again, and no snake poison could end me.

I emerged, finally free, the echoes of the past still ringing in my ears. I strained to listen, to make sense of the voices around me. It was dark. Where was I?

Mei's voice, uncharacteristically gentle.

"Benjamin, can you hear me?"

"Yeah, I'm here," I replied. "What... what happened?"

Someone's fingers brushed my face. "The poison." It was Mei. "It took your sight."

Blind. I stamped down on the panic that rose as the realisation sank in, the same terror that I had to fight when my hands had been broken. Fear that I couldn't do my job. Fear I couldn't pull my weight, that I could no longer do right by others. How could I be useful if I couldn't see?

Mei's voice broke through. "Be calm, Benjamin. I have arrested the worst of it. Your vision will be restored—I swear this."

Relief. Again I could smell the faint hint of flowers. Hope. But my heart yearned for something else, someone else.

"Adam?" I called out. "Is he okay?"

"I'm here, you idiot." His voice, then a hand cupping my cheek, brushing hair from my forehead. "I thought I lost you."

My heart thrummed. Perhaps it was the remnants of the poison, but I thought it was gladness. One thing had gone right in all this, at least. "Well, we're both idiots, then," I said. "Trying to save each other and ending up in this mess." I put a smile on my face, but inside, weeds of guilt carpeted the ground of my soul, multiplying out of my control. He had almost died, and it was my fault. I had gotten too comfortable having Adam around, relying on him, allowing my desire to have him around obscure the fact that this wasn't his responsibility.

No more, I promised myself. I wasn't going to put this man in any more danger. He meant too much to me.

Adam heard none of this. "We make a pretty lousy team," he said, laughing.

"I don't know how you guys got out of that," Jimmy said, cutting in. "But you did. We got out of a god's trap, guys. Give yourself some credit."

Just then, as we started to feel a little better about ourselves, my phone buzzed. Jimmy took it to relay the message to me, and he paused for a long moment before reading the message aloud.

"It's from Nadia. The jinni. She says that the favour you owe has come due. Tanglin Club, it says. Tonight, eight p.m. Dress to impress."

A silence fell over the room.

"We don't have a choice," I said. We really didn't.

"Does the invite say he can bring a plus one?" Adam asked.

"I'm not bringing you," I said. Then, more gently, "It's bad enough I have to go. The rest of you...please, stay here. Our priority must still be to deal with the incoming monsters, which means you have to figure out how to use the chintamani stone. It's still got power, even if it's cursed. We'll have a better shot at fixing this if you're all here."

I hesitated, imagining the thing pulsing with malice on the table. Imagining a second flare of the poison, when I wouldn't be there to protect them. Because I was at a stupid party.

"Just... stay sharp."

"Fine," Adam said. I heard Jimmy murmur agreement, too.

I exhaled. There was nothing good about this situation. I didn't want to abandon the team now, of all times, for Nadia's ill-timed interruption. But a jinni's debt is not something you left unpaid.

Now, blind and almost broken by the Nagamuthu's poison, all I had to do was survive Nadia's party and fulfil whatever favour she had in mind.

Piece of cake.

CHAPTER TWENTY-ONE

The Tanglin Club was one of the most prestigious and exclusive clubs in the country. All cream columns and stately architecture, it was nestled in a lush patch of manicured greenery right in the middle of the city, a sanctuary for the uber-wealthy to relax in, network, and cackle over how they were exploiting the proletariat.

That last part probably wasn't true, but how would I know? The basic membership cost two years of my salary, and no one I knew was anywhere in range of the right class to recommend me. I supposed I'd always been curious about the lifestyle of these folk, and here I was, standing before the club, about to be part of some high-society party.

I sure wished I could see something.

I'd left my glasses at home. Because what was the point? I knew that the Nagamuthu's poison had done more than blind me—it had turned my eyes strange and unnatural, a deep viridian that made it look like I was wearing those expensive

Korean contacts. I knew it looked unprofessional, but tonight, I didn't care enough to hide it. It was my little bit of rebellion against Nadia's commands.

Mei had done the best she could in the time we had, and between her magic and my accelerated Gardener regeneration, we'd made some progress on getting a bit of my vision back. But the poison contained the Nagamuthu's signature retrocausal malice. A clever thing, really. It opportunistically reached across time to make me blind and damaged not just here and now, but across a span of several years. The bright spot about this (pun intended) was that it paradoxically meant I'd had years to get used to navigating the world like this. It also meant that I'd been forced to hone my deep read, as I'd come to call the soul vision I learned from Mr. Tan. Between my partial healing and the deep read, I could make out enough shapes and blotches of colour and blurry souls that I didn't walk into people, but that was about my limit.

My patience, I'd admit, was also at my limit. This was yet another distraction from dealing with the incoming monsters, yet another bullshit side quest from the work that would actually save lives. I supposed I should have been a little more used to this—this was par for the course for civil servants. But still, the frustration of being stuck here instead of being with my team put me in too foul a mood to enjoy the Tanglin Club experience.

Nadia found me in the lobby, actively trying not to grind my teeth. She was dressed in green, with diamonds bright as stars at her throat and ears. The wasteland of her soul was lit by helices of pale fire.

"Ben!" she exclaimed. "So good of you to come!"

As if I had a choice. But politeness is our crutch in moments like this. Politeness and lies.

"Such a pleasure," I said. "And you look nice this evening."

She shifted slightly, and I imagined she must have smiled, blushed prettily, but no emotion touched her soul. For all that she was fire, she was as cold-blooded as the Nagamuthu, and even more ruthless.

"Always a sweet-talker," she said. "Anyway, this is just a small event my family hosts every year, a way for us to give back to the community, you know? Everyone here is a friend, so it's good to see you dressed so . . . comfortably."

God, she was insufferable. I was wearing my nicest suit (which, to be fair, was my only suit), but I supposed that couldn't compare to the price tags on what these other people had on. At least she'd made no mention of my strange eyes or my visual impairment—I guess it would have been too gauche. And then she linked her arm through mine, smelling like desert and roses, and tugged me along. "Why don't you come with me? There are people who are just *dying* to meet you."

Her tone made it clear that this was no request, so I followed dutifully as she made her way deeper into the club. What else was I to do?

She led me into what had to be the ballroom, because the

resonances changed subtly. When one sense is damaged, your others sharpen, as they say, and I heard the high ceilings from the faint echo of footsteps on carpet, the far walls from the acoustics of the music. A live orchestra was playing something light and jazzy. Overhead, the chandeliers were galaxies, and there must have been maybe fifty people standing below in small clusters. Mere blurs in my normal vision, but to my inner sight I saw hints of their souls, a wild variation of things in barren Gardens—pools of tar, lattices of bone, desolate twisted structures. Everyone here was an Other, even the waitstaff.

Then someone pressed a glass of wine into my hand, and I was thrust into contact with the movers and shakers of Singapore's supernatural world. "This is Madam Phua," Nadia said, introducing me to someone whose soul was thick with blood and weevils. "From Phua and Chan Securities, and an old family friend."

I got the impression that Madam Phua's glance skimmed over me like I was a waiter delivering her wine. "A pleasure," she said, in a tone that suggested it wasn't. Then, I felt her lean closer to Nadia, her voice low and conspiratorial. "I must say, you handled those labs beautifully. Su Ling will be furious, of course, but that woman should have known better. All that taxpayer money thrown at these startups—all flash, no staying power. Honestly, it was only a matter of time before someone . . . dealt with them. It is a good thing you did."

Wait, taxpayer-funded labs? *Senior Parliamentary Secretary*

Goh Su Ling? Were they talking about Vanguard? Was Vanguard a government project?

Then we were off again, and again Nadia was pushing me at someone, all runes and cold constellations. "Oh, Timothy, darling, I just love what you've done with your hair! Ben, you must meet Timothy—isn't he gorgeous? He's a *professor*." And then again. "Ben, this is my little brother Asif and his very shy wife. Say hello, dear. Don't worry, he won't bite."

I shook hands and kissed cheeks and bowed as required, my sense of vulnerability heightened by my inability to decipher the subtle cues that threaded through these conversations. Without sight, I could not tell whether the partygoers looked at me with interest or indifference, whether they glanced at one another and snickered as I passed. But what I could tell was this: Vanguard was the talk of the evening. I heard whispers, fragments of phrases—"all that money, up in flames," "pet project," "investors asking questions," "serious liability," "don't cross her."

Nadia basked in it. The burning of the Vanguard labs—the "favour" she'd done for us—had made her the most powerful player in the room.

And I—I was the cherry on her sundae tonight. She was showing me off, her tame DEUS officer, a trophy, my subordinate presence a statement of her power. Perhaps a younger me would have felt the humiliation more keenly, bucked off the metaphorical bridle, but I was wiser now, able to see how great a value this had to my own work. These folks she introduced me to were so important I never had a hope of meeting them normally, only interacting via their goons and minions and flunkies. I filed away names and job roles and who liked whom, enough information to start many new folders and keep Jimmy busy for a while.

And Vanguard. If even a fraction of the rumours I'd overheard tonight were true, it wasn't just a rogue startup gone wrong—they were connected to something big, perhaps even to some of our higher-ups. The puzzle pieces were there, and maybe Jimmy and I could put them together.

But that would have to wait. We still had to first deal with the sinking town and fish gods, and I had to finish playing this farce of making polite conversation and keeping a smile on my face.

Then, it was over. We found ourselves finally alone, standing next to an enormous ice sculpture I could not make out the details of, only that it was faceted to scatter the chandeliers' light in scintillating patterns. I sensed some enchantment in it, something in the dazzle that parsed sound and provided us with privacy. I was sure it was no accident we had ended our circuit of the room here.

"That was nice, wasn't it?" Nadia purred, an undertone of satiated pleasure in her voice. "I think they all found you very... interesting."

"You're too kind, Nadia." No harm being courteous. "I had a wonderful time, too. My only regret is that I'd never heard about this lovely event until today. Your networks are remarkably extensive, and your friends are impressive."

She made a dismissive sound, but I could tell she was pleased by the compliment. "Again with the sweet talk," she said. "We just didn't think DEUS would be interested in this little affair. Don't you usually work with...those of more modest means? And, to be honest, your predecessors were not exactly presentable. But you—you can come as my guest again next year, if you like. I'm sure we can find you something to wear that's more fitting for your station."

I wasn't sure if she meant I should dress more sharply or wear a leash, but either way, it was time to go. My obligation was discharged, and we had fishes to stop.

"Of course," I said. "I had a wonderful time, but if you don't need me for anything else..."

Nadia chuckled. "Oh, darling, why ever would you leave now? The evening's just begun. Stay! Have a little more to drink, enjoy the music, meet some people!"

"I—"

"We still have a little promise to discuss."

"What?"

She smiled. Even through my blindness, I saw the glitter of her teeth.

"You are so naive, it's adorable. Oh, I'm sorry, did you think that little tour was it?" She paused, waiting for me to ask her what the favour actually was.

I didn't want to give her the satisfaction, but I was too irritated to play this game right then. "Just tell me what you want."

"There's a woman sitting at the bar," Nadia said, her voice taking a wicked turn. "She's wearing a yellow top. Looks rather cheap, actually. I need you to seduce her."

"What?" This was not at all what I was expecting.

"Was that unclear?"

"No, but... why?"

"Did I ask this many questions when you asked of us a favour?"

"No, but—"

"Because you've been a good sport, have this, from my lips freely given. That woman—she's a witch with a particular piece of arcane knowledge, something that I'd like to find out. Your job is to charm her, get her to let down her guard. Our telepath-retainers are on standby, ready to do the rest."

"What knowledge are you stealing?"

"You don't need to know."

This was frustrating. If only I could see, I would have been able to get some read on Nadia. Did she look nervous? That would have told me about how dangerous this piece of information was. Who in the room was she looking at when she spoke? That would have given me clues on which factions this had to be kept from. But that data was denied to me.

"Why do you need *me* to do this?" I asked. "You have employees, and you could hire—"

"Two words: plausible deniability."

And I was disposable. I hated these games.

"Also," she continued, and even blind, I could feel the

pressure of her attention as she looked me up and down. "We've done some digging. You're just her type." Nadia reached out and prodded my arm appraisingly. "Fit, nerdy, good-looking in your Chinese boy sort of way. You'll do."

It was an odd feeling, being objectified so blatantly. Insulting, yes, but also a little flattering. Maybe it said something about how compliment-starved men are that even her cold assessment of me felt nice.

Then she wrapped something around my wrist, a watch of some sort. The weight of it felt substantial, expensive. "A gift," she said. "No strings attached. It'll read the witch's aura and warm against your skin when her shields are down. Just keep her in that state for at least a minute or two, and then you are free to go. Now... go fetch."

CHAPTER TWENTY-TWO

Well, this was all a big tub of horse shit. I didn't want to get involved in whatever nonsense this was between the jinn and the witches. But I hadn't figured out how to get out of it yet.

I felt my way to a stool at the bar and slid onto it, feeling distinctly out of my depth. "Hi," I said, though it felt more like a greeting to the void.

The woman—the target? The mark? I was really no good at this—sipped on something that smelled like cough syrup. In the realm of her soul, a knot of sparrows fluttered and spiralled, a dance of their own.

"Not interested," she shot back. "I have a boyfriend."

I could tell from her voice that she hadn't even bothered to turn in my direction. "Well, funny thing is, so do I."

At this, she finally shifted her attention to me, and all I could discern were vague outlines: curves, dark eyes, long hair framing a pale face. Her laugh was a delighted guffaw, very unladylike.

"Well, that's an unusual approach," she said. "What do you want?"

There was something familiar about her voice. It took me a moment, but then it clicked. The last time I'd seen her, she'd been in a robe, carrying a staff. She was the young woman at the pasar bayang, telling us where the trash bins were. The only Naga Sangam guard who'd been nice to us.

"You!" I said.

Silence. I had a hunch she might have raised an eyebrow. It was clear she didn't remember me, and I realised why.

"At the pasar bayang?" I said. "I had a glamour on, looked older. The guards... your friends... took us away to meet the Nagamuthu."

A quiet gasp from her. She shifted, and the birds of her soul whirled with great agitation. Her hands, uninvited, found mine and she turned them over, her fingertips tracing the scars that marred my palms, lines I knew to be faintly gleaming.

"Your hands." Her voice was thick with emotion. "They were... I saw what happened. From a distance. I'm glad you're okay. I'm... sorry."

I sensed her pity, and once, a part of me would have resented her for it. But the same ash and fires I'd used to heal my hands had burned that away. The same poison that had blinded my sight opened my eyes, let me see that what she said wasn't condescension or cruelty, just the ache of regret from glimpsing a ruin she could not repair.

"It's all right," I said, meaning it. "It's all right."

"And your eyes? Is that also . . . ?"

She was the first person here to mention my blindness. I was strangely grateful.

"Yes. Your boss again," I said. "Not your fault, either."

There was a pause, the silence stretching. Then, she gave my hands a gentle squeeze, a silent acknowledgement of this improbable connection, and I felt the watch on my wrist warm up. Despite myself, I'd managed to get her to relax her guard, and her shields were coming down.

What was my duty here? Was it to faithfully serve Nadia, the powerful and well-connected host of this party, who'd helped us ravage Vanguard? Or was it to protect the secrets of this woman whose name I didn't even know?

But Nadia treated me like a tool, and this woman treated me like a person. The choice, once I laid it out to myself, was clear.

"Your soul is birds," I said.

"Birds?" She drew back a little, and the watch cooled. Good.

"Yes, and they're lovely. But never mind. Listen." I grabbed a glass from the bar, raised it to cover my mouth like I imagined spies might do. Nadia probably had lip-readers around. Surely. "You have a secret the jinn want, and they've sent me to distract you while they pillage your mind. Don't let your guard down around me."

The watch pulsed with heat again, but this time unsteadily.

"You want me to believe you . . . to trust you that I shouldn't trust you." She sounded thoughtful, amused, curious. Unafraid.

It did sound ridiculous when she put it like that, but I nodded.

I heard her take a drink, heard her swallow.

"Why are you telling me this?"

"Because you reminded me just now that we are not our orders. I don't have to want what Nadia wants. You should leave."

"He's not my boss, by the way."

"What?"

"You called him my boss. The Nagamuthu. I just volunteer at the market. I have since I was a teenager, mostly to meet people. Speaking of which . . . the secret they want isn't worth much, you know."

"What do you mean?"

"The thing in my head that they're after. It's a name. The Nagamuthu's True Name."

"What? How can that not be worth . . . lots?"

"Well, first of all, it's not really secret. Most of us who are more senior in the Naga Sangam know it. Part of the history you pick up. Second, and this is the real secret, it no longer has power over him. He rid himself of that vulnerability centuries ago."

"And Nadia doesn't know this?"

"Apparently not, if she's sending a cute guy to steal it from me."

I couldn't afford to let that distract me. My mind was racing with the beginnings of a plan. "Do you know how the tiger got its stripes?"

"No idea where you're going with this," the woman said, a smile in her voice. "But go on."

"There's an old story of Sang Kancil," I said, formulating the plan as I spoke. The leaf of remembered story unfurled in my head. "The mousedeer. One day, he was being chased through the forest by his old enemy, Rajah Harimau, the tiger. Now remember, this was a long time ago, so Sang Kancil still had ugly grey fur, and Rajah Harimau was entirely the gorgeous orange of a sunrise.

"Anyway, Sang Kancil ran till he could run no more, so he turned around to bravely face the tiger. *Stop! Rajah Harimau*, the little mousedeer said. *Spare my life and I will give you my most precious possession.*

"*Give it to me, and I will spare your life*, the tiger said, ever greedy.

"*It is a pendant shaped like the sun*, the mousedeer said. *And I hid it under that tree.*

"So the tiger dashed off towards the giant tree, and it was a trap! The sticky sap of the tree held on to Rajah Harimau, and no matter how much he struggled, he could not free himself.

"*I will bring you the water from a coconut*, Sang Kancil said. *To wash the sticky sap right off. But you'll have to give me something in return.*

"*What do you want?* Rajah Harimau growled.

"*Give me some of your beautiful orange fur*, the mousedeer said. *And I will bring you a coconut.*

"Rajah Harimau roared with anger, but he had no choice

but to agree. And so, that's why mousedeers are orange, and tigers are only half-orange."

The woman laughed and clapped delightedly. "And here I thought it was because of variation and natural selection."

"The point I was trying to make is—"

"Disinformation," she said. "I got it. Selling it twice."

This woman was growing on me, I had to admit. "It has to be believable enough to work."

"Let me worry about that," she said. "I'll put together something that could plausibly be the True Name of an immortal snake god. Let them . . . steal it from my head."

The watch was cold against my wrist, only occasionally pulsing with heat. The flashes of trust were not enough for Nadia's telepaths to get through, I hoped.

"You'll have to lower your shields. It'll be suspicious otherwise."

I could see her shake her head. "Can't do that," she said. "If I did, they'd see what we intend to do. They'd see everything."

"And if you don't, they'll know what they get is fake."

We fell silent, thinking. Then I got it.

"Shall we dance?"

I'm a decent dancer, I knew. In my youth, before I learned to embrace my own dorkiness, I had big plans to become a suave international man of mystery, and had studied up on the moves and rhythms of a wide variety of styles. But where

I was technically proficient, this woman was a natural, effortlessly graceful. So I followed her lead, improvised some steps to complement her movements.

"Oh," she said, gripping my arm as I twirled her away and then reeled her back. "This is kind of nice, actually."

I grinned. She was right—this was nice. She was pliant and athletic, and her hair smelled fantastic, like sunlight and grass. However, our dancing was merely a cover. Concealed within the sleeve of my jacket was the chi disruptor, its power set low. We were experimenting, using it to alter her aura just enough to set off the detector in my watch, hoping it would fool whatever similar magic the jinn were using.

So I pulled her close, pressed her against me as I touched the chi disruptor to her lower back, the *qihai* acupuncture point, to veil the energies she expended to create her disinformation packet. I cradled the back of her neck, a sensual gesture, but also a way to activate the *fengchi* points and simulate the relaxation of her shields. I gripped her wrist, pressing on the *neiguan* and *shenmen*, hiding any signs that we were manipulating her aura. I had no actual expertise in such acupuncture, and was basing my attempts on a manual of traditional Chinese medicine I had flipped through years ago.

"Are you sure you're okay with this?" I asked, my focus divided between the acupuncture and the surrounding watchful eyes. As her knee rose to wrap around my waist, a daring move that must've raised a few eyebrows, I couldn't help but feel a twinge of distraction.

She gave me a level look, one I was familiar with from Mei. Was this a witch thing? "I've danced naked under the moon in more cities than you can imagine," she said. "This is nothing."

So that was certainly *something*, but I had to focus. Balancing the delicate act of applying pressure with the chi disruptor without inadvertently causing her harm required my full attention. And all the while, I had to maintain the appearance of having a good time, projecting to Nadia's observers the pretence that all this touching and groping indicated the wild success of my mission.

And in the midst of all this, my sole gauge of progress was my watch, its sporadic pulses of heat offering me feedback. With so much to manage and so many variables at play, I couldn't afford to let my focus waver.

"No need to hurry," the woman said. "It's been a long time since I got to do this."

I hurried anyway.

Then, it worked. The watch started radiating a steady warmth against my wrist, signalling the success of our illusion. Somewhere, I hoped, Nadia's hired telepaths had received the same signal and were now grabbing for the faked True Name of the Nagamuthu that my dancing partner had prepared.

"We're live," I whispered into her ear.

"Perfect." This close, I could see that she had a crooked, endearing smile. "I'm glad we met again."

And then she pulled away, making a little sound of surprise.

"Oh, I think I've had a bit too much to drink," she exclaimed, her voice projecting enough for others to hear. "Excuse me."

I heard her stumble backwards, as if losing her balance, and I heard a murmur of concern sweep through the crowd. I imagined that a path must have cleared for her to exit the dance floor, because I heard her footsteps as she tottered out. From the scandalised gasps and muttered conversations near me, I gathered that she had somehow managed to snag a glass of wine and spill it on not one but two elderly gentlemen before she vanished outside.

The intensity of the moment gradually subsided, and it was only after a few moments that I realised she had slipped her business card into the inside pocket of my jacket. Her name, I would later find out, was Tessa, and she was a software engineer at Google. Intriguing. But it was the words scrawled on the back that would catch my attention. *Had fun, owe you one,* accompanied by a cartoon drawing of a bird.

By the time I made my way back to Nadia, reclining on a divan beneath a tapestry so large and so brightly coloured even I could see it, she was beaming with satisfaction. I assumed it was because her pet telepaths had already notified her of their success. She ran a tight ship, I'd give her that.

There were no chairs, I noticed, across from her. By tradition, as the host, she was the queen, and anyone who spoke with her was a petitioner, forced to stand uncomfortably by design.

I was beat, dead on my feet, exhausted by the deception and the intrigue and the socialising, drained by the last few days. Even the verdant energy given to me by the trees inside had limits. I really just wanted a chair, or better yet, a bed I could collapse into for a few hours. But now was not the time. There was still work to be done, so I stood, straight and tall, channelling a little bit of Adam for just the right amount of insouciance.

"Excellent work, Benjamin," Nadia purred. "You've got game."

"I'm glad to be of service to your family. Is my debt discharged?"

"Yes, yes, of course," she said, her voice husky. "I did enjoy watching you work, though. We'll have to do this more often."

Was she flirting with me? Or did she want something?

I hated these games. The great factions, they all did it, pretending one thing was another. The Nagamuthu hid terrifying violence behind philosophy. Vanguard masked ambition behind science and progress. Nadia gilded her plays for power with mutually beneficial contracts and deals. For all of them, these were just games, just ways to pass the time while they accumulated more money, more power, more status. But they held all the cards, so the rest of us had to play as well.

As much as I hated it, DEUS had to play, too. Nadia's patronage would be invaluable for our work. She was connected to people with power—a word from her, in the right ear, could do more than any number of policy papers I could write or government programmes I could propose. That avatar of Annapurna who was still on my to-do list, who was dealing with racist landlords? The jinn could flash enough cash to make the landlords care about the colour of money, not the colour of skin. That goblin family who couldn't afford to send their child to school? Nadia's family could give the kid a full scholarship and not feel the pinch. And there was another, more personal, issue that Nadia could help me with.

I flashed her my best grin, the effect likely marred by my having to guess where exactly she was. "There's one other matter," I said. "I have one more trade to propose."

Even without my vision, I could feel the sudden sharpening of her interest, as if a predator had just focused its sights on me. Which was, I supposed, exactly what happened.

"Go on," Nadia said.

"Two pieces of information for you. One free, one not. The free one is that what your telepaths just picked up is fake. That's not the Nagamuthu's True Name."

"How do you know this?"

"I sensed the deception from that witch you had me speak with. But it doesn't matter. What matters is that I can give you his True Name, if you do me a small personal favour in return."

"The Nagamuthu's True Name, on your honour?" I heard the greed in her voice, the craving.

"On my honour."

"Then speak. What is the favour you would have of me?"

I hesitated. The thought had occurred to me, of course, to

ask for information on Vanguard. It was exactly the kind of pragmatic, for-the-greater-good kind of decision the government expected me to make.

But I had another promise to keep. To Seng.

Maybe it was the memory, so recently dredged up, of how Seng had looked at me, twenty-something years ago, as he sat at the canteen table with the older boys. Maybe it was that there were a dozen other ways we could investigate Vanguard, but if I wanted to help out Seng's nephew...a favour from the leader of one of the major jinn families didn't happen every day.

I smiled a little, grimly. "There's a girl. A jinni. She's in love with a human boy, and her family doesn't approve. It should be easy for you to—"

I was going to say that it would have been easy for her to find out who they were and put some pressure on, but Nadia started chuckling darkly, her amusement tinged with a note of disbelief.

"You're talking about Asif's daughter. Izzati. My own niece."

"Yes." Sheer luck, but no reason to let her know.

"And what would you have me do?"

"Merely speak with your brother and your sister-in-law. No more. Ask them to let the two kids try things out."

The silence stretched.

"We are not a modern people, Benjamin," Nadia said at last. "Many in my family would think that you are sticking your nose where it doesn't belong, trying to upend millennia of tradition and dilute our culture. They would say that you are mud, trying to interfere with fire."

But I heard something in her voice. Something between sorrow and regret. I waited, let the silence in the space bloom.

She sighed. "Do you know I'm the only one in the family who still keeps in touch with Miriam? That's Fizah's mother, my sister. She's cast out, because she loves a human. A human! Mud! I will not have Izzy throw her life away just like that."

"You can't protect her forever," I said. "Let her make her own choice."

In her soul, the helices of fire slowed, seemed to hesitate, spun, hesitated again.

"So be it," Nadia said. "Give me the name, and my niece will get to have her fun."

I told her the name Tessa had told me, all sibilants, then made my escape from the party. Being Sang Kancil was tiring work.

CHAPTER TWENTY-THREE

There's nothing quite like a late-night biryani to make you feel better about things, especially after you've spent hours picking at fancy hors d'oeuvres and amuse-bouches and other things rich people eat. Give me warm spiced rice and a good mutton curry any day.

So there we were again at our favourite eatery. It was late—almost ten. Everything else in the shopping centre was closed, but the team was all there. Even Fizah, who must have wheedled the time and place of this meeting from, I assume, Jimmy. I really didn't like that she was present, but there was little I could do. And Jimmy seemed to find her helpful, the two of them hunched over their laptops, digging into the depths of Binder Two for information to help us against what we'd started calling the Shoal, capital *S*. Adam was sitting in a ring of thinned reality, half-submerged in the Outside, keeping an eye out for its approach. Mei had been in the back of the restaurant for the last few hours, somehow having managed to commandeer the kitchen from the shop owner, who sat at an adjacent table, watching something loud and musical on her phone.

"I made you soup," Mei said, emerging. She placed a large plastic bowl in front of me, and I could smell chicken, ginseng, dried wolfberries.

"Just call it a healing potion," Jimmy said without looking up from his screen.

I took a sip, then raised the whole bowl and downed half of it. "I'll take whatever you call it, Mei. This is delicious."

She glared at me like that was a mortal insult. "That is entirely irrelevant. This is medicine for your eyes, old magic to neutralise the poison. You have to finish it."

I did. It was genuinely very good, but I pretended to grimace a little, just for Mei's benefit. Immediately, my vision started to clear, as if by magic. Scratch that, definitely by magic. It was clearly no ordinary chicken soup.

I couldn't help but let out a short laugh of elation at my returned vision. Jimmy and Fizah gave me a delighted thumbs up, and Adam came over to give me a long hug from behind, and to steal some of the biryani. The ghost cat, who must have followed us from the office, appeared to rub his sides against my leg in congratulations. Even Mei pressed her lips together in what was clearly a suppressed but satisfied smile.

With a team like this, we could take on anything.

"All right, folks," I said, pushing the plates aside. The warmth of the soup was settling in, and this was a nice moment of calm. Not really a luxury we could afford. "The Diviner said we had three days. Less now. What have we got?"

Jimmy placed a bundle on the table. Wrapped in fine black cloth and silver wire, it looked incongruous next to the plastic plates and food. "The chintamani stone," he said. "It's still locked behind the poison, still unfriendly, still wild. That Nagamuthu is a real piece of work, but it's the real deal."

"We still need three things," Mei said. She removed three charms from her bracelet and laid them out in a line. "An eye," she said, tapping on a blue bead with concentric circles, a *nazar*. "Someone to find their way through the chintamani's trap. James can see more than the rest of us. He can do this.

"A heart." She touched a charm in the shape of a knife. "Someone to take the released power and channel it outwards. I can do this.

"And finally, a hand." This was a small golden palm, open, a mudra of some kind. "Someone to go to the Shoal's realm and strike it with that power. Adam can do this."

Jimmy shifted uncomfortably. "I think I can—" he started, but I had heard enough. My earlier good mood had evaporated.

"Unacceptable, folks. This is too dangerous. I thought we agreed, no stunts like this."

Adam started to say something, and I cut him off sharply. Started counting things off on my fingers.

"Jimmy—you haven't even encountered the poison before. You don't *know* if you can find your way through the trap. Think of your wife and kids. Mei—we can't risk you burning out with all that power. If this doesn't work, you'll have to find a spell to fix it. And Adam—you just...can't. It's too dangerous. It's not your job. We need another plan."

They looked at me, faces unreadable. Nobody moved. Then Adam turned to his left and right, seeking support from the others, but Jimmy glanced away and Mei stared stonily forward. Even Fizah just fidgeted with her tudung.

Another moment of silence, fraught. Cords stood out on Adam's neck as he faced me again. "There is no other plan," he said. His voice was hard and edged as glass.

Why was he getting frustrated? He wasn't the one who had to deal with daredevil teammates.

Then the knowledge settled inside me. I knew what we had to do.

"There is," I said. "I'll do it. I've faced the poison, and survived. I've seen the Shoal and come back alive. I can do this, be the eye, the heart, the hand. I mean, look." I paused, searched for an argument, trying to sound reasonable. "It makes no sense to risk three of you when we can just risk one."

"You can't do this," Adam said. "I'm going."

"Adam," I said. "I'm not letting you go."

His face hardened. "I'm not asking for your permission, Ben. I'm going, whether you like it or not."

The words hung suspended in the still air, frozen in that moment. Before this, the closest we'd come to fighting was when he'd booked a pair of very expensive tickets for a helicopter tour of Singapore, a few weeks ago, before the world was nearly ending. He'd meant it as a surprise for that weekend, but there was the department budget I had to clear and a speech for our Minister I had to vet, and I did not have the mental or emotional room to do a new thing. I'd snapped at him, triggered by the stress from work and some amount of guilt at how much the tickets cost, and he'd apologised and then I'd apologised and we'd had a fun time making up.

That time, I could admit, had been my fault. But this time? He was being unreasonable. Why was he so insistent on putting himself into danger? Why did he have to pick this, of all things, to be so stubborn about? Couldn't he see I was trying to protect him?

"You're not part of this team," I said. "You don't know how we do things. You can't just waltz in here and try to be a hero."

His hands knotted in the hem of his shirt. "You think *I'm* trying to be a hero? I'm just trying to help. It's pointless to risk you, when you know so much about everything. I'm going, I'm more expendable," he repeated. "End of discussion."

His voice was low, a growl. But I caught it, just for a heartbeat, the way his chin was tucked, as though flinching from a blow. The way there was just the slightest crack in his voice, something no one else would have noticed.

I caught it because I knew him. Because we were… together.

And that was also why I could not allow him to do this.

"No," I said. I had a flash of a memory, Adam moving

helplessly towards the Shoal's light. "You're not expendable. Not at all. It's because I have the most knowledge that I need to go. Not you. I'll take you down if I have to."

Adam leaned forward, then tore his gaze away from me, like he couldn't even look at me. He was trembling with fury. "I'd like to watch you try."

"Whoa, whoa, whoa," Jimmy said. "Guys, can you both stop it with the macho bullshit? We don't have time for your egos here. We have things we need to do."

The silence between us felt like a wire pulled too tight. Like a string of shadow, hooked into the soft places of my heart. Adam's shoulders rose and fell with his breathing, and I willed with all my might that he would just look at me.

The only sound was the tinny music coming from the shop owner's phone.

Then Adam shoved his chair back and stood, his movements tight and controlled. "Yes," he said, his tone flat with anger, still not meeting my eyes. "Let's stop with the macho bullshit. I have better things to do."

And then he was gone.

Silence hung heavily in the air in his wake. I felt the weight of the team's gaze on me, waiting for my reaction. Jimmy quietly cleared the dirty plates and cups from the table. No one said a word. Weeds grew in my soul—anger, guilt, worry—but they were still small shoots. We had a mission to do, so I ignored both them and my team's concern, and picked up the cloth-wrapped chintamani stone.

We didn't have any time. We didn't have the luxury of being human right then. "Let's do this," I said, and before anyone could stop me, I slid one finger under the cloth to touch the stone.

Poison, potent and overwhelming, once again washed over me. But this time, I was ready for it. I knew there was a path through. Again I held back what I could with barricades of trees, and again I leached what I could from the soil and transmuted it into something harmless.

Just as it had before, the poison leaked out along my lines of connection, but this time I couldn't send it out across time and space. The network couldn't take another round of it.

So I threw my soul in its path—virtues I'd cultivated, skills I'd honed, memories that defined me—all set up as dams to stem the flow. The poison corroded them, broke through, but I flung more of myself at it, lavishly, avoiding thinking about the cost. But I was always a little too slow, a little too late. Where Jimmy might have used his sensitivity to guide the poison into petering out along subtle paths, I could only bludgeon ahead, always one step behind the curse.

I didn't know how long it went on for, but it felt like hours. Long, exhausting hours, fighting with my body and soul against the virulence of a snake god. Each time, I threw what was surely the last of my energy at it, but then new channels of poison were revealed, more deadly, more subtle, and

I would somehow find the reserves to steel my will for one last round. Then another last round. And another. I'd been called pig-headed by colleagues, friends, family, ex-lovers, but that stubbornness held me together here. Stubbornness, and my knowledge that the trite phrase, so loved by motivational speakers and Rebecca, was true.

Failure was not an option.

And then, after one last wave, everything was still. The curse had spent itself, and the poison was contained. Across my soul, what was once healthy rainforest and mangrove was now blighted, the trees at the borders had withered, fallen and rotted where they lay. It was devastation, and while I was sure I could recover, it would take time.

A faint hint of something acrid twinged on the edge of my awareness. There was still poison left, pooled under the soil of my soul, slowly eating away at who I was. I knew I should clean up these last dregs, but I was out of gas.

I opened my eyes, caught my breath, saw everyone watching me. Every inch of me ached, like I'd just emerged from a fever. My vision swam, the room tilting for just an instant, but I ignored it, this lingering shadow of the curse. No time for doubt now. I drew on my already depleted resources one more time to give the team my best smile. Confident, in control, definitely not feeling like I was about to keel over.

"We're good," I said, unwrapping the chintamani stone. With the curse defanged, its glow was gentle instead of malevolent. "Now to frighten off some fish."

Jimmy nudged a coffee over to me. It smelled awful, but I drank gratefully. "Are you"—he paused, swallowed a little nervously—"are you sure you're okay? I know your magic is strong, but you just broke the Nagamuthu's curse by yourself. Maybe you should rest...I mean, we can wait. I mean, I can—"

"We can't wait, Jimmy," I said, gently as I could. I forced down more of the coffee, buying myself a few more seconds before I had to get up. "We only have two days, remember? We have to do it now."

They all followed me with their eyes as I walked over to where Adam had been sitting. I thought I caught a whiff of the soap he used, but perhaps that was just wishful thinking. Where he had been, reality still felt thin, the waters of the Outside closer than usual. Just as I hoped.

I wasn't sure I could do it until I did it. It felt like remembering a dream, like activating muscles I didn't know I had, like flexing invisible wings, like remembering Adam wrapped around me, his self, cradling me when he had pulled me Out.

I slipped through, once again connecting to the many-limbed thing that was me in the noumenal realm. In one of my hands rested the blazing chintamani stone, and in the far distance, a fainter light shone. The Shoal.

I swam towards it, slow and clumsy without Adam to guide me. The dark water felt even more alien, colder now I was alone. At least this part of the plan was straightforward. I'd get close enough to the Shoal, channel the magic of the chintamani into a spike, a bomb powerful enough to nuke the heart of the swarm, and hopefully convince the creatures that the pain of coming any closer wasn't worth it. It would work exactly like some of those videos I'd seen where people use explosives to blow fish right out of the water.

I was totally fixed on the plan when a current, frigid and merciless, seized me. It swept me sideways, down a long stretch of empty ocean, and I tumbled, unfamiliar limbs in an unfamiliar body. Disorientation. I was flailing, I was drowning, I couldn't understand how I was breathing, how I was supposed to breathe. In that instant of distraction, runners of panic wormed through me, drawing toxic sustenance from the poison still left inside that I hadn't had the strength to completely neutralise. As always before, I fought for control, but my exhausted will sputtered and failed.

In desperation, I grasped for the last shreds of my previous experience in the Outside, when Adam had taken me on that magic carpet ride. But, try as I might, I could no longer hear the music of his voice. Everything was overwhelmed by a silent expanse of meaningless water. All I could remember was the hurt on his face as he turned to walk away.

I was sinking, falling away. I couldn't breathe.

This was it. Here in the black, alone, was where it would end for me. I thought of my father. My mother. Adam. Mei and Jimmy and Fizah. The ghost cat, oddly enough. But those were merely images. I couldn't parse the complexity of my emotions: regret and sorrow and, for some reason, an overwhelming sense of affection for everyone I'd ever known and loved. Then the images slowed, and they slowed, and they slowed. The water was cold and dark.

This was it.

And then the cavalry came storming in. Jimmy, following a thread only he could see, pulling himself to me. Mei beside him, pale and grimly muttering incantations, holding a bubble of air and radiance and reality around them both through pure willpower. They came from an unfathomable distance, and they took me, those colleagues of mine, those teammates, those friends, and they dragged me through alien water towards home. We were a single spot of illuminated safety streaking through the nightmare water, an impossible rescue, plucking back from the Outside a single life. Mine.

But they were two people against an ocean, and Mei's sphere of protection was faltering. The Outside came pressing in, not just the pressure of water but the entire weight of a dimension beyond ours, and Jimmy was reeling us back along his line as quickly as he could, kind Jimmy, Jimmy who never took risks, Jimmy with daughters and his wife waiting for him, he was pulling as fast as he could, but not fast enough. We would not make it.

If they died for me, I would not be able to bear it. But there was nothing I could do to protect them. I had nothing left. I was worthless.

The barrier cracked further, the ocean seeping in through the fissures. Inside the bubble, the Outside's reality was a crushing weight reimposing itself. Light was rapidly turning to darkness, air turning to water. Breathing was drowning.

And then, when the light had almost entirely faded and the air was gone—

We made it.

Fluorescent lights. Air conditioning. The smell of curry in the air.

But Jimmy was retching, vomiting out nothing we could see, lungs waterlogged from an unreal sea. Each heave further diminished him, as if he was expelling not just the contents of his stomach but a more vital substance. His skin had an unhealthy green tinge, and he smiled weakly, started to say something, then his eyelids fluttered and he slipped into unconsciousness.

Mei was by his side immediately. She felt his pulse, and when she looked up at me her face was stricken.

"He is fading, Benjamin. He was too exposed." Her voice broke. "He will pass."

I stared dumbly at her. She was lying. Except I knew she wasn't.

Something fell to the ground. My hands felt numb, and I must have lost my grip. The chintamani stone rolled to a stop against a plastic table leg.

The chintamani stone! I scrabbled for it, thrust it at Mei.

"Use it!" I said. "Use it. Save him."

She nodded. No hesitation. She placed the stone against Jimmy's chest, struck it hard with the heel of her hand.

A flare of magic, blindingly bright. Jimmy coughed, his colour returned. We were out of danger. But the stone, our one hope for saving the city, the only source we had strong enough to even faze the Shoal, no longer glimmered. It was dark, powerless. Like us. Spent.

CHAPTER TWENTY-FOUR

I took a moment to catch my breath, leaning against the wall, my legs trembling. The fluorescent lights overhead seemed too bright, too harsh, casting an unforgiving glare on our exhausted faces, on our failure. Mei was by Jimmy's side, her hand on his forehead.

"Thank you, Mei," I said, my voice hoarse. "Thank you for saving me."

She looked over at me, gave me the slightest of nods, and went back to taking care of Jimmy.

There was no recrimination in her look, no accusation. She didn't blame me for forcing them to go out there on a suicide mission, into a place neither she nor Jimmy knew, to pull me back from death. She didn't blame me for driving Adam away. She didn't blame me for not leaving Mr. Tan with Vanguard, for not killing him, either of which might have let us avoid this.

She didn't blame me for Jimmy, and I couldn't bear it.

I might have made a sound, or perhaps it was some

expression on my face, because Fizah came over and hugged me, burying her head in my chest. She was crying, perhaps from relief, from exhaustion, from despair. I held her for a while as she worked through emotions I shared but couldn't let out. Not now.

Then Jimmy groaned. He opened his eyes and looked around, confusion clouding his face.

"How are you feeling, James?" Mei asked.

Jimmy blinked. "Like butterflies and rainbows," he replied weakly. "But I'm alivc, right?"

I couldn't help but smile. "Yes, you're alive," I said. "We all are. We made it back."

The ghost cat leapt onto the table and batted at the chintamani stone first with one front paw, then the other. I started to stop him, but thought better of it. What was the point? The stone was inert now, powerless, no more than a rock. Let the cat play.

Despair settled in. We had lost our mightiest weapon, our only hope. Without that source of deity-level power, we were doomed.

Outside, I heard the drumbeat of a light rain starting. Through the eatery's dingy little window, I saw people running for shelter, the glow of lights from cars and streetlights, a whole city unaware of the danger approaching. We had failed to protect them. Overhead, the half-moon was momentarily obscured by a cloud, but then it shone on, serene and unconcerned about such mortal affairs.

Wait.

The moon!

"Mei!" I said, unwrapping Fizah from myself and setting her down on a chair. "If the moon were full, you said you could draw enough energy to scare the Shoal off?"

"Yes," she said, settling into a chair now that Jimmy was no longer in danger. "But it will not be full in time. And I will need the old man."

"Mr. Tan? Okay. So, just to make sure we're clear: *If* it were full, you *could* do it? Is there a special place you need to be to do the ritual?"

"Somewhere high up. Close to the sky."

Jimmy, still slouched in his chair, was watching me the whole time. "You have that look again, Ben," he said. "You have a plan?"

I grinned at him, a little giddy with manic energy. "We've got ourselves one last shot, buddy. Let me help you downstairs. Everyone else, pack up. We're moving."

This might yet work. We'd failed when Adam and I went in with the *Dapur Nala Wahi* spear. We'd failed when I went in with the chintamani stone.

Third time's the charm, right?

At almost three hundred metres, Guoco Tower at Tanjong Pagar was the highest point in Singapore. As luck would have it, it also had a roof garden open to the public. That was where we found ourselves, after a brief detour to pick up Mr. Tan and some masking tape from Dr. Kamini. We also had with us an additional team member—the ghost cat had somehow followed us from the eatery, and was comfortably perched on Jimmy's shoulder.

The garden was pretty, all low shrubbery and flowers, open to the night sky. What I hadn't expected, though, was how popular it proved to be as a late-night hangout spot for young people. Various groups sat on the wooden deck playing cards, couples played kissy-face in the darker corners, and someone, off in a corner, was strumming on a guitar poorly. Scattered everywhere were schoolbags and briefcases, the remnants of fast food and potato chips and some of those fish-skin things Jimmy loved so much. This, here, was a place for friendship, for youth, for love.

We found ourselves a clear spot, sandwiched between two groups of teenagers engaged in their own arcane social affairs. As far as I could tell, it mostly involved watching videos together, scandalised laughing, and then one person getting up to do an entirely age-inappropriate dance. I guessed I was getting old.

"So," I said, turning to face the team. Mr. Tan was sitting on the floor, muttering to himself, but I didn't have the energy to corral him. "Here's the plan. Mei can do this when the moon is full. It's not full now, and a common misconception is that moon phases are caused by the shadow of the Earth. Actually, they're... You know what, it doesn't matter. The moon's not full because a part of it is dark, right? In shadow?"

"Yes, Mr. Toh," Jimmy said. "I promise I'll try harder for my science midterm."

I ignored him. I had the punchline to deliver.

"Since that episode with Vanguard, I can move shadows. So...I should be able to change the phase of the moon."

They all stared at me.

"From this distance?" Jimmy said sceptically. "The moon is, like, how many millions of kilometres away—"

"Three hundred eighty-four thousand. But I don't have to do it from here." I turned to Mei. "Um, I need your shoes."

She gave me a withering look, the same one Tessa had given me, and then I watched understanding dawn on her face. Jimmy's face, always more expressive, went from confusion to delight to dismay in that order.

"You're"—he choked out—"you're teleporting to the fucking moon? This is mad. How do you even know that Mei's shoes will fit you?"

I was pleased to see Mei turn her glare on Jimmy. She looked almost insulted.

"The Unseen Step is not the only enchantment I have on these," she said, slipping off her heels and handing them to me. "They will fit Benjamin."

She was right. They were snug, but comfortable, or as comfortable as stiletto heels could be. I imagined I must have looked somewhat ridiculous in my blazer and khakis and white heels, and they made my glutes ache immediately. Why did women put up with this?

"There will be enough magic for two trips, Benjamin," Mei said. "There and back, no more. Do not dally."

What did she think I was going to do, hop around and explore the lunar surface, like I'd wanted to do ever since I was a child? Okay, maybe, but we didn't have time for that, so I just nodded.

"I've worked it out scientifically—" I started to say.

Jimmy groaned. "There's nothing scientific about this! You're going to use Mei's five-inch pumps to—"

"Six," Mei said.

"—*six*-inch pumps to get to the moon, move the shadow of a whole planet, then make it back here before you explode or implode or whatever it is space does to you?"

"I just told you it's not the shadow of the planet. Anyway, I've thought this through. There's no atmosphere to conduct heat, so as long as I'm not touching the regolith, I won't burn or freeze too quickly. I'll empty my lungs so the lower pressure doesn't rupture them, and I got this to tape up my nose and mouth. To keep the air in my body." I waved the roll of masking tape at them.

Fizah snorted, a little harsher than her usual giggle. "Cutting-edge government technology. Now I know what my taxes are paying for."

"You don't pay taxes," I said, eyeing her. She'd parked herself by Mr. Tan and was stroking his hair, her notebook abandoned on the floor. It was a little weird. "Are you okay?"

"What?" she said sharply, tucking her hands back into her pockets. "I'm fine."

Whatever this was, I didn't have time to deal with it.

"I'll have about a minute," I said, ripping out pieces of tape. Realistically, it was probably closer to twenty seconds, but I didn't want them to worry. "But once you see the moon is full, start the ritual. I don't know how long the moved shadows will last. Got it?"

What went unsaid was that they shouldn't wait for me to come back. Because I might not make it.

They nodded. I breathed in, then out all the way. Laid tape across my nose, across my mouth, then a few more layers for good measure. Jimmy gave me a fist bump, I looked up at the moon, and then I stepped.

Across.

The.

Void.

Of.

Space.

A.

Long.

Stretched.

Moment.

Bitter cold. I'd chosen to go to the shadowed part of the moon's face, figuring that it was better to avoid any radiation burns, and there I was, the pockmarked landscape of our companion rock stretching out before me. I had dreamed of this moment all my life, but I didn't have time to marvel. My body was already crying for air, and my eyes felt like they were on fire, probably from the fluid membranes congealing. My tongue felt like it was swelling into a very, very large and floppy fish. Incredibly inconvenient for the screaming I'd probably need to do soon.

So, instead, I reached out with the tiny seed of darkness in my soul, planted there by Semar, and I *pulled.*

Across the sere ground, the distant line demarcating light from dark remained unmoving.

I heaved again, felt the black seed in my soul plunge deep, its roots spreading.

The line shifted. Or perhaps it was my imagination, my brain playing tricks before I died.

Again. I pulled with all I had, the world's heaviest carpet. The seed drew deeper, its roots burrowing into the trees felled by the chintamani poison trap; they fed off the rot, drained the corruption.

A tiny black shoot, like a finger, poked above the ground.

The line rolled towards me, shadow shrinking, a vast field of white brilliance approaching from the horizon. Then the shadow sped past me, and I was standing in the sunlight, bleached radiance all around me, the face of the moon shining in full glory.

I'd done it!

Time to go home. I looked up, searching for the Earth, for somewhere to step back to. But my eyes were swollen and burning, the sunlight blinding, and everything was bright, so bright, there was no way I could find one blue planet in a sky full of fire.

I was desperate for air. Already, darkness was creeping into my vision, competing with the light from the blazing sky. Panic grew inside.

Then I remembered. I'd been blind before, only recently. And I'd learned to see with more than my eyes. So, I shut my stinging eyes, and I saw, far away, the blooming of uncountable trillions of souls, human and animal and plant, the vast interconnected web of the Earth. From this distance, everything was beautiful, perfect, each life worth protecting. I looked for the souls I knew, the ones connected to mine. I looked for home.

Then I stepped.

To where it was warm again, where a guitar melody filled the air, where Jimmy was patting me on the back, helping me remove the heels, exclaiming, "It worked! It worked!" The cat was ramming my ankle with his forehead and purring like an engine, clearly pleased with my return. As my eyes recovered, I located the moon hanging in the sky, luminous, perfectly full. But already I saw a sliver of shadow creep from the edges of the circle, a reassertion of physics. We didn't have long.

"It's time," Mei said, and started singing.

I'd heard her sing before, of course. Jimmy was very fond of dragging us all out for karaoke, and Mei would do very technically impressive renditions of Zhou Xuan and Stevie Nicks, but I'd never heard her do it in *communion*. It started with humming, her eyes closed, hips swaying. Then, the beginnings of a wordless song, personal and haunting, incongruous there on that rooftop of teenagers and leftover food. Here was something sacred, something transcendent and holy, something private between a woman and her goddess.

No one else was paying attention to us. They were steadfastly ignoring the magic and the beauty there among them, in favour of gossip and social media. Typical.

Still singing, Mei moved her hand to her abdomen, fingers weaving, pulling silken strands from her navel. Filaments of silver, gently luminescent and barely visible, were bound together with dark threads slick as blood. And she was knotting them even as she braided the cord, intricate loops and whorls that bound ethereal moonlight into usable power.

The cord grew, and with each knot Mei grew paler, lines of weariness and age etching themselves on her face. She was using a vital resource, drawing from the same well that had allowed her to maintain her youth, aging before our eyes. It felt like everything—the moon, the night air—held its breath to acknowledge the magnitude of the magic wrought, to witness her sacrifice.

Finally, she fell silent, her hands trembling with exhaustion, her breath ragged. She turned to look at us, and she was an old woman, her flesh loose, her skin dull and wrinkled. Her expression was triumphant, fierce, bitter.

"What?" she said, brooking no pity. "You are the only one who can play hero?"

"Did you know the magic would do this?" Jimmy asked, tentatively.

"Of course, you dolt. But it is irrelevant." She held up the knotted cord. "We have what we need. This is enough."

In the sky, the moon narrowed back to a semicircle. My manipulation of its shadow had run its course.

Mei strode to Mr. Tan barefooted, pointed imperiously at him. "Get up," she commanded, and I remembered Mei arguing that we should kill him.

Apparently, I was not the only one who remembered, because there was a sudden frenzy of motion, and Fizah flung herself in front of the old man, her face twisted. "You can't—"

"Get out of the way," Mei said. "He is my conduit to—"

But she didn't get a chance to finish. Fizah screamed, launching herself at Mei. Frail as she was, shorn of her preservative magics, Mei stood no chance. Fizah knocked her to the ground and snatched the rope of moonlight from her hands, standing crouched and snarling at us.

There was a wrongness to Fizah—the way she was hunched, like someone older. The way she held her mouth in a snarl. Even the way she crouched by Mr. Tan, her hip against his shoulder. Close, protective, too familiar. Not Fizah.

A prickle at the back of my brain. The shadow of recognition, something I had seen in Mr. Tan's memories, back in his flat. A young woman in a mustard-yellow polka-dotted dress, at a child's birthday party, crouched just like this and pretending to be a monster for the giggling children . . . Mrs. Tan?

Oh my god. Possession.

Fizah had been with me when we first spoke with Mr. Tan

in his flat, back before we had any idea he was responsible for any of this. The memory-seeds must have been planted then, but I had been too busy dealing with everything else to notice. I'd driven Fizah away for her own safety, thinking I was protecting her, but really all I'd done was hide the changes from us. Given the seed time to grow, to take over.

Fizah's eyes blazed, and someone else looked out of them at us. "Leave us alone!" Her voice was older, unfamiliar.

Then came the fire.

A blast of heat, so hot as to be invisible, drove us back, knocked us to the ground. My lungs, already battered from the trip to the moon, were burning, and all I could do was scramble to shield my face from the flames.

I forced myself to look up. In her hand, the moonlight cord that had cost us so much, the cord that represented our third try, our final hope, smouldered. Then, it burned, for an instant glowing before it was consumed completely.

The burned remains spilled from Fizah's fingers.

Crushed by the fire, I watched as she picked up Mr. Tan, as she turned and left.

I should have done something. Thought of something. Fought past the fire. Run after her. But I didn't.

What was the point?

The ash of the moonlight cord settled on the floor. Without Adam, without the chintamani stone, without the rope of lunar magic, we truly had nothing left.

CHAPTER TWENTY-FIVE

It was over. We were tired, beaten, out of options. The Shoal was coming. The sharks would feast on the defenceless population of the city, from them and their children and their children's children, and there was nothing we could do to stop it.

At least we could say we tried, but that wasn't saving any lives.

I'd sent the team home. They needed a break, after all this. Jimmy had risked his life to save me, and he deserved to go home to his wife, hug his kids, do whatever it is good fathers do. And Mei—Mei had sacrificed years of her life, her vitality, for nothing. And Fizah. Fizah wasn't even herself anymore.

We were no closer to saving the city than we had been days ago. In fact, we were further away. We'd taken two steps forward, and five steps back.

I was the one who'd failed them all.

If I had paid a bit more attention when I was Outside with

Adam, I might have been able to make it to the Shoal with the chintamani stone. Mei and Jimmy wouldn't have had to come bail me out. Jimmy wouldn't have been hurt.

If I'd put the pieces together better, I would've noticed something was off with Fizah. I would've remembered that she was there with me when we spoke with Mr. Tan that first time. I would have extracted that rotten seed from her before it took root. I could have saved her.

If I'd been smarter. Worked harder. Had more willpower, more strength, more endurance, more wisdom, I could have fixed this, protected everyone.

I would have kept Adam.

I would have been enough.

My thoughts as I got home were dark, and I hadn't expected my father to still be up. But he was awake, and he had a few dishes on the kitchen table waiting for me. Bean sprouts with salted fish. Cai po omelette with honey instead of sugar. A soup with pork bones and lotus root. Simple fare, family recipes.

I didn't have much of an appetite, but I had to eat something, and this was good. My father sat at the table and watched me eat, something I would have found irritating any other time, but this time I was glad not to be alone.

"Eat more," he said. "You're getting skinny."

"Okay."

He watched silently for a few minutes.

"I went swimming today," he said.

I looked up, surprised. He had been very resistant to trying it, complaining about how the pool downstairs was too small, the chlorine too strong, and so on.

"That's good!" I said around a mouthful of rice. "How was it?"

"The lifeguard is new, wanted to ask me a lot of questions. So I only swam a few rounds. Getting old is like that, everyone thinks you can't do anything."

"Mmm," I said. The food was *really* good, and I was hungrier than I realised.

"You're very busy," he said, falling back on familiar rituals.

For a moment, my mind blanked. I couldn't remember how I usually replied to this. I was too tired, too overwhelmed, my heart too broken by failure.

"It's... it's hard," I said. My voice might have cracked, or maybe it was some food stuck in my throat.

He sighed, sat silently while I continued to eat.

"You were always like this, you know," he said. "Even when you were little. Always taking on everybody's responsibilities. Do you remember, your teacher had to call us in because you were completing all your classmates' science homework for them?"

This made me laugh, despite myself. I did remember.

"Because they didn't know how to do it!" I protested.

"You have to let them learn. Have to trust them. Have to accept that—"

He didn't finish, but we both understood. He was talking

about my mother, the time she was sick, our fights about what she needed, how to take care of her. I was young then, with a young man's certainty about what was right and proper.

We fell silent again, unwilling to reopen an old wound any further. But when I sneaked a peek at him, I saw his hands were relaxed on the table, his eyes soft with memory. There was no rancour there, no blame. I already knew what he would say if I tried to apologise for what I'd done so many years ago. "Nothing, nothing." He'd dismiss it. "So long ago already."

He watched me eat, then seemed to remember something.

"Where's your friend?" he said. "Adam. Should tell him to come over to eat more."

"Okay."

Again, silence.

"*Ba*," I said, after a while. "You know we are... together, right?"

He nudged a dish closer to me, the bean sprouts. His face was expressionless as always, the mien of a stoic stone lion. "Not everything we have to say. You're my son, you're together means he's my son also. No need to say everything.

"Anyway," he said, getting up, "I'm going to sleep. Whatever you can't finish, just put in the fridge. I'll eat it tomorrow. You get some rest."

I watched him shuffle to his room, struck in that moment by his age, his frailty. When did my father become an old man? What the lifeguard did, it wasn't right. I didn't even know we had a lifeguard, but I'd have a talk with them tomorrow, get them to recognise their ageist actions. If they weren't receptive, I'd go look for management.

I shook my head. Realised I was thinking about all this—solutions and plans for smaller things—all to avoid thinking about things that were more painful and more important. Looking for things in the world to blame so I didn't have to look inside.

Just as the Nagamuthu said we humans did.

My father was right. I was still the kid who did everyone's homework for them, whether they liked it or not. Still convinced that if I was strong enough, smart enough, tried hard enough, carried enough weight, I could...what, save the world?

I couldn't even save my team. They had saved *me*.

The roots of my failure had been there all along. When I'd taken on too much, and refused to stop. When I had insisted I could be the eye, heart, and hand of our plan. When I had been so focused on moving forward I didn't look back, and missed Fizah's infection. When I drove Adam away.

Something hung heavy in my chest, in my throat. How could this be failure when it was the path the world had laid out for me, the one every leadership course had taught me, the same path as the Nagamuthu, Vanguard, Nadia? Always moving forward, always having a scheme, a plan, an answer. Always growing in power, always in control. Always with a clear vision of what the goal was, letting nothing stand in the way. This was the path of strength. This was the path of winners.

But the Nagamuthu, for all his near-immortality, was clever rather than wise, small of soul, full of spite and grudges.

Vanguard, with all their knowledge and power, no longer understood anything *but* knowledge and power. They were so sure about the rightness of their actions they'd become ruthless, harsh, immoral.

Nadia, for all her refinement and cunning, was greedy, vain, always grasping for more, for advantage, for anything, her beauty hiding deep insecurity.

There was another path.

I thought of what it had been like on the moon, my running out of breath, my desperate search for the Earth, and the blaze being too much to bear. I thought of how, sometimes, too much light is not illuminating, but blinding.

I thought of Mr. Tan, the look on his face as he spoke about his wife. I thought of the million million copies of her trapped in nectar and sweet fruit, replicas growing stagnant and toxic on the vine. I thought of how, sometimes, too clear a memory is poison.

I thought of Adam, and what we were to each other. I thought of him as he had looked on that stage at the bar, flushed from singing, with that dumb grin on his face as he searched the crowd for me. I thought of him following me to the pasar bayang, to Mr. Tan's flat, to Vanguard, to the Outside. How he was always by my side—never in front shielding me, never behind hiding—always a partner, a friend. I thought of how, sometimes, we must learn to return the trust we are given.

I thought of my father, the way he'd always been. A quiet man, patient, humble, forgiving, a role model of a gentler kind of love. A love that could trust, could free, could let go.

I'd gone inside my soul and outside the world. I'd gone to the goddamn moon.

Perhaps it was time to stop going somewhere.

Perhaps, just for a while, it was time to stay still.

All these realisations merged in my mind into a single epiphany, one I could not easily articulate. But as it settled, I felt something inside me shift.

The sun inside, the one I had pinned to the middle of the sky for as long as I could remember, was setting. Always before, I had forced a noon blaze. I had demanded growth from the rainforest, from the mangroves, because growth was how I grew stronger than I had been the day before. Growth was how I became better at protecting those who needed protecting. There had always been a gale, guarding the boundaries of my heart.

But I couldn't do that any longer. It was too much. For the first time in my life, I let the light dim, the winds fully die.

A heartbeat.

Then twilight flooded in through the sky and through the trees, a blanketing tide. Through cracks in my walls where the Nagamuthu's poison had breached my defences, shadows powerful and silent poured through, swelled my soul with the darkness I had always kept out.

Except the darkness was not failure. Nor was it weakness or despair. It was gentler, dotted with stars, vast and deep. It was respite and refuge, balm for a weary heart.

In my soul, finally, night fell, unassuming as a father's love.

And quietly, one by one, the trees of my Garden broke into flower. Reds and purples and pinks and whites, yellows, a profusion of vibrant colour muted and rendered ethereal by the night.

Lilies, my mother's favourite. Given this moment of stillness, there in the secret grove in the depths of my heart, they finally bloomed.

CHAPTER TWENTY-SIX

Monday morning. I got myself a good night's sleep, the first in what felt like a long time. The Diviner had told us we had three days—well, two now—to deal with the Shoal, which had put us into full panic mode. We should have realised that it meant *we still have two days*. We could afford to take one morning to recover. So I messaged the team that I was taking the morning off, and suggested they do the same. It'd been just about a week since this all began, and we'd been going flat out. They'd earned the break many times over.

In any case, we could figure out next steps together after lunch, when we were all back in the office.

I shaved and showered, had a long leisurely breakfast with my father. We didn't say much, but then out of nowhere he told me he needed a new belt, could I get one for him just like mine, but not too expensive. This was as close as he was ever going to get to expressing vulnerability, and when I teased him about giving him a makeover he declared he was going for a swim and left.

My role model, everybody.

And then I had before me the hardest task.

Hey, I texted to Adam.

Hey, he sent back immediately.

Can we talk? Please?

Blue tick. He'd read it. Several minutes passed. My stomach hurt.

Are you home? Adam said. Can I come over?

Okay, I said, suddenly nervous. Several times, I started planning what I wanted to say, rehearsed a speech, but I stopped myself. This wasn't a negotiation with the Nagamuthu or with Nadia. This was real.

You know that feeling you have on a roller coaster when you're at the top of the track and about to plunge? You know everything's going to be okay, because you trust the universe and more importantly the mechanics who maintain the rides, but you're still terrified because of that tiny, tiny chance it could be a catastrophe and your life could end? Yeah, that's how I felt.

By the time Adam arrived, I was on edge and feeling nauseous, my soul a jumble of anxiety and worry. To be fair, he looked a mess, too, his clothes rumpled, his eyes puffy from lack of sleep.

"Hey," he said, standing at the door, looking for all the world like a lost puppy.

"I'm—" I said, and then he was holding me, his arms wrapped around me, his cheek pressed against mine, and maybe I was hugging him back, fiercely, desperately, and maybe we were crying, but it was relief, it was vindication, it was affirmation.

We pulled ourselves apart and went to the kitchen table, where I poured him some coffee and myself some water.

"Listen," I said. "I've been a little bit of a dick."

"It's not that little."

I gave him my best glare. "I'm serious. I've been thinking, and I realised I've been a really shitty... uh, boyfriend. I've been—"

"You're not—"

"Wait, let me finish. Not just to you, but, like... everybody. I keep trying to carry everything, to push ahead without caring what you think, treating you like you're some weak, fragile thing. Pretending like I'm some kind of hero—"

"You're *my* hero."

"Really?"

Adam reached over and squeezed my knee. "Yes, you dummy. You always want to do what's right. You throw yourself in front of us again and again like a self-sacrificing idiot. You try to save everybody. It doesn't even cross your mind that we could have passed on the Clementi issue and let someone else deal with it. You're responsible, and you're brave, and you're kinda cute. That's why I want to face the world with you, side by side. That's why I love you. Your heart's in the right place, even if you're an ass about it sometimes."

But I was frozen. Did he say...?

"I—" And then I stuttered to a halt.

"It's okay," he said, smiling, understanding. "We'll get there."

Patient, forgiving, kind. What had I done to deserve this man?

"I . . . I missed you," I said.

There, I said it. Not everything I wanted to say, but it was something.

"I missed you, too," he said, his voice barely above a whisper. "I missed us."

We reached across the table at the same time, squeezed each other's hand, holding on as if trying to anchor ourselves to the certainty of the other.

Then he grinned. "You know it's only been like twelve hours since we saw each other, right?"

I kicked him under the table.

"You look like garbage," I said. "Smell like it, too. Want to hop in the shower, and then I can catch you up on the way to the office, to meet the team?"

"You sure you want me there?" he said.

"I'm sure."

Adam was the kind of guy who could take two hours to get ready in the morning—more this time because I kept distracting him—so by the time he was out of the shower, my father had come back from his morning swim. He made us stay for lunch, and when we agreed, we received a list of stuff to get from the NTUC nearby while he prepped the other ingredients. He spent the next hour puttering happily around the kitchen, cooking, shooing us away whenever Adam and I tried to help. There was shrimp and snow peas, black bean fish, some kailan with oyster sauce, steamed egg, chicken corn soup. It was a ridiculous feast, especially for lunch.

"No pork," he assured Adam.

"We know, *Ba*," I said. "We were the ones who got this, remember?"

He ignored me, focusing on stacking more food on Adam's plate. "Eat more," he said. "Not like Ben, he's too skinny."

I sighed, resigned to being the second-favourite son. But finally, full to bursting, we managed to escape and made our way to the office.

Mei and Jimmy were already there in the meeting room with the projector. Jimmy didn't look on the verge of death anymore, and Mei wasn't as decrepit as she'd been—the rest had done us all good, it seemed.

They looked up from their laptops when we arrived, expressions shifting to relief when they saw Adam come in with me.

"Well, well, well," Jimmy said. "Look who decided to rejoin the land of the living." He turned to Mei, extending a palm. "Pay up. I told you they'd be back together."

"I did not take your foolish bet," Mei said, but I thought I detected the slightest ghost of a smile. She was glad, too. "We still have a city to save, remember?"

She was right, of course. For all the gladness in my heart, we had work to do.

"So what are we going to do?" I asked, finding myself a seat.

They stared at me.

"Don't you have a plan?" Jimmy said. "You always have a plan."

"I... I don't. I was hoping we could figure that out together."

Jimmy made a face. "I'd have brought some snacks if I'd known this was going to take a while." He paused, putting some real thought to the matter. "But wait, hold up. Let me see if I have things clear."

I nodded, leaned back to give him the space. Jimmy played the fool sometimes, but his just-some-dumb-questions were often helpful for getting clarity on the heart of the real issue.

"So, this started because Mr. Tan was very sad," he said. "He planted a memory tree of his wife, and there were so many fruits that they began dragging things down into the Outside. Vanguard used their shadow magic thing to make him grieve harder and faster, hoping to bore a hole in this dimension, so we kicked their asses and they stopped. After that, we had to get the chintamani stone and the moon-rope as power sources, because we realised Mr. Tan was drawing monsters here, this metaphorical Shoal, and we had to— Why are you guys looking at me like that?"

"It's a real shoal, Jimmy," I said.

"Like... *real* real? Real fish?"

"The same way the Nagamuthu is a real snake. It's accurate, but inadequate."

"Oh." Jimmy was quiet for a while. "The whole time, I thought it was a, what do you call it, a metaphor. For danger from this Outside, generic monsters or something. Like when people say, 'Oh, when you invest, watch out for the sharks!' Or when you get married, people say, 'Avoid the relationship barracudas!' "

Adam let out a snort. "No one says that. Literally no one."

"Fine," Jimmy said. "If it's real fish, then why have we been trying to zap it with magic? Why can't we, like, lure them away with fish food?"

"The only bait we have is Mr. Tan, and he..." I paused, suddenly struck with painful clarity. I was remembering something Jimmy had said, days ago.

"You have that look again, Ben."

"Jimmy," I said. "Before, at the clinic. You asked if we could convince Mr. Tan to let go, detach him from his attachments, let him sink free. Do you remember?"

"Yeah! I thought, like, the whole metaphor was about the dangers we make up to keep from letting go. But you said it wouldn't work."

"I say dumb things," I said. My mind was racing.

I had been holding on, against all reason, to my belief that we could somehow save Mr. Tan and fix everything. That *I* could save Mr. Tan and fix everything.

But maybe we didn't have to save Mr. Tan.

Maybe Mr. Tan could save *us*.

I closed my eyes and focused on how to say what I was

thinking. This was new territory for me. "We don't have to be the heroes here. Mr. Tan can be the hero. He's been grieving for so long, stuck in his pain. If he lets go, he could draw the Shoal away."

"You..." Jimmy said, confusion on his face. "You want us to abandon him? To let him die?"

"I want us to give him a choice."

Mei crossed her arms. "And if he doesn't want to?"

"Then that's his choice," I said. "But we have to give him the chance to make it."

Jimmy was nodding thoughtfully, turning the idea over in his mind. Mei's face was unreadable, but slowly, she uncrossed her arms. Adam...Adam gave me a look I couldn't parse at first.

It was pride. He was proud of me.

"So how do we do it?" Jimmy said.

"Adam," I said. He was still looking at me in that way, that half-smile on his stupidly handsome face. But I had to focus. "Can you get to Mr. Tan from the Outside? Find a way through the pollution and unknot whatever he's hooked on to?"

He held my gaze for a heartbeat. He didn't say anything about what had happened before. Just nodded. "Yeah," he said. "I'll do it."

"Then that's what we do," I said. "We locate Mr. Tan, wherever he is. Adam releases him from the Outside, makes sure that he's not tangled up with his flat, his neighbourhood, his remaining family. The rest of us, we talk to him. Help him understand that it's okay to let go."

"It might not work," Jimmy said.

"It might not," I agreed. "But he's a good man. We have to trust him."

"We do," Adam said, softly. "And we trust you, too."

"Fizah," Mei said. "She will be there. We will save her as well."

And so, like that, it was decided.

I could feel it now, a new energy in the room, and in my soul a new flower blossomed in response, pink tamarisk, a precious gift from another life. It was hope, beautiful, invincible hope, not just the feeling but the truth of it, a transforming of the world into something worth hoping for. I let the perfume of it drift from me, offered it to my team, my friends, my companions, driving back despair.

Jimmy unfolded the large map he used, then unspooled his dowsing pendulum. "I'll find them," he said. "Then we trust him to be the hero we need."

We took a break to get ready. One does not simply walk into Mordor.

When we came back together, everyone had geared up in their own way. Mei had somehow found time to change. She was now in full make-up, wearing a stunning cheongsam of midnight-blue silk embroidered with silver peonies, winding rivers, dragons in flight. She had a scarf around her shoulders, pale yellow, and even from a distance I could sense the sorceries woven into it. This was her war paint, her armour. She was beautiful, owning her new look as an older woman, but my heart ached for her loss—her youth, even the scarf we had yet to recover from the ghost cat. In the face of calamity, the small indignities stung all the more.

Adam looked much the same as he had when he'd left my place—dark jeans slightly distressed, stylish sneakers, a cream henley shirt he'd borrowed from me. But there was something about him, a sense of a presence behind what we could see, something gargantuan, many-limbed. He must have done whatever it was he does on the Outside, prepared himself with whatever other-dimensional warm-ups he did.

Me, I had spent the time making calls to some people I knew. I still didn't like putting my friends in danger, and even asking for help still felt new and uncomfortable. But I reminded myself that they could make their own decisions, and I knew I would have, without hesitation, done the same for them.

I also took time to slowly, gently tune my soul back to daytime. For what was coming, I would need the strength. Oh, and I managed to convince the IT folks (Sandra, actually) to let us sign out an array of earpieces and collar microphones. One for each of us, plus an extra for when we rescued Fizah.

Jimmy had with him six umbrellas, not the small foldable kind normal people used, but great golf umbrellas with handles hooked like shepherds' crooks. Each one was enormous and eye-wateringly yellow.

"Hey, boss," he said, waving the umbrellas at me and coming quite close to puncturing an organ. "I bought these for later, but I forgot to get the receipt. Also, I forgot to do the email submission for the cost. I'll do it later and claim retroactively, okay?"

"What? Yes, I mean, sure," I said. "But...why?"

He looked at me like I was insane.

"Because I've been very stressed, between trying to save lives and, oh yeah, *almost dying*!"

"I meant, why are you bringing... You know what? Never mind."

He grinned victoriously, tucking the umbrellas under his arm like a bundle of sticks. "Let's go already!"

We'd never encountered a possession like the Mrs. Tan one before, so we didn't have an established vocabulary for talking about it. I'd just been thinking of them as memory ghosts. Like ghosts, just made of memories instead of ectoplasm.

Ghosts were still not particularly well understood, despite how common hauntings were. One reason for this was that the term seemed to be a catch-all for a wide variety of underlying things, from alien spirits to demons to the undead. There were hauntings that brought with them retinues of dark entities, those that came unconnected to anything else, those capable of growth and change, those that were just mechanical echoes winding down.

Just like memories, I supposed.

I'd met Mr. Tan, seen into his soul. I knew the sort of ghosts he'd spawned, the sort of memories he'd captured. His error, the reason why the tree of his memories leaked cloying sap and his fruits of remembrance putrefied on the vine, wasn't that he neglected to tend them. His error was that he held on to them, refused to let them change as they had to. He prized a perfect remembrance of Mrs. Tan, every hair, every smile, and in so doing lost the spirit of her.

Too much light can blind. Too much clarity can obscure.

These memory ghosts, they grew too much, but in another sense, they couldn't grow at all. They were stuck repeating the same patterns again and again, just stimulus and response on a fixed template. They would gravitate to where was most familiar, where they could endlessly rerun the past. Where they were, Mr. Tan would be, too. And Fizah, the intern I'd failed.

And that was where Jimmy found them.

Clementi, Block 375, where this all began.

CHAPTER TWENTY-SEVEN

We all crammed into one cab, Mei in the front, the rest of us squeezed together in the back. Few cars dotted the roads at this time on a Monday afternoon, so the driver uncle tried to start some conversation with us, but even Adam and Jimmy were too tense to respond with much beyond monosyllabic grunts. Eventually, the uncle stopped trying, and we rode towards our destination in silence.

He dropped us off a block away from Block 375, and the moment we got out we could feel it—the first drops of rain, heralds of a coming storm. Clouds were massing overhead, the wind rising. People hurried to find shelter, but there was something more at play. Everything felt paper thin, unreal, the light watery and oppressive, the air heavy with a strange stillness. The only sound was the rustle of leaves, too loud, and the wind gusting past the flats around us.

Jimmy handed out his yellow umbrellas, one for each of us, and when we opened them the burst of colour was shocking, almost taboo. But it broke a little of the pall the place and the weather had cast over us. We could do this—free Mr. Tan, turn the Shoal away, save Fizah.

Jimmy, we'd always known, could work a special sort of magic.

More rain fell as we walked towards Block 375, scattered and sporadic at first, tapping gently against the pavement. Then it got heavier, the rhythm turning into a hiss, a downpour, veils of water through which we had to cross, leaving the normal world behind us. Even the blocks of flats around us were barely visible, only dark and hulking towers, their features obliterated. All we could see were one another, faces grim, the only bright spot in the world the impossible yellow of our umbrellas.

At least the earpieces were working. We knew this because Adam started singing, out of nowhere, some song about an improbable family of sharks, the devices transmitting the song clearly, through the rain, to our ears.

At first it was ridiculous, his upbeat *doo-doo doo-doo doo-doo* juxtaposed to the weather, to all our failures, to the severity of our mission, but by the middle of the first stanza we were all smiling and singing along. Even Mei, I noticed, was bobbing her head to the rhythm.

It would've been nice to sing our way to our destination and carry out our plan. But, as they say: Man plans, and stakeholders laugh.

We were three generations deep into the shark family tree

when, through the rain, shapes appeared. People? They emerged through the deluge, too close together, and then we saw that they were not people but horrors: figures with eyeless faces and limbs that bent wrong, who had too many fingers, whose mouths were gaping holes. They were detritus. Sand, gravel, branches, plastic bags, twisted bicycle racks, a child's toy tractor, all struggling to hold a human shape—five, maybe six of them reaching through the rain for us, but more came from behind them, shapes hidden by water.

What were these? Some new nightmare from the Vanguard labs? But I had no time to figure it out. They were lurching at us, violence written in their mishappen bodies. I took a moment to focus, burning away hesitation and fear, and I stepped *towards* them, rotating to slam a shoulder into one of the golems.

I was motion. I was power. Inside me, verdant force surged—I was a blinding arc of lightning, I was the blistering heat of the afternoon sun—and I flung the creature into the one behind it. Both of them disintegrated on impact, broken junk sluiced away in torrents of rain.

Next to me, Mei stood like a queen commanding an army, brow furrowed in concentration. Her finger was pointed magisterially at another golem, one she had pinned in a halo of moonlight, silver filaments shearing through it like wind through paper. To my right, Adam vanished, dragging a creature with him, while Jimmy stabbed at another with a spare umbrella.

Ah, so that was why he'd brought extra.

The team had it under control. And it felt good to let loose. The sun inside suffused me with strength and new growth, reinforcing tendon and muscle and bone, body realigned to the soul's design. I abandoned my umbrella and spun among our attackers, my fists the rain's rhythm. No fear. No wasted moves. Water streamed down my face and tracked rivulets on my glasses, but I trusted my reflexes, the pulse of the Garden. I wove through them like roots through concrete, like a monsoon.

The world was chaos and violence, so I let my strikes become meditation. My movements become mantra. Inside, I found a clearing, still and quiet. And from there, deep read active, I looked out.

Possession. It was all possession. The seeds Mr. Tan had been spreading, the poisonous spores of his dead wife, had infected people first, because people were the most vulnerable. Their hearts were soft, easiest to hook. But over time, the seeds had settled into the ground, into other things. Because leaves and brick and trash accrete memories. Because stones remember.

What we were fighting, these golems, were all copies of Mrs. Tan, driven mad by the unfamiliar forms she found herself in, knowing only that she had to guard this place. Against people like us.

Individually, they were nothing, clumsy things easily destroyed. But they were legion, their numbers uncountable.

Each time we broke one, the rain washed the pieces away to re-form somewhere else. I saw pieces of a park bench I'd broken incorporated into new golems.

What we were doing... This was unsustainable.

"Let's go, people," I said into the microphone on my collar. "Follow my lead."

We fought through them, through the pelting rain, advancing slowly towards our destination. Block 375. But I saw that Mei was flagging. Her face was etched with lines of strain, and she was relying more and more on Jimmy to keep the golems off her with his umbrella. Whatever she had spent channelling the moon's power had cost her more than she showed, and sheer willpower could take her only so far.

Before I could think of a solution, I felt sand under my feet. Ahead of us loomed a scaffold of bars, a plastic fort. The playground! This was where I had met Fizah that first time we came here, and perhaps that was a good omen. We could hold our ground here, take a breather.

Wordlessly, the team found our natural formation—Mei and Jimmy sheltering together in the central fort, Adam and I circling the perimeter to repel attackers. It worked well for a while, Mei slinging hexes, Jimmy using his extra umbrella to drive back golems who got too close, Adam drowning them, and me trying my best to keep the area clear.

And then the people appeared. Human people. In between waves of golems, aunties and uncles came at us, drenched from the rain, clothes waterlogged, all with the same raw desperation on their faces. These were the block's residents—also possessed, but unlike the golems they weren't unhinged by their concatenated bodies. They weren't crazed, they didn't foam at the mouth, but they were convinced we were there to do bad things to their husband, to their family. I knew they'd do anything to stop us, and they came wielding knives, rocks, and bamboo rods normally used for hanging laundry.

In theory, they should have posed little trouble for us. They had none of the material durability of the golems, nor the strength, and they couldn't reconstruct themselves from scattered pieces. But these were real people, someone's sister, someone's grandfather, someone's neighbour, many of them frail, none of them trained combatants. The tactics that had worked against the golems would seriously injure them.

We had to slow down. Mei, I noticed, switched to stunning spells. Adam and I desperately disarmed them as quickly as we could. I used the chi disruptor to take a few down, but then we had to take time away from defence to carry the unconscious folks back to the fort, lay them down carefully so they wouldn't get trampled. All the while, the golems kept coming.

"Look out!" Jimmy shouted, and even through the rain I heard a low rumble, not thunder but something closer. Then I saw it, and I was running, hurling myself between the playground fort and an incoming car.

The vehicle rammed into me, just as the wyvern had. A screech of tires on sand, the windshield shattering, the front of the car crumpling against me. In the driver's seat was a middle-aged man, bleeding from a cut on his forehead, passed out from the shock of the collision.

The possessed were getting creative. We couldn't handle much more of this.

Then out of the deluge, like a vision, they appeared. Four avian shapes, splashing gleefully through puddles, the glint of their eyes visible through the rain. Behind them strode a slight figure in a charcoal suit, his black umbrella obviously high-quality and expensive even from this distance. And next to him was a woman with a crooked smile.

"You're late," I said. It was Seng, his duckling *toyols*, and Tessa—the friends I'd called for help. They'd come.

"I wasn't sure I should show up," Seng said with an infuriating smile. "I didn't have an appointment. But hey, friends against the world, right?"

Tessa laughed, gestured behind her. "We met back there, figured we were both here for you. Seng here told me how you helped his nephew, and I thought, well, anyone who likes birds, undead or otherwise, can't be all bad."

Last time I'd seen her, I had been mostly blind. I hadn't realised how young she was.

"This is Jun Seng and Tessa," I explained to the team over the comms. "Old friends. They're on our side."

But that explanation wasn't necessary. Even as I spoke, the ducklings got to work. They snuck through the battlefield, tiny fluffy dots of yellow in the chaos. One flapped madly as it latched on to a stone limb, twisting the whole thing like a bottle cap until it popped right off. Another wedged itself into a golem's torso and, quacking with delight, wrestled the creature to the ground. They fought like feral toddlers on a sugar high, completely unreasonable and unstoppable. And right now, I wasn't complaining.

Seng, meanwhile, focused on the possessed aunties and uncles. He wove energies with his hands, graceful as a conductor at an orchestra, the necromantic powers he controlled attenuated to bring not death but sleep. One by one, the Clementi residents slumped onto the wet ground, drawn into deep, dreamless slumber.

And Tessa, her magic was hard to see, darting through the ranks of golems like...sparrows? Flying worms? Surely that couldn't be right. She did arcane things with her fingers, whispered secret words, and golems just collapsed into piles of debris.

"We got this," Seng called out, and I knew he and Tessa wouldn't let us down.

The rain eased off just a bit, the gale temporarily blowing the rain sideways against the buildings instead of into our faces. Suddenly, in that break in the storm, Jimmy was shouting, waving and pointing, almost incoherent in his excitement.

"Fizah!" he screamed, too loud for the earpieces. "Here! We're here! She's...I see...There!"

For an instant, I thought I saw her, a familiar face illuminated by the white glare of sudden lightning, but then the rain came crashing down again.

"We have to go get her," Jimmy said, almost hysterical.

"Yes," I said, peering into the rain. Nothing beyond a few metres was visible.

Adam grabbed my shoulders, turned me to face him.

"I'll come with you," he said, a little tentatively.

A stab of shame. I knew why he hesitated. Just a day ago, I would have said no.

"I'd like that," I said, honestly. "Cover me?"

His smile was radiant.

Fighting again, Adam and I advanced side by side, pushing our way through golems, through the battering storm, through our own insecurities.

Quickly, naturally, we fell into a pattern.

I pushed forward, aiming directly for where we'd seen Fizah. What golems got in our way, I cut a line straight through. Some I shoved stumbling aside. Others I tossed bodily into the rain, threw them—tumbling and broken—to be lost behind curtains of falling water.

Adam warded my back and my flank, flickering away to take care of attackers that got too close, seizing them with the tendrils of his extended self and casting them away into an otherworldly ocean. But always, he returned, back to the shelter of the umbrella and the warmth of my side.

I was a dagger—unyielding, all forward motion, a single-minded thrust towards the goal. He was a net—fluid and reactive, catching what I couldn't. Like a *secutor* and a *retiarius*, not opposites but complements, we made our way forward together, step by slow step.

If that wasn't a hell of a metaphor for us, I didn't know what was.

Without warning, a jet of flame roared past us in a near miss, turning the rain to sizzling steam. Fizah.

Fortunately, the ghost inside her was clumsy. She'd revealed her position, and let us get too close. We sprinted forward, ducking wild streams and gouts of fire. Broke past a few remaining golems. Glimpsed Fizah through sheeting water.

Almost there.

An inferno blossomed ahead. Nuclear fire, colourless, unfurled like petals. Not the controlled jinn-magic I'd seen before from Nadia's crew, but something wild. Crazed. This was her last desperate attempt to keep us away, and she'd thrown everything into it. Already, the heat warped the air, too strong, too massive.

It would swallow us all—Adam, Jimmy, Mei, all the golems and the possessed aunties and uncles. Everyone. There was nowhere to run.

And I wasn't close enough to Fizah to stop her.

Then, impossibly—

The flames stalled midair.

Another heartbeat, and the fire was jerked off course, plucked from the air like a disc intercepted mid-throw. It was dragged *elsewhere*, pulled into dark waters where it guttered and died.

Adam emerged beside me, panting.

Smooth.

Also, effing hot. Guess all that stupid Frisbee playing had paid off after all.

The rain thinned, and there was Fizah, her face caught in the same expression I'd seen on the other possessed people. Fury, determination, and a fierce love. The same snarling expression that was on her face last night, there on the rooftop of Guoco Tower.

Her hand was outstretched towards us, perhaps to burn us, perhaps to ask for help.

But she was out of fire.

I stepped in, touched the chi disruptor to her side, caught her as she sagged.

We made our way back to the playground fort, Adam carrying Fizah in his arms. Past the *toyols*, still brutalising the golems, untiring as only the undead could be. Past the skin-tingling perimeter of a ward Mei or Tessa must have found time to set up while we were gone, slowing and weakening the attackers.

Adam sat Fizah on one of the pogo-pony rides while Jimmy and Mei both hurried down from the fort. Under several umbrellas, we stood looking at Fizah, who was slumped and unmoving. She was soaked to the bone, tudung and T-shirt plastered to her, and I found myself fussing how she was going to catch a cold.

Ridiculous under the circumstances, I know.

"I can try to draw the possession out," I said, moving to sit on the pogo-pony right next to her. "But she's a strong soul, and the possession has had a while to take root. I...I'll need help."

"You're learning," Mei said dryly. But she gave me a nod.

I closed my eyes and went inside myself. And I lowered all my guards.

It was easier this time. The mangroves that shielded me from harm opened up. The winds that protected me quieted down. I gathered sunlight, readied it into brilliant spears, and I waited.

From Fizah's soul came what I expected: the uncoiling creepers that were the ghosts of Mrs. Tan. A spiritual cancer, preserved past her death and kept alive by a husband who couldn't let go, each twisted vine blurry with fractal sickness, blunt and heavy with recursive memories. Questing towards me, seeking the new fertile ground of my soul to plant more copies and to grow.

And farther out, I could sense even greater danger. Opened as I was, vulnerable and arable, the parasitic mycelia in the residents and in the golems found me irresistible. From all around, an ingrowth of ghosts, focusing on me.

I put them out of my mind. Fizah was my priority. I let the tendrils from her reach into me, groping, and I made myself be patient as trees, patient as earth, patient as my father.

I waited.

I made myself wait. Even as the ghosts twined through me, seeking the deepest parts of me, I waited.

Then, when I could bear the violation no more, I set loose

the lances of fire I'd been holding back, cascades of white heat to incinerate Fizah's infection. I would scour her clean.

But . . . nothing?

The vines from her soul, fed on her jinn-magic, would not burn. They writhed through my flames, growing stronger and thicker. Hungrier.

I panicked then. The lessons I'd learned recently would be of no help here—patience, gentleness, trust would do no good against these invaders. Already, they were reached past my offence, snaking greedily into soil, strangling the trees of who I was, drinking of my substance. And just beyond them, the vines from the other possessed, converging.

Somewhere near, I felt Mei's presence, cool as moonlight, and then she was there, in the space of my soul, luminous and young. She danced among my fires, between my trees, graceful as a song, turning the encroaching tendrils away with gentle sorcery, giving me the space to do what I needed to do.

She was here, young in a way she no longer was in the world outside. She was here even though what I did had cost her.

I understood now what that meant.

We don't fight ghosts with fire. We call them to rest with forgiveness.

I remembered that one tree in the rainforest of my soul, stunted and hidden, one I'd neglected for too long—Forgiveness. For one another, for mistakes, for truths, for holding on, for letting go. For ourselves.

And so, for the second time in as many days, I let the fires die down, let night come once again to the space inside me. Let the vines of these ghosts pierce me, let them come all the way into the hollow places, let them draw from the small, stubborn tree of forgiveness I had nearly forgotten.

Let them be transformed.

I don't know where memories go when they fade away. Do they evaporate like dew into the Anima Mundi, the world-soul? Do they decay into the loam of our dreams, the raw materials for new memories? Or does the act of forgetting free them?

I don't know. But I know that when these memories, these ghosts, came and drew from the tree at my heart, most of them faded. Because to forgive was to be released, to free yourself from someone's power over you. A few remained, patient, silent. They were waiting for something. I didn't know what.

I opened my eyes. The storm was letting up, and just beyond the edges of the playground, I saw a circle of detritus and unconscious bodies. What we had done had exorcised the golems and people nearest to us. Except for the rain drumming on the sand, on the umbrellas over me, all else was quiet.

Fizah coughed, sat up, looked around at us with wide eyes. "That," she said, "really sucked."

CHAPTER TWENTY-EIGHT

Jimmy handed Fizah the sixth umbrella, and we spent a few moments huddling under their inadequate protection. We could have gone to the void decks of the surrounding blocks to take shelter, but it felt like we'd fought for every inch of progress, and none of us wanted to go backwards even now that many of the golems were gone. We also weren't yet quite ready to go forward to Block 375 to face what waited for us there, so we all squatted there in the playground, in the rain.

"I saw what you did." Seng walked up, while behind him his duckling terrors continued to keep the perimeter clear. "It's not so different from some of my vitality transference spells. I can do the same for the others, draw out the extra life force in these people and stop the... what did you call it? Possessions. Leave it to me."

"I can help," Tessa said, joining us under the umbrellas. She looked soaked but otherwise unharmed. "What Mei did, I can copy some of it."

What they were suggesting could work. Necromancers, I knew, had esoteric ways of rooting out spirits, and Tessa had the power and skill to support Seng. They would be more useful here, protecting our backs once we went into Block 375, the den of the beast. And someone had to move all the unconscious uncles and aunties to shelter, which I was sure Seng would do professionally, given his day job.

"All right," I said. "Thank you."

~

The storm was easing up. Eventually, it was Fizah who broke the silence.

"We should do this, right?" she said, peering into the rain.

"Listen, you can..." I was going to say that she could back out still, they all could. She was an intern, they were just public officers, this wasn't even Adam's job. But I knew better. I understood now that they had to see this through the same way I did. We knew the stakes, and leaving was not an option for any of us.

"...do it!" I finished, feebly. "We can all do it!"

Jimmy gave me an odd look, but he was the first to stand.

~

The rain had almost stopped by the time we got to the lift lobby of Block 375. That's just how thunderstorms in Singapore are—they come and go as they please. But what relief we may have gained was offset by an intensification of the feeling we'd had when we exited the cab earlier. The thinness of the world, the sense that everything was precarious, poised over a drop into something deep, was even stronger here. It was clear that we were approaching its source.

"Sorry about this," Adam said, when he noticed our discomfort. An absurd apology, as if this was his fault. "Everything here is half-submerged. Might make it a bit hard to breathe."

"Can you take us through?" I asked. I was thinking of how he'd led me before, wrapped his self around me like a cocoon.

He grinned at me, perhaps thinking of the same thing. But then he shook his head. "Better not. It's strange out there, too, something wrong with the currents. And there are . . . things. Scavengers, coming to feed on whatever Mr. Tan is giving off. The Shoal's scouts. It's safer for you all here. I'll go take a look and let you know what's ahead."

"Hold on," Jimmy said to Adam. "Give me your earpiece."

He held it for a few seconds, concentrating intensely, then gave it back. "Just drawing the threads together, making sure it's all connected," he said, almost embarrassed. "So we can, y'know, talk when you're Outside."

Adam smiled, gave us a wave, and vanished.

Stay safe, I tried to whisper to him, but the words caught in my throat. He was swimming knowingly into danger, towards a poison he had no hope of escaping unscathed. But he was just doing what needed to be done, the same thing I was doing. The same thing we all do to keep the world turning.

None of us trusted the lifts, so we took the stairs. For the first two floors, it felt like we were descending rather than ascending, as if the pressure of the air and the pull of gravity grew as we climbed. At the same time, the stairs seemed increasingly flimsier, as if they were made of paper and we would just fall through with any misstep. It was disorienting, but we pressed on. Determined.

By the third floor, the strain was getting to everyone. It felt like we were climbing not a block of flats but a mountain, every step on the stairs impossibly far, the cracks in the walls and in the stairs revealing gargantuan knotted roots and jagged stone. The Outside was here, too close and yet not close enough. We were in between, neither walking nor swimming, neither wholly breathing nor drowning, slowed by a liquid we couldn't see or feel.

The air on the fourth floor smelled like poison, sickly-sweet and rotting, too thick to breathe. We stumbled back, choking and panting.

"I see you," Adam said, his voice in our earpieces but somehow still sounding very far away. "You're nearly there."

"We can't go on," I replied.

"We have to," Mei said. She spread her arms, muttered something, and from her blossomed a hazy sphere, an uncompromising argent light that pushed back the rising waters of the Outside and established a measure of normal reality. I knew this spell. I'd seen it before, the bubble she had around herself and Jimmy when they rescued me from the Outside.

But I knew also that it took a lot from Mei and from her unseen spirit allies, and that it wouldn't last.

We climbed, Mei holding our world through sheer force of will. Fourth floor. Fifth. But she was already faltering, the light dimming. She stared straight ahead, eyes fierce as ever, but her outstretched hands trembled almost imperceptibly, and perspiration beaded on her forehead. We weren't going to make it.

"Do something!" Jimmy hissed, but I wasn't a witch. What could I do? I didn't know the words to the ritual, didn't have the right bonds with the right spirits—

But, I realised, I didn't need to. I might not have known the ritual, but I knew Mei. She'd saved my life more than once, and I had seen her, her soul in mine. Whatever bonds allowed her to draw power from her spirits, she and I had a bond like that, too. She could draw from me.

So I gave her my strength. The same way Mr. Tan had given seeds to his neighbours, the same way the Mesopotamian woman in my vision had given pink tamarisk to her clients, I poured sunlight into Mei. I sent her leaves, and flowers, and soft breezes, a clumsy jumble of everything I could draw from my own soul. Vitality, or qi, or mana—whatever she needed.

Then it struck me: There was another person I was bonded with. Perhaps not in the same way as Mei and her allies, but he'd said I was his *boyfriend*, and that counted for something, right? Across space, across dimensions, I extended the light and blossoms of my soul to Adam, swimming so bravely in an alien world towards the cloud of poison he meant to face alone.

I couldn't see how Adam reacted, but Mei turned to me and gave me a tight smile. The spell around us stabilised, tinted now the faintest shade of gold and ash.

We pushed past the fifth floor onto the sixth.

I remembered this place. The discarded pair of slippers was still there on the landing between floors. The corridor still had the row of plants, the same bicycle locked to a rack. The brightly coloured blankets we'd seen the first time weren't there anymore, but that wasn't the only difference. The area around Mr. Tan's flat, I could see, was thick with a haze of spores.

More memories of Mrs. Tan that had not yet taken root, eddying in the disturbed air. They were seeds, and without possessing someone or something they were not yet semi-sentient vines, had not yet matured into ghosts of Mrs. Tan. I wouldn't be able to lure them in the same way I had with the others. But we couldn't pass.

A shriek of wind, a last gasp from a dying storm, and a portion of the spores swept outwards, scattering. Some of them would drift far, I knew, and some would be carried by the rain into the drains and reservoirs and from there perhaps infect more people. And I was sure this wasn't the first wave of it. These possessions were no longer a localised problem.

I pulled Mei back, preventing her from walking into something she couldn't see.

"There's—" I said, trying to explain what was going on.

Jimmy interrupted. "I see it. Can you get through, yourself?"

"Yes, but—"

"Then go," he said, glancing over at Fizah and Mei. "Go save us. We can handle all... this."

Later, I would learn that Jimmy let Fizah possess him, use his eyes, and together they learned to send out jinn-fire along the connections Jimmy could see, burning out every seed from the sky and the water, all while Mei held the world steady around them.

But in the present, I trusted them and dashed through the spores, my mangroves holding at bay the memory-seeds that sought purchase in my soul.

The door burst open as I drove into it with my shoulder, slamming violently against the inside wall. The flat was as I remembered it—again sofa, piano, ceiling fan. The old man was seated with his hands loose on his lap, at the same dinner table where he had served us tea. He was not a monster, not a lunatic. Just an old man.

He looked up when I entered, and I sat down by him.

"Calvin?" he asked, uncertain and hopeful. Again, he thought I was his son.

"Yes," I said. "I'm here."

"I'm here, too." Adam's voice in my ear.

My heart at my throat. "Are you—"

"I'm okay. The poison... It stings, but it's not too bad. Did you do something? Anyway, I think I can do it—untangle him from everything going on. But he has to make the final decision. You have to help him see, Ben. Help him choose."

Mr. Tan was searching my face, his eyes soft with fondness.

"Do you remember," he said, "when you were little, there was this girl you liked? You asked me how I got your *ma* to like me—I think you said how I did it a hundred years ago, and I had to explain to you that I'm not that old."

He laughed, quietly. "I told you to just tell her how you felt. Just be genuine, I told you. But she said no. You were heartbroken for days—couldn't eat, couldn't sleep. Do you remember?"

For me it had been something else, someone else, but I understood.

"I remember," I said.

He smiled to himself, a tender and private smile.

"Mr. Tan," I said, hesitantly. "*Ba*..." It didn't feel like I was pretending. "How did Calvin...how did I get over it?"

"I don't know," he said.

Silence, save for the clicking of the turning fan overhead, revolution after revolution through all the years in between.

"Can you...?" I paused. Swallowed. Started again. "Can you get over *Ma*?"

"I don't know," he said. His eyes were full of pain. One man's pain, but enough to drown the world.

I reached out, took his wrinkled hand like Fizah would have. Shored up my courage, met his eyes like Adam would have. Found Jimmy's empathy and Mei's steel in my voice. "Let her go, *Ba*."

He clutched at me, and there was a heart-wrenching need in his grasp. His eyes, when he met mine, were wet but lucid. He recognised me now, knew I was someone else's son.

"I'm hurting people, aren't I?" His voice cracked. "It's just...we had thirty-two years. But it wasn't enough. I still miss her."

And with that, something rose up in me, vast and aching, a tide of feeling I couldn't name, and with that also rose the remaining echoes of Mrs. Tan, looking through my eyes at the man they loved, whispering something, something I couldn't understand. Clearly Mr. Tan did, because his eyes were shining and he had a smile on his face, and I looked past him at the photograph I remembered on the piano, Mrs. Tan in her mustard-coloured polka-dotted dress, and she was smiling there, too, that same smile.

Then Adam was in my ear, awed. "It's happening."

Mr. Tan exhaled, long and slow, and began to sink. Slowly, gently, he slipped away into the Outside, pulled under by the million frozen memories of his wife that we had thought were burdens but were, in truth, anchors. He was fading from this world, receding into the distance of another universe, loved, unmoored from everything but memories of the woman he could not live without, those memories ablaze like a constellation of stars around him and within him as he fell away into dark water. I had a sudden vision of him adrift in the vast ocean of the Outside, the seed of a new bubble, a new reality where his family was alive and together and beautiful.

But here, in this world, all that was left was a profound silence, a sweet and ebbing sadness.

"Did we win?" Jimmy said as he and Mei and Fizah entered through the broken door. Normal reality had reasserted itself once Mr. Tan left, and the world was solid again.

"I'm not sure," I said.

"I'm not sure," Adam said at the same time, through the earpieces. "The Shoal . . . I can see it. It's hesitating."

Mutely, we reached out, held hands in a circle. We had gambled it all on this. Far off, I imagined the monstrous school of predatory fish hanging there where the deep ocean transitioned to the shallow waters of our world. I imagined hundreds, thousands of hungry shapes poised, uncertain, strange and alien considerations going through their minds.

On such small things our fate hung.

A breathless moment passed. Then another. Still, the Shoal wavered.

And then, from behind me, a familiar sound.

A tiny, squeaky meow.

On the sofa, looking entirely unconcerned about the impending end of the world, was the ghost cat, legs extended in a long and tail-curling stretch. The cat that had plagued the office, that had stolen Mei's scarf. The cat I'd secretly been feeding in the mornings. The cat that interacted with time in weird ways.

It gave us the reproachful look that only cats and teenagers could manage and hopped onto the coffee table. In his mouth was something luminous, pulsing.

Fizah gasped. "Is that—"

The cat trotted to the coffee table, dropped the object unceremoniously. The chintamani stone.

The *chintamani stone.*

From a point in time after we had undone the curse but before we'd used up its magic. Somehow, impossibly, the cat had found it and retrieved it.

And then, as we watched, the cat hooked his paw around something we could not see, batting it onto the table. Another stone, faintly glowing. Then another, each from the same moment in time.

And then, as if to mock us, he reached into whatever temporal pocket he had access to and dragged out another object. A knotted rope, silvery with the power of the full moon. Unburnt.

"Mei?" I said, faintly.

But she was already on it. Power erupted from the stones and the cord as she took them, and she was its master. With impossible finesse she wove a part of that lashing energy into the brilliant form of a spear, then bound into it layer after layer of radiant potential, each layer more dazzling than the last, until the spear hummed with the blinding power.

Then Fizah was there, next to her, notebook clutched tightly to her chest, fire pouring from her into the nascent weapon. *Jinn-fire.* Pure and young and irrepressible, winding through the cold puissance of the chintamani stone, through the ageless radiance of the moonlight cord, a refusal to bow before what had seemed inevitable.

Then Jimmy was there, too, face scrunched up in concentration, pulling on threads only he could see, speeding Adam home, pulling him back to our reality the same way he had drawn me back.

Then Adam. Adam was there, briefly surfacing to take the weapon, meeting my eyes for a moment before he Dived again. The light illuminated everything, turned the Outside temporarily visible, and we could all see Adam fling the spear like a stroke of lightning, like a bolt of insight, a shattering and final answer. A distant thunder, a madness of shadows like moths before a light, and the swarm receded. The monsters before which we had cowered for so long scattered and vanished back into the cold and empty darkness.

We had driven off the Shoal. It was over.

CHAPTER TWENTY-NINE

The newspapers blamed the whole thing—torn-up pavements, broken trees, unconscious people—on a "localised weather phenomenon," and the climate activists had a field day reminding people of the consequences of unmitigated climate change. The Clementi regional town council received overwhelming donations of food, clothes, and toys, as if this had been some sort of natural disaster, and I heard the residents bounced back quickly with that help.

People can surprise you with their generosity and resilience when you don't get in their way.

The papers had one other major report that week, on a restructuring of a major government-linked entity. Ujong Holdings announced that they were shutting down some of their more experimental divisions to "focus on [their] core mission and value-add to clients." The rumour mills on the conspiracy-focused internet forums were awash with images and videos of what looked like a fire in one of their satellite research offices, and there was speculation that experiments gone wrong were the cause of the restructuring. Aliens, as a theory, were very popular. Whatever the truth was, I suspected that we hadn't seen the last of whoever was behind Vanguard.

Mei managed to siphon off some of the ambient magic from the unleashed chintamani stones, and with it she restored the spells that maintained her youth and vigour. Enough was left over that she crystallised it into a new stone, which we sent back to the Nagamuthu with our regards. It was untampered with, sent in good faith, but I suspect he might not have trusted us enough to absorb it. We see outside what we don't want to see inside, I suppose.

Jimmy made a full recovery under the care of Dr. Kamini. He had to talk his wife (and daughters) down from their plan to find me and murder me for putting him in danger, but they eventually got over it... mostly. His brief possession experience when Fizah took over his body seemed to have left no lasting harm, and might actually have improved the range and sensitivity of his powers.

The rest of Fizah's internship passed mostly uneventfully. In the end-of-internship report she had to submit to her university, she wrote that she had "a meaningful experience with a wonderful team of genuinely passionate people," but she also gave us a rating of one out of seven for "Relevance of this internship experience to your academic work." I guess that was fair.

Nadia sent a very nice box of chocolates to the office, along with a note of thanks and a coy reminder to me to save the date for next year's Tanglin Club event. Seemed like Fizah's assessment was right, that the jinn didn't in fact hold grudges. All this manipulation and counter-manipulation was as much a game to them as it was business, and nothing was personal. She even pulled some strings to get that avatar of Annapurna a nice flat in Bishan and that goblin kid a place in a public school.

Last I heard, Seng's nephew and the jinn girl were still together, and they were considering doing a throuple thing. Seng's expression had curdled a little when he told me that. I think he wasn't sure how he should feel about it—I supposed even people like him who wanted a change in the structure of society could balk at other changes they didn't expect.

Tessa really hit it off with Mei, and apparently they had long lunches where they got into screaming fights about feminist principles and then went shopping for shoes together afterwards.

The seed of darkness in my soul continued to grow, slowly, but I had yet to hear it speak to me as Sem had. Instead, it occasionally bombarded me with dreams populated by shadows, nightmares where I absolutely had to avert some catastrophe but a succession of people kept stealing away my tools, then my arms, my legs, my eyes. Always, I would wake up just as I realised those thieves were all the same person. One day soon, we would have to mount a mission to rescue the shard of

Semar that was in the effigy, still with Vanguard or the jinn, and get ourselves some answers.

The cat, which we named Simba, became a permanent fixture within our team, or as much a permanent fixture as he could have been, given his odd relationship with time. Once we started feeding him regularly, he returned Mei's scarf and even stopped messing with the other divisions. Mostly.

Father really liked the belt I got him. Still no luck on the makeover.

Adam and I found our rhythm again. We hadn't quite figured out why our magics—his Outside and my Inside—felt so familiar to each other, but we had plenty of fun arguing about it. On the work front, he had become a full-fledged honorary DEUS member at this point, and he regularly popped by for team lunch or just to play with Simba. Once or twice a week, he joined my father and me for dinner, entertaining my father with stories of his entirely implausible adventures around the world. Then, sometimes, we went out for drinks, or we would stay in and watch ridiculous movies, or we just got some bubble tea and took a walk along the green paths of Singapore in the evening twilight. Once, on one of those walks, months after the Shoal incident, he asked me how I had explained the whole thing to our management.

So I told him about the report we had to put together, all the annexes, the PowerPoint decks, the clearance chains and the back-and-forth between multiple levels of bosses. I told him about a verbal update we had to give Rebecca, and I was wrapping up with a description of how I had valiantly tried to cast all our missteps in the best possible light.

"Then I told her," I said, "that we all played a part there at the end. Or, as I put it, it was a synchronised effort wherein each and every team member contributed their expertise and resources to effectively address and resolve the prevailing challenge at hand. I basically told her we beat the monster with the power of—"

"Are you going to say the power of friendship? Because if you say the power of friendship, I will mock you forever."

I was in fact going to say the power of friendship. But I couldn't very well say it now.

"Actually," I said, "I was going to say the power of love."

"Oh."

"Yeah."

We walked for a bit more, in a companionable quiet. Some kids ran past us, screaming, chasing something made-up but that was entirely real to them. The humid air held us close.

"Really?" Adam said, after a while. "Now is when you decide to use that word?"

"Who said it's about you?" I shot back. "Maybe I met someone else. Someone who orders bubble tea with the sugar level they want instead of just stealing mine."

"Oh, who's this totally real person? Tell me their name, I'm willing to take out the competition."

"And here they say romance is dead."

The moon was visible in the darkening sky, a crescent just

over the tops of the flats nearby. We gazed up at it for a while, and I remembered how cold and alone I had felt when I was there.

Adam looked over at me, very serious. “I just want to note, for the record, that you said *love* first.”

“That’s bullshit. You said it that day at my place, when you were being all emo.”

“That was under duress. Doesn’t count.”

“Totally does.”

“Does not.”

“Does too.”

“Does not.”

And so we went, bubble teas in hands, bumping shoulders, walking out into the night.

The story continues in . . .

Book TWO of the DEUS Files

ACKNOWLEDGMENTS

Gratitude is a tall tree with a hundred branches. It's a river fed from a thousand streams.

Enormous thank you to the team at Orbit—Angelica Chong, whose sharp eye plucked the weeds and whose gentle hand nurtured the flowers, fielding all my first-timer questions and requests with such aplomb. To Rachel Goldstein, Vivian Kirklin, Xian Lee, Crystal Shelley, Bryn A. McDonald, Alexia Mazis Pereira, Lauren Panepinto, Natassja Haught, Ellen Wright, Angela Man, and all the rest of the crew for their incredible expertise and friendliness, who made this an adventure and not a disaster. And a billion thank-yous to my wonderful agent, Maddy Belton, who believed in this when it was still a seed, and who I'm still convinced has real magic.

To the friends on this journey—Derrick, for that initial burst of ideas years ago, the constant encouragement since, and for being one of the first to read the earliest draft; Tze Min, for conversations about books and magic; Zul, for Semar and theology from Ibn Taymiyyah; Liyana, for answering my random questions about Islamic thought and language; Abhi and Alicia, for helping me get the Ultimate chapter not-so-wrong; Minyi and Anie, for all the brainstorming on ghosts and Indonesian folklore; Letch, for naming the Nagamuthu and the Naga Sangam; Fuad and Kevin, for the inspiration and writing tips; the whole Singapore SFF Writers group—Yi-Sheng, Megan, Zubin, Daryl, Jon, Nicholas, Wayne, and others—for feedback and camaraderie and community.

To the Mage (I know we probably should update the name) bunch—Del, Serena, Paulo, Tim, Kel (we miss you!)—for the absurd adventures we go on, for helping me understand character work and plot structures, for briefly inhabiting the pasar bayang, for all the laughs. We made worlds together, didn't we?

To the early readers, Lynette Teo and Joe Nassise, whose advice shaped the early roots of the story.

To ex-colleagues and old friends, for being a source of stories (and sorry about that).

To my mother and my father, for the unquestioning support even for silly things. For nagging me to not be too inflammatory in a book about the government. For all the books you read me as a kid, even if you had to pick up a whole new language to do it. I know this is love.

To Tim, Pascal, Cantor, for being baby corns.

Thank you, all of you, for helping me grow this wild, weird thing. My world would have been dimmer without you.

MEET THE AUTHOR

Jared Poon

Jared Poon is a philosopher, futurist, and facilitator working with governments in Southeast Asia and around the world to improve policymaking through storytelling, imagination, and cocreation. He's a recovering public servant and lives in Singapore with his husband and two very silly cats.

Find out more about Jared Poon and other Orbit authors by registering for the free monthly newsletter at orbitbooks.net.

Follow us:

/orbitbooksUS

/orbitbooks

/orbitbooks

Join our mailing list
to receive alerts on our
latest releases and deals.

orbitbooks.net

Enter our monthly
giveaway for the chance
to win some epic prizes.

orbitloot.com